BLOOD RAGE

ANTHONY GIANGREGORIO

OTHER LIVING DEAD PRESS BOOKS

BLOOD RAGE

Chapter 1

Chad Mitchell stretched out on his couch and picked up the television remote.

It was a warm summer's day and the Red Sox were playing at home today. They were about to take on their arch rivals, the New York Yankees.

On the coffee table next to where the remote had sat, was a beer, pretzels and chips. Kicking off his shoes, he flipped them into the corner of the room and smiled as they flopped to the floor like tiny, dead animals.

Ah, this was the life, he thought.

Divorced for almost three weeks, he'd had a better lawyer than his bitch of an ex-wife and he got the house and she got the dog. Fine with him, he hated that damn dog. It was one of those small ones with a weird name and even after three years with the little mutt, he still couldn't pronounce it.

In his mind, it wasn't a dog at all; it was a large rat with hair.

If you could kick the dog like a football and watch it sail away it was a rat, not a dog.

She didn't agree with his assessment and that was one of the many reasons why they had gotten a divorce. Well, that and he had cheated on her. But he wasn't a bad guy, he told himself. She had become distant for more than a year and a man needs attention.

And if she wasn't going to give it to him, well goddammit, there were plenty of women out there in the big wide world who would.

He looked up when the front door opened and who should it be, but his ex-wife.

"Well, well, sitting on the couch, there's a shock," Sandy Mitchell snapped as she crossed her arms over her chest.

"Screw you, Sandy, this is my house and I'll do what I want in it. What're you doing here, anyway?"

"Giving you your house keys back, asshole, that's what," she said, tossing the keys across the room. Her aim was off and the keys almost hit his head, but he ducked, the keys hitting the wall instead.

"Hey, that almost hit me, dammit!"

She pursed her lips in the way he'd always hated. "Well, they didn't, so get over it."

She looked around the first floor. "I have a few things I want to get, is it okay?"

Chad considered telling her to fuck off but decided to be magnanimous in victory.

"Sure, knock yourself out," he grinned.

"What a gentleman, thanks so much," she replied sarcastically. Without waiting for his reply, she stomped up the stairs to the second floor.

Chad watched her go, admiring her ass. Sure, he divorced her, but she still had a great ass. Hell, that was why he'd had the affair, because she wouldn't let him touch that ass.

With a sigh, he pressed the ON button on the TV remote. He began skimming channels, knowing he still had a few minutes before the game started. The screen went to the news channel and he paused for a second, seeing if there was something good going on.

Maybe there was another shooting/suicide. In the past few days, there were five already, and no one knew what was the cause.

He turned up the volume.

"...standing here on the corner of 5th and Main where two unidentified men began attacking passersby for no apparent reason. One man wielded a butcher knife and the other was using what appeared to be a garden hoe."

Chad chuckled when the man said *hoe*, finding it funny for some reason.

"More than ten people were seriously wounded and we have reports that another victim was killed but at this time there is no

word on that. Police were called to the scene and after repeated warnings; the two males refused to surrender and actually attacked the police. The two men were gunned down and pronounced dead just a few moments ago."

Chad could see behind the reporter on the screen to see two body bags and an ambulance. So that must be the two nutjobs. Serves the idiots right, he thought. You don't go attacking police with knives, shit, they got guns, and they know how to use 'em.

The screen flicked and there was the inside of the news station soundstage, another anchorman at his desk.

"We'll have more on this terrible attack at six, so please stay with us, now a word from our sponsors," the man said.

"Not!" Chad yelled at the television and changed the channel. He shook his head as he thought about what he seen. Seems lately people were going crazy for the stupidest reasons. Why, just the other day a woman got pissed at another woman in the supermarket. Apparently the victim had eleven items in the ten items or less line and the second woman was so upset she tossed her groceries to the floor, left the supermarket, and then waited in her car for the victim to appear. As the woman stepped off the curb, the angry woman stepped on the gas and drove over the hapless woman. She was later caught thanks to someone getting the license number of the hit and run but just imagining someone getting that angry over an extra can of soup was mind boggling.

Then he remembered another incident that had happened last week.

A nineteen-year-old girl had flipped out when an old lady had cut her off on the highway. The girl had followed the old lady off the highway, and when the old lady was at a stop light, the girl jumped out of her car and dragged the poor woman out the window and began to beat the living shit out of her. If it wasn't for a few Good Samaritans, the old woman would have been killed.

The girl had been brought down and the cops called in.

Madness, Chad thought, *utter madness.*

He had the sports channel on and he waited for the ads to end, while a bar of soap danced in the shower, telling the world how clean one could get if they used this particular soap, and it was while this commercial was on, and Chad leaned over and picked up his beer, that he began to hear raised voices coming from outside in the street.

At first he ignored them; after all, there were many times he would hear voices from outside. He lived on a street where the homes were no more than six to ten feet from the property lines. On any given day neighbors would run in to each other and would chat it up for a few minutes. Of course, sometimes that would be the opposite, such as what he was hearing outside at the moment.

He recognized the two male voices immediately. It was Charlie from across the street and Bob to the left side of him. The two men had been having a disagreement about parking on the street. It seemed Charlie, who lived across the street, continued parking in Bob's spot in front of his house and of course that pissed Bob off.

So, the two could be seen arguing about it on any given day. Bob had even called the cops once or twice, hoping to get Charlie towed, but the man was parked legally and there was nothing the police could do about it. This was a turf war, and though Charlie wasn't doing anything technically illegal, perhaps morally it was a little petty of him. If Charlie wanted, he could park on his own side of the street, or in his driveway, which fit two cars, but he just didn't want to have to move his wife's car every time he wanted to get out if she was parked behind him.

Bob could have cared less about Charlie's woes, and the two men who had once been friends were now bitter rivals as Chad tried to tune out the two arguing voices and enjoy the game, he realized it wasn't going to happen, especially when he heard Charlie cry out in what was obviously pain.

At first Chad tried to ignore it, not wanting to get involved, but then Charlie yelled out again and it was obvious the man was in distress.

Now that was something new, Chad thought as he glanced out the window overlooking the street. But the two men were to the side and he couldn't see what was happening.

With a muttering of curses, Chad stood up and walked to the front door. As he crossed the hallway, he glanced up the stairs to where Sandy had gone. He could hear her up there tinkering around and he almost went upstairs to see what she was doing, and maybe talk to her a little more about the divorce. Despite everything that they had gone through, he still cared for her and deep down he still loved her.

But he decided the hell with it and reached out for the front doorknob, opening it and stepping outside onto his front porch. The instant he opened the door and stepped outside, Charlie's voice grew in pitch and the man definitely sounded like he was in pain.

Chad grunted as he strode down his walkway to the street, figuring Bob had finally gone and done it and punched Charlie in the nose.

It hadn't surprised him one bit, the two going at it for so long, eventually something had to give. So when Chad reached the sidewalk and gazed down the street, his mouth fell open at the gruesome sight before him.

Charlie was prone in the middle of the street, Bob standing over him, and it looked like the lower half of Charlie's torso had been sliced into bloody hamburger.

Bob was swinging a machete in a chopping motion, like he was hacking at a tree stump, and the feral glee on the man's face was absolutely shocking. Chad recognized the machete immediately. Bob would use the long blade to trim the wild kudzu that grew untamed on the edge of his land like living snakes.

He was probably doing this distasteful chore when he began arguing with Bob for the thousandth time.

Charlie was gagging on his own blood as his insides were chopped into confetti. Bob was like a maniac, hacking away as blood shot up into the air and danced only to fall back to the earth. Bob's upper torso and face were bathed in crimson, like he had picked up a bucket and doused himself with it, letting the warm, viscous fluid dribble down his body from his head to his toes.

The blood stuck to him, congealing as fast as it hit him, and as Chad stared in utter shock, it looked to him like Bob had been dipped in red paint, now only his eyes peering through the paint. When Bob snarled, his white teeth were a sharp contrast to the bright scarlet.

Charlie turned his head and his mouth opened and closed like a landed fish, his right hand reaching out to Chad, begging Chad to help him. But no sooner did the arm rise into the air then Bob sliced it off, first the fingers and then the limb just above the elbow.

More blood shot out and now Chad could see the white of Charlie's ulna sticking out as the severed arm sprayed crimson. Chad couldn't help but be amazed how much blood was still flowing inside Charlie's mangled form.

With a few more hacks to makes sure Charlie was good and dead, Bob stopped what he was doing and turn to stare at Chad with that feral gaze. The blood-red man's chest heaved from the exertion of chopping his neighbor into bite-sized chunks and his teeth clicked like he was sending Morse code.

Chad's eyes locked with Bob's and Chad realized then that whoever Bob had once been, friend, neighbor, confidant, now he was nothing but a wild animal.

A wild animal that knew how to use tools to kill.

"Uhm, now take it easy, Bob, this shit is none of my business," Chad said as he took a step backwards. He didn't want to turn around for fear of turning his back on Bob and find himself with a back full of machete. It was like when you corner a wild animal, you would never turn your back on it. That was how Chad felt now.

Bob was breathing heavily, and as he glared at Chad, he raised the machete to his mouth and stuck out his tongue. With a demonic smile, he licked the blade, the blood sliding down his chin like maple syrup.

At Bob's feet, Charlie expired, his eyes glazed over in death as his open body cavity glistened in the sun. Then, before Chad knew what was happening, Bob spun and sprinted at Chad, screaming at the top of his lungs.

As the wild man ran, the machete swung back and forth in his hand, small droplets of blood dancing in the air before they dropped to the pavement. Chad, staring at the man as he came for him, at first was paralyzed with fear.

With the exception of getting into a few fights when he was a kid, he had really never seen true violence. He had lived in the suburbs where the street crime of inner city Chicago never stretched its slimy tentacles and his shocked mind was still trying to process what was happening.

But when Bob was only a few feet away from him, Chad snapped out of his stupor and the fight or flight reflex kicked in. Spinning around, Chad took off for his house, assuming there would be safety inside its familiar walls.

Once inside, with the front door safely locked, Chad could call the police and have the cops come and get Bob before he killed him or someone else.

Poor Charlie, it was too late for him.

Bob wailed like a psychopath as his tongue lolled out of the side of his mouth, his eyes wide with...what? What did Chad see in there?

Was it anger, lunacy? No, that's not what it was.

While Chad ran back to his house he realized he knew the emotion dancing within those wild orbs.

It was rage. Pure...unadulterated...rage.

With his heart pumping in his chest like a trip-hammer, Chad let out a scream of his own, only his was manifested from fear, not rage.

Bob was growling like an animal now, his head shaking as he ran, his balance slightly off and causing him to go slower than he would have normally been capable of.

Chad used this advantage and ran as fast as he could, reaching his open front door and thanking God he hadn't bothered to put the screen door on yet for the onset of spring.

He had no pets so the door was ajar and he bolted into the house, slamming the door and turning the bolt. No sooner did the door close than the thudding of fists began to pound on the door, but then, as fast as they began, they stopped.

Gasping for air, Chad didn't know what to do. Did Bob leave? Realizing he couldn't get in?

Then, coming from the front room, there was a crash of glass and Chad dashed to see what happened, only to stop in mid-stride at the entrance to the room.

The front window was now shattered, a large decorative stone, one of many from his front lawn, now lying on the carpeting in the middle of the room.

And at the window, eyes wide with rage, stood Bob. When he spotted Chad, Bob screamed as loud as his lungs would allow and he climbed into the room, cutting his palms on the exposed glass shards still in the frame. If the wild man cared he was wounded, he paid it no mind, and now dripping blood from the gashes in his hands, he fell into the room and rolled to his feet.

"Oh, sweet Jesus," Chad whispered as his former neighbor came for him again.

Backpedaling, Chad spun and ran for the second floor stairs, not knowing where else to go. Adrenalin surged through his circulatory system, giving him the extra strength he needed to take the stairs three at a time.

Behind him, Bob screamed as he charged up the stairs, his tongue hanging out, saliva dripping off the tip to fall onto the planks of the stairs.

Bob reached the top landing in seconds and his eyes darted back and forth, not knowing were he should go, or what he should do.

Within an instant, he saw his open bedroom door and he ran for it, for the moment forgetting Sandy was up there somewhere.

Just as he reached the door and was about to charge inside the bedroom, the bathroom door opened and Sandy stepped out. Behind her the toilet swirled in a downward spiral, the tank already filling up again.

"Chad, what on earth?" Sandy gasped, not understanding what was going on. "I heard a crash, are you all right?"

"Get back into the bathroom, Sandy, now!" Chad screamed. "Bob's gone fucking crazy!" Then he had to run into his bedroom as Bob reached the top landing.

Chad was just closing the door when he caught a glimpse of Bob, the hallway, and Sandy, who was standing perfectly still, dumbstruck.

Then the door slammed closed and Chad was kneeling down to peer out the keyhole to see into the hallway.

"Sandy, what the fuck are you doing! Get into the bathroom, he's crazy!" Chad screamed at her, but she was frozen to the spot.

Bob stared at the locked bedroom door and then at Sandy, his breath coming in short pants like a tiger. His face was covered in blood and his matted hair was plastered to his skull, giving him a desiccated look. Bob's rage-filled mind was working overtime as he decided what to do next, but the answer was obvious.

With a throaty roar that shook the walls, he charged at Sandy who at the last second, screamed for help.

The machete was raised overhead, the tip scraping the low ceiling as Bob brought it down in an overhand chop that had the blade connecting to the top of Sandy's head.

Her head was sliced in two like a ripe melon, the awesome power of the blow slicing through the cranium like it was made of cordwood. Sandy was still on her feet, as blood geysered from the massive wound to spray the walls and ceiling with dark arterial blood.

But Bob wasn't finished, and as he pulled the blade free, he yanked the spasming body to the floor and began hacking at it with abandon, the meaty *thwacks* filling the small hallway.

"Oh my God, no!" Chad screamed as he watched Bob now begin hacking at Sandy like she was a wooden log being prepared for firewood. The machete came down again and her left arm was taken off, the blow so heavy the machete sank a quarter inch into the hardwood floor before Bob yanked it out. Then he sliced off the other arm, and as he looked up and around, wondering where Chad's voice was coming from, he forgot about it and went back to work. Raising the machete over his head with the point facing down, he slammed it into Sandy's breastbone and then began sawing and cutting as he eviscerated her like she was on a slab at the morgue for an autopsy.

When he had made his incision, he dropped the machete and reached into the cavity and spread the ribcage wide, the cracks of the ribs filling the hallway like small firecrackers. Mixed with the cracking of bones were the soupy sounds of splashing beef stew as Bob swirled his hands in the warm organs and began pulling them from her torso. Chad was in tears now as he watched Bob take out Sandy's heart, the wild man having to use the machete to cut a few nasty muscles and tendons that were giving him some difficulty.

Blood was covering the floor like the toilet had overflowed and the water had turned crimson.

With each slide of his feet that Bob took as he moved about the body, his sneakers splashed more blood onto the walls.

"Jesus Christ, no! Sandy! Sandy!" Chad screamed, banging on the bedroom door as he wept for his lost ex-wife. Sure, they'd had their problems, but he'd still loved her. And to watch her massacred in front of him, like a hunter cleaning his kill, made him want to vomit.

Chad squeezed his eyes closed, tears running down his cheeks, and when he opened his left eye and put it back to the keyhole, he realized he couldn't see Sandy any more. At first he didn't understand why it was so dark, but a second later he knew it wasn't dark in the hallway, but he was staring at Bob's pant leg.

Chad blinked once and then jumped back and screamed when the door shook in its frame.

Bob was pounding on the bedroom door, and with each blow the door rattled just a little more. It was a decorative door, hollow, and wasn't built for security.

Chad scurried a few feet away until his back struck the foot of the bed. Then he just stopped and stared at the bedroom door with terror-filled eyes.

The pounding continued, but miraculously, the door was holding and Chad was about to breathe a sigh of relief when the sound of chopping wood carried to his ears, the door vibrating anew.

"Jesus, Christ, what the fuck?" Chad screamed. "Leave me alone, Bob, get the fuck out of here! I've got a gun! I'll shoot you dead if you come in here!"

If Bob was worried, he didn't show it, but continued to chop at the door with the dark-red machete coated in a thin layer of gore. Chad counted the seconds in his head and at the twentieth second, the tip of the machete appeared in the middle of the door, the wood splintering under the impact.

Then the tip was withdrawn to be brought back again, this time the hole growing larger.

Time seemed to stand still as Chad watched small splinters of wood cascade to the carpeting below the widening hole. His civilized mind was upset about the bits of wood, knowing he would need to get the vacuum cleaner or else risk getting a splinter in his bare feet when he went the bathroom in the middle of the night.

The sounds of chopping wood continued and Bob began to scream. It was a low, guttural howl, like a wolf would make.

Chad was shaking in terror, not knowing what to do when his eyes rested on the window at the front of the room. He knew there was a small roof below the window, the roof leading to the front porch, built to give the house some architecture.

The middle of the bedroom door was now gone and Bob was reaching inside with his free hand, trying to find the doorknob.

Realizing his only chance of escape was the window; Chad climbed over the bed like a toddler and almost fell head first to the floor. Reaching up, he pulled the drapes and shade from the window frame and opened it as wide as he could, then with one last glance over his shoulder to see Bob's hand reaching through the hole to open the door, Chad kicked out the screen and climbed onto the roof.

It was unstable on the roof, the shingles slippery due to the steep angle, and he imagined his body tumbling head over heels to land on the hard cement walkway below. He imagined his neck snapping, the dull crack filling the street as he slumped to the ground, dead.

But then he had to focus on the here and now as he crawled across the roof and to the edge. Bob reached the window and he howled in anger at his lost prey, but for some reason he didn't want to follow Chad onto the roof.

Chad was too busy maintaining his footing to worry about Bob at the moment.

When Chad reached the gutter, he swung his legs over and then let his body slide down. He scraped his stomach on the gutter but he ignored it, and then he was hanging by his fingers.

The drop was about six feet and he let go and landed hard. He didn't bend at the knees and the impact shot up to his teeth, causing him to cry out. As he fell to the walkway, he found himself staring up at the blue sky. There were a few fluffy clouds and it made him think of when he was a kid and he use to lay on the grass and try to see if there were shapes he knew in those clouds.

But then Bob screamed at him from the window and Chad's focus went there. Bob pointed the machete at him, and with a snarl, Bob pulled his head back into the bedroom, leaving the opening empty.

Chad realized Bob was going to go through the house and come out the front door, so picking himself up and running away, he headed for the backyard. His right leg pained him a little and he limped, but it didn't feel too serious.

By the time Bob had made it to the front walkway, Chad was long gone.

Bob stood in the front of Chad's house, looking back and forth on the street, and he raised his arms into the air and howled.

A second later, other savage howls replied to his and he nodded, understanding he wasn't alone. Across the street, an old woman was peeking through her side window, her face a mask of fear and terror as she watched Bob.

The old woman was clumsy and she accidentally hit the shade on the window. In an instant the window shade rolled up, flapping at the top, the movement catching Bob's eye.

With a scream of rage, Bob bolted from Chad's house and across the street. There was a picture window to the left of the front door and he ran at it like it was made of paper, his full body weight connecting with the center glass. Shards went flying as Bob rolled into the living room of the old woman's house. Rolling to his feet, he ignored the large gash in his side where a particularly sharp piece of glass had found his flesh.

The old woman screamed and stared at Bob, not understanding what was happening. This was a man who had taken her barrels in when she was sick and had given her mail delivered to his home by mistake.

Bob went over and picked up his machete which had fallen when he landed in the house. Now he grasped it with a blood-soaked hand, and with a howl and a bark, as if he was now nothing than a dog, he charged at the old woman.

The poor hapless geriatric had just enough time to put up her hands to defend herself, but then the hands were falling to the carpet, severed from her wrists. As she bled out from her devastating wounds, Bob lunged in and began chopping and hacking at her body until there was nothing left to recognize as a human being.

Breathing heavily from the exertion, Bob turned and walked to the front door. It took him a second to figure out how to open it, as if his intelligence was slipping away with each tick of the clock, but eventually he figured it out.

Stepping out on the walkway, he howled again, and when another scream came to his ears, his head snapped in that direction and he bolted, loping off like a gorilla, the machete still swinging in his hand as droplets of blood flew through the air to land on the sidewalk.

He didn't know where he was going next, but wherever it was, his blade would be busy.

Even in his rage-dampened mind, he knew that for a fact.

Chapter 2

Chad's breath came in gasps while he ran. His vision was cloudy and he fought off the fainting spell that wanted to consume him. Running into his driveway with a limp, he jumped over a lawn chair and onto the grass. The lawn was mostly weeds, interspersed with large dead spots where only gray dirt peeked through. He had never been much of a gardener and the lawn attested to this.

As he ran to the six foot wooden fence bordering his yard, at first he didn't notice the sirens and sounds of chaos filling the air. But as he reached the fence and glanced over his shoulder to see it was devoid of Bob, he paused for a moment, bending over with hands on his knees as he tried to catch his breath.

Looking up at the sky, he stared at those same clouds and wondered what was happening to him.

Hell, what happened to Bob? The man had gone insane, much like the incidents he'd heard about on the news.

Sounds of fire trucks and police sirens floated on the wind like a symphony of doom and he knew what had happened to him wasn't isolated.

Not with so many sirens. He cocked his head to the side when he heard a few yells and screams drifting on the wind, and he jumped slightly when he heard a faint *pop*, followed by a few more. It sounded like someone was playing with firecrackers or a dozen cars were backfiring, but that was implausible.

Could it actually be gunshots? Here, in Andover, Illinois?

No way, he thought. Andover had always been a quiet town. It was a little over six miles from Chicago, and you could see parts of the city if you were on elevated land. Sometimes, when he was driving home from work and it was dark, if he was on the right road he could see the flashing lights of the Sears Tower blinking at him like a silent banner in the night.

But the street crime that filled Chicago's seedy parts had never found their way to his neighborhood before.

Yes, that's what was happening. Gangs had ventured out from the city and were now attacking innocent civilians. It had to be.

But then how to explain what happened to Bob? The man had gone completely mad, like a psychotic killer on speed.

Chad looked up when the sound of breaking glass came to his ears, but from the backyard he couldn't see that Bob had just jumped through his neighbor's front picture window.

Deciding he needed to go somewhere, anywhere, other than where he was, he climbed the fence and landed in his neighbor's backyard, wincing when his right foot came down too hard. Maybe he was wrong about his leg; maybe he had sprained it or worse.

At first he only heard the pounding of his heart in his ears, but after a few seconds of inactivity, he began to calm down, if only slightly.

Images of Bob hacking Sandy to bloody chunks invaded the front of his mind and he fell to the ground on all fours, his face creased with grief.

How could this be happening? What the fuck was going on?

He squeezed his eyes tight and shook his head, feelings of pity and loss overwhelming him. He stayed that way for almost five minutes until he heard a loud boom.

Looking up, he was able to peer through the tree line to see Chicago in the distance. Just to the right of the towering rooftops of office buildings, he saw smoke wafting into the sky and what looked like a news helicopter circling the effected zone.

Whatever was happening in his small town was also happening in Chicago.

With so many people crammed into such a small area, he could only imagine the chaos, the violence.

For the thousandth time, he was glad he lived in the suburbs.

To the left of him, was the opened gate that would lead to the street, and to the right was his neighbor's house.

Trish was a pleasant woman in her late thirties with two kids. Many times he would come out to his backyard to see a whiffle ball or a birdie from a batmitten set on his lawn, tossed over the fence by her kids when they played in their small yard.

The oldest child was ten, with light brown hair and dark blue eyes. She was the kind of little girl who had such beautiful features it looked like she would grow up to be a super model. The youngest was a boy of six, with light blonde hair and piercing eyes that always made the child look like he was up to something sneaky. He had a mischievous smile that was as endearing as it was aggravating to any adult who knew him.

Chad looked around the toy-strewn yard seeing the discarded playthings of the two children. To the left were a few abandoned toy construction vehicles, the hook on the crane swaying back and forth thanks to the gentle breeze blowing in from the north. To the right of him were a few old dolls, more than one with missing limbs, their bodies looking like the relics from an old zombie movie.

Chad crossed the yard and walked up the three steps leading to the back door of the house.

It was the middle of the day and Chad was fairly certain she would be home. Trish worked weekdays and relished her weekends with a passion.

When he knocked on the door, it opened slightly when his knuckle's connected with the wood, and with a soft squeaking of a rusty hinge, the door swung inward.

"Hello? Trish? Anyone home?" Chad called out, but not too loud.

It felt almost insane after what he'd been through to be casually knocking on his neighbor's door, as if he just wanted to borrow a cup of sugar.

There was no answer and he frowned. But as he was still pumped on adrenalin and needed someplace safe to go, he stepped into the house. If Trish wasn't home at the moment and she came home to find him in standing in her kitchen, well, he'd deal with that when it happened.

His eyes went to the sink, and he moved to it like a man dying of thirst in the desert spotting an oasis. Turning on the tap, he let the water run for all of two seconds and then plunged his hands into the cool spray. He then cupped his palms and splashed his face as he closed his eyes and tried to calm down. Each time he tried to calm down however, visions of Sandy being slaughtered flooded his mind and he had to open his eyes or else he would go mad.

As mad as Bob?

"Oh, Christ," he muttered. He hadn't thought of that at all. What if whatever had turned Bob into a homicidal maniac affected him, too? Would he go on a rampage as well? Would he slaughter his friends like they were animals that were rabid and needed to be put down without mercy?

It seemed Bob was the rabid animal now. Chad remembered the unadulterated rage he'd seen swimming in the man's eyes, the pure anger festering within like a bomb about to detonate.

Shivers went down his spine and he shook his head to clear it, then plunged his entire head under the cool spray. The sink was deep and his head fit with room to spare, despite the cereal bowls and plastic cups already on the bottom.

As the water sluiced off his scalp and ran into his ears, at first he didn't hear the strange sounds emanating from the opposite end of the house. But when he finally turned off the water and reached for a dish towel to wipe his hair and face, ignoring his now wet shirt collar, the noise wafted through the house again and this time he did notice it.

It was an odd sound, like rubbing two pieces of raw steak together, and for the life of him he had no idea what it could be.

From outside the house, a police car roared by, its siren piercing the day.

Chad turned and stared at the back door, wondering if he should just leave.

But he didn't know where to go if he did leave. He sure as hell wasn't going back to his house, not with Bob outside somewhere. Plus, he wasn't feeling exactly safe at the moment. He realized at that precise moment that the common house with its doors and windows wasn't the best place to go for safety. With its dozen or more exposed windows and multiple exits, it would be very hard to defend, even if he thought he was cleaver and attempted to board up all the openings.

Besides, all an attacker would have to do is set the house on fire and he'd either have to leave its safety or burn to death.

No, his house wasn't the place to be if whatever happened to Bob was affecting others in the neighborhood. And from the sounds of sirens, muffled gunshots, and the occasion explosion, it seemed that was the case.

As to what was causing it he could only imagine. News programs about terrorism and biological attacks came to him, but were quickly dismissed as implausible. He had to face the truth that he had no idea what was happening and it was very possible he might never know.

The noise filtered through the house again and Chad was pulled from his thoughts. So, swallowing the knot in his throat, he went to investigate, not knowing what he would find, but his curiosity getting the better of him.

Chapter 3

Chad moved through the house like a prowler searching for valuables. The quaint home was filled with light, each window wide open, the shades up and curtains pushed to the sides to maximize the sunlight.

It was odd moving through the house like this, Chad thought. It should have been dark, with thunder and sheets of rain pounding the roof as he slowly searched the home.

The squishy sounds grew as he left the kitchen and walked down a hallway that would lead to the front of the house. He'd been in Trish's home in the past and so knew the layout well.

Off on his left was the living and dining room, and if he continued forward, there was a den for the kids and a small room Trish used as a sewing room or office, depending on her mood.

Reaching the doorway to the living room, he peeked inside, but there was nothing unusual there. A few toys were on the floor and a TV Guide sat on the coffee table next to a ceramic mug which was half full with what looked like coffee or tea. Looking to his right, he was able to see into the dining room and here, too, nothing was amiss.

Then more sounds came to his ears, but then a new one was added to it. A low guttural sound like what an animal makes when it's feeding on a kill. Walking into the dining room, Chad looked around for something to use as a weapon, his eyes resting on a pair of candelabras. They were made of heavy steel, plated in gold, and he hefted one to see how it felt.

He was satisfied it would protect him if he needed it to. His heart was in his throat as he moved through the house, each foot carefully placed in front of the other.

His adrenalin was pumping again and he felt sick. He was never one for heroics and now he was being forced time after time to either act or die.

He debated calling out, wanting to see if someone would hear him, but the thought of Bob made him hold back.

No, if there was someone in the house he wouldn't want to meet, then calling out would be a very bad idea. Moving to the front of the house, the squishy noises now became more prevalent and he was able to pinpoint the source.

It was the den, where the children would play after school and before bed. Chad knew the room well from previous visits. There was a nineteen inch television with a VCR in there. A game system was connected to the TV and sat on the floor in front of it. To the left was the couch, an old one Trish had gotten cheap from a yard sale, and to the right was a stack of board games that were now never touched. The children favored the video games over the older board games and Trish had commented in the past how she needed to get rid of them.

The floor was carpeted with a brown, six-by-nine throw rug she'd had in another room upstairs and had gotten the idea to reuse it, not wanting to waste it. Besides, with the kids eating in the den, she knew putting a new rug in there would be a waste, as neither kid was a neat eater and stains were sure to follow.

A week after installing the carpet, her assumption was correct and a grape juice stain was soon followed by a ketchup one, then followed by a mustard stain.

Chad moved to the open doorway to the den and knew immediately he was correct in assuming the noise was coming from there.

It was as he stepped up and turned at the doorway, so he was standing in the middle of the opening, that his jaw dropped open and he felt his stomach heaving inside him, threatening to rise up and spew its contents all over Trish's brown carpeting.

But even if he had thrown up, the vomit wouldn't have mattered too much as the carpeting was now stained a dark red. A red so deep that if someone were to step on it, an inch of liquid would squirt out of the sides of the footprint.

Chad was speechless as he stared at the visceral scene of carnage in front of him, his mind not wanting to believe it was true. His sinuses reeled with the redolence of death and bile.

It couldn't be true, for no mother could ever do what Trish was doing at this precise moment in the middle of the den.

The video game system was knocked askew, the wires connecting it to the television now pulled out. The board games were pulled from their place on the shelves to be strewn across the floor, the boxes now open, different pieces from different games mixing together. Chad couldn't help but think what a pain it would be to have to figure out what game piece went where.

But that wouldn't be a problem, now or ever.

And the reason for that was the unbelievable sight Chad was looking down on.

On the floor, in the middle of the den, were the two children, but now they were nothing but a mangled mess of meat and bones. Bits of their clothing hung off the small bodies in rags, and with the sunlight streaming into the windows, the internal organs, now exposed to the air, glistened like snow-encrusted ice on a cold winter's day.

Their heads were all but severed from their small forms, only bits of gristle and tendons still defiantly holding on. The girl's body was in five pieces; all the limbs hacked off to be spread across the room like the limbs of a dismembered doll. The small boy's eyes were still open, the mouth gaping wide in a silent scream, and Chad felt his legs growing weak and felt like he was going to faint.

And it was possible he would have if not for the raging woman that came out from the corner of the room where she was hiding behind a partially open closet door.

With the guttural shriek from his attacker, Chad's head turned in the same direction and he immediately knew it was Trish, though only just.

She was covered from head to toe in congealing blood and in her right hand she wielded a wicked looking butcher's knife. Her eyes were manic, her mouth twisted up in a rictus of rage, the tendons on her neck taut.

When Chad turned to see her coming at him, he froze in shock, forgetting the candelabra he was still holding in his hand.

Trish screamed like a demon and slashed downward with the knife. Only dumb luck saved Chad from half the blade slicing into his chest.

As Trish came at him, Chad stepped away from her on instinct, like when someone throws a baseball at a person's face, and Trish was moving too fast and loose to shift her aim. Instead of the knife plunging into Chad's chest, the blade merely scraped along his ribs, leaving a dark red furrow that caused Chad to cry out in pain and surprise.

As he fell away from her, his feet became entangled and he fell, his left hip pummeling the floor, only the carpet saving him from true injury.

Trish was still moving, her eyes even wider now that she felt she had her prey within her sights. The blade came up again and then it was dropping directly for Chad's left eye.

It was like the next few seconds happened in slow motion for Chad. As the blade came downward, his vision could actually see the tip of the knife glinting in the sunlight filtering through the den windows as the tip moved ever closer to his eye.

But at the last second, he rolled away, the knife missing his head by a hairsbreadth, the tip sinking into the carpet with a muffled thunk.

Trish was still moving with abandon and she fell heavily to the carpet as Chad rolled away. But Chad didn't see where he was going, only wanting to escape Trish's viscous attack, and he ended up landing in the soupy goo that was the two children.

His right hand went up to his elbow in intestines, and even in his panic he could feel how the organs were still warm, the children murdered only minutes before he arrived. As he came up in a crouch, he was looking down at the small, severed head of the young boy, and Chad's mouth opened in a scream as he pulled his arm free of the viscous goo, stringy tendrils of red mucous clinging to his skin.

And then he had no time for squeamishness as Trish rolled onto her knees and charged him, the knife coming for his face.

Acting on pure instinct, Chad weaved away from the blade, the knife's edge missing his nose by an inch, and as he backpedaled, he realized he was still holding the candelabra.

But before he could lift it to defend himself, Trish screamed and threw the knife at him, the blade flying past his head to stick in the wall behind him. Then she was jumping on him, her body landing on top of him like a pro wrestler on crack.

Chad was forced to the carpeting, the sticky blood beneath him soaking into the back of his clothing and matting his hair to his scalp. Letting go of the candelabra, he raised his hands to defend himself as Trish began punching and kicking him, her hands curled into claws.

Unknown to Chad, his only saving grace was that Trish was so insane she had no formative ideas on how to attack him. Otherwise, she never would have thrown her knife at him. Her blood lust was so unimaginable, she had no rational thoughts, only images of violent death filling her mind to overwhelm her.

Chad knew none of this, all he knew was there was a maniac trying to kill him.

Trish managed to get in a few punches, her manic strength enough to cause him to see stars, but he was still stronger than her, and once he gained a small amount of his composure, realizing if he didn't fight back, she would eventually kill him, the battle turned in his favor.

Slapping her arms away, he reached up with his right hand palm-open, and sort of half-punched, half-slapped her under the chin. The gesture caused Trish's chin to rise up and her head to snap back. As this happened, Chad punched her in the throat with his left fist, causing Trish to gag as something fragile broke inside her neck.

When her eyes opened wider to suck in a breath of precious air, Chad bucked his hips and tossed her off him. But no sooner did Trish fall away, then she was rolling back on her knees, heedless of her now blue-colored face as she was slowly starved of oxygen. But she was slower now as spots filled her vision and Chad used the chance to reach out and pick up the candelabra once more. As Trish wheezed and came for him, he raised it high and brought it downward, the heavy metal bottom cracking Trish on the top of the head.

At the back of Chad's mind, he was surprised at how anticlimactic the entire incident was. When the weighted base of the candelabra connected with Trish's skull, there was a dull *smack* and the woman dropped to the carpet, a massive dent now in her scalp, pink brains peering out the sides to slip out. She dropped like a sack of potatoes, and other than a few twitches of her fingers and toes, the body remained still.

Breathing heavily, Chad was amazed at how quiet it now seemed to have become in the house, at least until the blood stopped surging in his ears and his pulse lessened. Once this happened, he could hear the steady sirens filtering in from outside and the occasional gunshot echoing through the landscaped yards.

He sat immobile for a while, time becoming meaningless. He might have stayed that way forever if not for Trish beginning to move again, as well as a low growl emanating from her damaged throat. She groaned loudly and her hands made fists in the rug, the blood-soaked carpeting squishing around her fingers.

Chad realized she wasn't dead yet, and not knowing what to do, and certainly not a murderer, he stood on shaky legs and headed for the front door.

Before he left, he glanced back one last time to see into the den. Sure enough, Trish's head was moving and her arms were shaking.

Totally freaked out to a degree he could never believe possible, he opened the front door and ran out into the waning daylight.

As he ran, he gazed up at the darkening sky, realizing he'd been inside Trish's house for hours. How many he wasn't sure, but he must have zoned out like a zombie as he sat in the pool of blood from the two children slaughtered by their mother.

Glancing down at his clothing, he saw he was covered in dark brown and reds, the congealing blood crusting in some places, his body heat keeping it soft in others.

He knew he was covered from head to toe in blood, but he didn't care, all he did was run, not knowing where to go but just wanting to escape.

So with his mind a complete blank, and sounds of violence and destruction all around him, he ran to parts unknown.

Chapter 4

Stacy Lewis sighed as she shuffled the papers on her desk. Glancing at the clock on the wall, she saw it was only eleven in the morning and she had a good six hours to go before she could clock out for the day.

The intercom beeped and she pressed the receive button.

"Yes, Mr. Masters?"

"Stacy, I need you, will you come into my office, please? And bring your notepad."

"Yes, sir," she said, opening the drawer on her left and taking out her notepad for dictation as well as two pens. Her boss must have something for her to take down and then type.

After all, she was his secretary and it was her job, as well as getting him coffee and some times picking up his dry-cleaning on the way to work. The last one might have upset her if not for the fact Mr. Masters was probably the only boss in the Chicago financial district she had worked for who had never tried anything funny with her. He was the perfect gentleman and she loved him for it.

As far as she knew, he was a happily married man of over twenty years with three kids now in college and a wife who kept busy in the charity circle.

If he was any other man, Stacy had no doubt he would have tried something by now. She had worked for him for a little over three months and so far he always treated her with the utmost respect.

Sure, she had caught him casting glances at her lithe frame, her firm breasts, her light-blonde, shoulder length hair that caressed her neck when she moved. Sure, she had seen him sneaking a glance at her buttocks as she exited the room, but that was all and Stacy had learned long ago not to take men looking at her in that way personally. From the age of twelve, when she began to blossom, boys had begun to look at her differently than her other friends. Her mother had explained to her how men were basically animals who were wired to spread their seed wherever possible. But most men knew how to control their urges, and though they might look with lecherous gazes, that was all they would do and most men never knew they were doing it, as it was so hardwired into their psyche.

So she considered herself lucky, and though Mr. Masters would eye her admiringly, that was all he did and she was okay with that. Sometimes she wondered if he took the images he was processing home and thought of her when he was making love to his wife. She didn't know why she thought these things, but she had an idea. The more someone wasn't interested and didn't pay you attention, the more you would want them to do that exact thing. So, though Mr. Masters was a perfect gentleman, deep inside she wished he would be a lecher, even if it was just for a few seconds.

With another weary sigh, she pushed away from her desk and went to the door leading to Mr. Masters' office. As she was invited, she didn't knock, but turned the doorknob and entered.

Mr. Masters was sitting behind his desk, his tie slightly loose as he talked on the phone. She knew to sit down in one of the two chairs in front of his desk and wait for him to finish. Once done, he would rattle off something and she would write it down and then type it up; he would sign it and off it would go.

Yes, she knew it wasn't the most challenging job in the world, but it was easy for her to do and it paid pretty well.

As she waited for her boss to finish his call, she couldn't help but study him. He was a handsome man in his late forties with strong arms and a strong chin. His hair was slightly receding, but not so much that he still wasn't handsome in her eyes, and by that she meant she wasn't attracted to bald guys. She liked her men with a full head of hair. He had piercing brown eyes and a smile that would make any woman melt, despite being ten years her senior.

Sometimes, Stacy wondered if he ever did try anything, if she would go along with it, even if it was just for a little while. Perhaps an office fling to break up the monotony, though she had learned the hard way they usually ended with her out of a job. Sure she would get a handsome severance package so she wouldn't scream sexual harassment, but once the affair was over, her boss would usually figure out a way to let her go.

That's why she was so glad Mr. Masters had never tried anything. She needed her job, having just gotten a new apartment downtown near The Loop, and she needed the paycheck to pay the rent. Chicago was an expensive city to live in.

Mr. Masters finished his call and spun in his chair to look at her as he set the phone back on its receiver.

"Ah, I see you're all ready to go," he smiled and she nodded.

With a shifting in his chair to get more comfortable, he leaned back; steepled his hands over his chest, and began dictating a letter for one of the investors while Stacy jotted it down in shorthand word for word.

As she worked she sighed. Just another day in the wonderful world of high finance.

Oh, well, she thought. *Maybe one of these days something interesting would happen to spice things up.*

Mr. Masters was finishing up dictating his letter to Stacy when suddenly he stopped in mid-sentence, his mouth falling open like he was in shock.

At first Stacy didn't know anything was amiss, but when her boss hadn't said anything for more than thirty seconds, she looked up at him and saw his weird expression.

"Sir, are you all right?" Stacy asked as she stopped writing and stared at her boss' face.

Mr. Masters didn't move, and Stacy thought he looked like a statue.

"Sir? Mr. Masters? What's wrong?"

She had images of him clutching his chest and falling over as he succumbed to a massive heart attack. Already her mind was racing with what she would do if that happened and she was setting her notebook on the edge of the desk so she could go to him.

But Mr. Masters didn't reach for his chest; instead he slowly closed his mouth and turned his head so he was staring directly at Stacy.

"Oh, there you are. You had me worried there for a second," she said as she began to calm down. "What happened, you lose your train of thought?"

He didn't reply, but looked at her with a blank expression.

Stacy locked eyes with her boss and she actually *saw* his orbs shift from a blank slate to something...what was the word...*off*, was the closest she could think of.

And there was now a hunger there she had never seen before.

"Mr. Masters? What's wrong?" she stammered, unsure of what to do or how to act. This wasn't proper office protocol right now, this was something else.

Oh, God, was he finally going to do it? Was he going to pass right by sexual harassment and go right to rape? she thought.

He could if he wanted to. His office was down the end of a long hallway, off the beaten path of the rest of the floor. She knew he paid extra for the office space; he liked being away from the general population, he said. Of course, he hadn't said this to her, she'd accidentally overheard it one time when an associate was in his office and the door was cracked a little.

So she could scream and call out for help but no one would hear her, no matter how loud she shrieked.

"Mr. Masters? James?" she stuttered.

Mr. Masters continued to stare at her, as if he was thinking of what to do next. And then, before Stacy realized what was happening, her boss jumped up and crawled over his desk like a gorilla, his eyes never wavering, his piercing gaze seeming to bore straight into her soul.

His face curled up into a snarl as a growl slid from his open mouth, and Stacy was awestruck, not understanding what was happening. This was so out of character for her boss it just didn't make sense, and a part of her refused to believe this scenario could truly be occurring.

But when Mr. Masters flew over the desk and crashed into her, causing her to tip over in her chair, her head striking the floor as her boss landed on top of her, she knew this was really happening and it had turned very dangerous to her well-being.

When he landed on her chest, her breath whooshed out of her lungs and she gasped for another taste of oxygen, all the while trying to fend off her boss.

Mr. Masters was snarling now, drool sliding out the corner of his mouth to drip onto her forehead while his hands tried to wrap themselves around her throat.

"James, what the hell is wrong with you?" Stacy gasped as she fought him from securing a killer grip on her neck; but it was no use. Mr. Masters was a strong man and it didn't take him long to push her arms aside and finally get her throat in his hands. Immediately, he began to squeeze, his eyes manic with anger and rage and Stacy's mouth opened and closed like a fish as she tried to breathe.

Despite all this, she felt something rub her stomach and realized her boss had a raging hard-on, the throbbing member pushing against her abdomen like it was going to burst out of his pants and impale her.

Her vision was growing cloudy and she could feel her pulse pounding in her head as loss of oxygen took its toll on her. As she gagged for air, she had visions of what would happen to her unconscious, or worse, dead body. She imagined Mr. Masters ripping her pants suit off and then fucking her like a wild animal, all the while her prone body helpless to do anything to prevent him.

These images gave her a much needed boost of adrenalin and she used that one last ounce of strength to do something to stop him from either knocking her out or killing her.

Letting go of his arms, immediately feeling his grip tighten on her throat, her arms went to her sides as she tried to find some sort of weapon. At first there was nothing but a few scattered pieces of paper, and then her left hand found her dictation pen. Her frantic fingers wrapped around it in desperation, and without slowing, no hesitation on what she was about to do, she brought up the pen and jammed the tip into Mr. Masters' right eye.

The orb was punctured like a hardboiled egg and the man screamed louder than before, only now his voice was filled with pain, not anger. A milky-white solution dribbled down his cheek to fly off as he shook his head back and forth. The pen lodged in deep, more than halfway, and his remaining eye flared with agony. Now distracted from pain, he let go of her throat.

Stacy bucked her hips and rolled away as Mr. Masters fell off her, his hands reaching for his wounded eye. His left hand wrapped around the tip of the pen and yanked, the pen sliding out, the clip at the end catching the orb and pulling it out with the pen, the deflated eye now looking like a flattened marble. The empty socket was now a red hole filled with a clear, pinkish, viscous fluid that seeped out of the hole to drip down his face; but he barely noticed.

Stacy got on all fours and began to crawl across the office floor while Mr. Masters roared in pain. But no sooner did he let out his first wail then he was turning and searching for Stacy again, his remaining eye flicking back and forth to try and compensate for the decreased depth perception.

Upon spotting Stacy crawling away from him, he leapt on all fours, like a jungle cat pouncing on prey. His right hand snatched at her ankle and began pulling her back to him.

Yelping in terror, she fell to the floor, her chin hitting so hard she felt her teeth rattle. She was just glad her tongue had been inside her mouth or no doubt she would have bitten it in half and died drowning in blood.

Mr. Masters yanked her back and screamed in rage as he prepared to fall on top of her. His face was a mask of blood now, the empty socket making him look like some kind of humanoid monster only seen in horror movies. With her one ankle trapped in Mr. Masters' grip, her other leg was free and she used it now, kicking out with the sole of her shoe.

The heel of her right shoe connected with his testicles and Stacy cringed inwardly when she felt them collapse under her blow like two small balloons filled with tapioca pudding.

This time Mr. Masters roared in pain so loud the paintings on the walls seemed to shake. When he released her foot to cup his shattered groin, Stacy turned over and crawled away again. Mr. Masters was on his knees as he looked down at his crotch with his remaining eye. There was now a large wet spot there, the remnants of his family jewels. The man wouldn't be fathering children now or ever again.

When he looked up again to stare at Stacy's retreating backside, his face twisted into a mask of absolute insanity. His once perfectly combed hair was now a matted rug from sweat and his blood-coated his face like clown makeup. His teeth were bright white beneath his trembling lips, and with a howl of rage that boarded on prehistoric, he launched himself at Stacy, who had made it to the office door and was reaching up with her hand, fingers prepared to grasp the doorknob.

Just before he reached her, she yanked the door open and tumbled into the long hallway. Mr. Masters was off balance in his anxiousness to grab and tear her apart and his head whacked the edge of the door as it popped open, right where the lock was. As he fell way, there was now an indentation of the locking mechanism on his forehead and he shook off the blow, feeling slightly dizzy for a second.

But seconds later, he was okay and was charging through the door and into the hallway, Stacy just now climbing to her feet in hopes of escaping. He laughed, knowing he had her trapped and Stacy began to back away, like she was being stalked by a lion. Her back came up against the wall, but she wasn't flush with it, and as her hand reached behind her, she found out why.

The bright-red fire extinguisher she passed every day before she entered the office was now pressing into her back, and as Mr. Masters moved closer to her, now slowing down, thinking he had her trapped, Stacy slid her arm behind her, trembling, fumbling fingers trying to disconnect the extinguisher from the wall bracket.

The gleam in her boss' remaining eye was enough to make her legs want to collapse under her. There was no mercy in that twitching orb, only pain and death.

"Please, James, don't do this, what's wrong with you?" Stacy pleaded as she fiddled with the small plastic strap holding the extinguisher. It was difficult as she couldn't see what she was doing; only being able to go by touch.

Mr. Masters didn't reply, but instead licked his lips. His hands curled into claws and then he was coming for her, his mouth hanging open, his tongue lolling out like a rabid dog.

Stacy screamed as adrenalin flooded her system for the hundredth time in the past five minutes. And then her fingers found their target and she was pulling the fire extinguisher off the wall, swinging it around to block Mr. Masters' charge.

As he came for her, she never slowed and her hand squeezed the trigger, breaking the small pin in the handle and sending white foam out of the nozzle directly into her boss' face.

Mr. Masters was thrown off balance and blinded as he swerved to the left, missing Stacy as he ran into the wall next to her. Rebounding hard, he bounced and dropped to the floor, his hands already wiping his one eye clear.

But Stacy knew this was her only chance to save herself and she sucked up every ounce of strength and fortitude she could muster and went on the attack, Mr. Masters now on the floor in front of her.

As the wild man looked up with his now irritated one eye, thanks to the foam, he blinked when he saw the bottom of the fire extinguisher coming straight for his face.

There was a meaty *crunch* as the bottom of the canister connected with his nose, flattening cartilage and pulping his features into mush. That was followed by a dull *clang* of metal on bone when the canister connected with his forehead and Mr. Masters was knocked to the floor, his brains rattling around in his skull like he was on a tilt-a-whirl at the carnival.

Stacy was lost in revenge now, her fear and terror at being a victim overriding her compassionate nature. With Mr. Masters on the floor, she began to pound his face and head repeatedly with the canister, each clang of metal on bone becoming slightly less loud, the impacts soon taking on a more meaty sound, squishy in nature.

This was due to the fact Mr. Masters' skull was becoming flattened, like his head had been jammed under a car tire as it rolled over him or better yet, placed in a vice and compressed. Stacy screamed now, Mr. Masters' blood spraying up to land on her face and chest, covering her in a scarlet solution that tasted coppery and had her blinking to see.

When she was finally done, her arms heavy from exertion, Mr. Masters' head resembled road kill, the skull now flattened with pinkish brains and dark red blood spread out in a semi-circle like a spilt bowl of tripe bathed in marinara sauce.

Stacy looked down on the mangled head of what was her boss only a minute ago and she stopped hitting him. The extinguisher fell from weak hands to land next to the now twitching body, and she stumbled backwards to the wall, sliding down to the floor with her head on her knees, which were pulled up tight to her chest.

It was over, she was safe, he was dead, but she had killed him.

She'd killed her boss, no one would believe what had happened and why should they? She had just murdered her boss and though it was self defense, she would have a hard time proving that to a jury of her peers.

In a nutshell, she was so fucked it was scary.

As she peered over her crossed arms at the bloody body, she began to cry, her body now shaking as the adrenalin drained from her system, her body now sensing the danger was over.

Putting her head down to her arms, she sat in a tight ball and cried, not caring that she was covered in sticky, congealing blood.

As she cried, she barely heard the ruckus coming from down the long hallway, where the rest of the office personnel had their cubicles. No, all Stacy was worried about was herself and her now shattered world, one that would never be the same again.

If she only knew how right she was, because Stacy's world would soon be altered into something resembling a nightmare from the darkest pit of her soul.

Chapter 5

Stacy stared at the corpse of her former boss as she sat huddled against the wall.

Her eyes were immobile, and if someone were to have watched her for more than a minute, they would have wondered if she was still alive.

But if that same someone had been diligent and didn't let their eyes waver, they would have caught the hint of Stacy's upper lip quivering. They might have noticed the few tears she shed that slowly crept down her cheeks to pool on the floor beside her. They might have seen the look of utter shock in her glazed eyes as she tried to rationalize what happened to her.

More than an hour passed without incident. No one came down the hallway from the outer floor to see what had happened. No one came to visit, which was odd. The mail boy, Rob, should have arrived by now with the day's deliveries.

Any other day Stacy might have noticed this, but not today. Today she was lost in a world of despair as she stared at the cooling body of James Masters.

Wiping her eyes clear, she sniffed and tried to regain some composure. Looking directly at the flattened pudding that was James Masters' face, she cleared her throat.

"Uhm, Mr. Masters...James, if you didn't know this already, I quit," she whispered to herself and then began to laugh. But not a normal laugh. This was a laugh of insanity as she tried to grasp what little bit of rationality within herself still remained.

She heard more cries and screams, mixed in with pounding, coming from the end of the hallway and her head snapped in the same direction. As she listened, she realized the noises had been going on ever since she collapsed to the floor, but in her unsettled state, she hadn't noticed until now.

What was going on out there? Were there people going crazy like Mr. Masters had? That seemed unlikely.

Well, she knew she didn't want to remain where she was.

Looking down at herself, she saw she was covered in blood, and when she touched her face with her fingers, she felt the stickiness there also.

Standing up, she felt her head swim for a second, and when things smoothed out, she took a step away from the corpse. She had to step over the wide pool of blood and she tittered again, thinking it funny how she didn't want to step in it even though she was now covered in it.

After a few steps, she was clear and she paused at a picture hanging on the hallway wall. The glass in the frame was easy to use as a mirror, and when she looked at the reflection therein, she was shocked to see not herself but a blood-coated shape that resembled her in form only.

My God, how much blood is on me? she wondered.

She tried to think back to when she was bludgeoning Mr. Masters, and she faintly recalled the blood shooting out of the man to spray her like a sliced garden hose filled with plasma instead of water. But in her terror she had ignored it.

Her hair was now matted to her skull and her eyes peeked through the red like two white marbles. When she opened her mouth her white teeth peered through her red lips like two pieces of Styrofoam.

It was uncomfortable to feel the stickiness, but the bathroom was back in the office and she didn't want to go back there. No, she would use the one out on the main floor, where there were other people who could help her.

As she stumbled away, her right hand leaning on the wall and leaving a red streak behind, she wondered how the hell she was going to explain this to the authorities.

At the end of the hallway, she paused at the double doors. Now the sounds of a ruckus grew louder and she almost didn't push the side bar down and open the door. If she had been thinking clearly, no doubt she wouldn't have, but she was still in shock from killing Mr. Masters and her reasoning skills were muddled.

Holding back the sobs welling up in her throat, she pushed open the doors and stepped out onto the main floor.

The door swung inward, and the sounds of violence grew in pitch as Stacy stared with openmouthed shock at the carnage before her.

She stood perfectly still in the doorway and watched silently as one of the temps, Amy was her name, stumbled up to Stacy, her arms held out pleadingly for help.

Stacy couldn't believe what she was seeing.

The woman was partially clothed, most now hanging from her body like rags. The left breast could be seen through the torn blouse, the pink nipple jutting outward defiantly.

Where Amy's eyes once were, there was now two gaping cavities, each dripping viscous fluid down her cheeks, the pinkish fluid a mockery of tears. Her left ear was missing and her bright red hair was hanging by bloody ribbons, as if someone had taken an interest in tearing it out strand by strand.

The wounded woman opened her mouth and Stacy saw her tongue was missing; the severed edge where the tip once was now looked like it had been bitten off. Blood seeped from the corners of her mouth whenever the woman wasn't swallowing, and Stacy felt her insides turning with sickness from the visceral sight.

Stacy didn't know what to do to help the poor woman, but Amy then veered to the left and wandered away, her arms forever reaching in front of her as she tried to find her way around the shattered main floor.

Stacy remained perfectly still, not wanting to move and call attention to herself.

All across the main floor, where there was once neat cubicles, there was now wreckage and gore. The cubicles had been knocked flat, the desks hiding behind them now overturned. Bodies were everywhere, pools of blood looking like small coy ponds. Arms and legs, severed from their owners, were spread across the commercial carpeting. Stacy saw a hand holding on to a cubicle wall that was still upright and as she watched, the fingers fell away. The hand dropped near the end of the small wall and she saw it was connected to nothing, the death grip on the cubicle finally releasing as blood dripped out of the open wrist.

A woman, a temp, was at a doorway to the supply closet, and three people were dragging her inside. Her hands grabbed fitfully to the frame to try and halt her progress, only her upper body visible as she screamed for help. Then she was yanked into the room and a second later a gallon of blood shot out of the opening and the screaming ceased, quickly followed by the sound of flesh being rent apart like splitting the legs from a cooked chicken.

And there were more living people here as well. All across the floor, men and women in disheveled office attire moved about, most carrying assorted limbs.

Their faces were covered in gore and more than one looked her way. She expected them to come for her but they didn't and she held her breath in anticipation of the assault.

To her right there was the mail boy, but he was most definitely through for the day as his torso was now a bloody mound of hamburger. Two men and a woman had used scissors and a stapler to carve out the young man's chest, cracking his ribcage and tearing out the organs within. Intestines were strewn across the floor like long, dead eels and she tried to hold her nausea back, not wanting to give her position away to any of these *people* that hadn't noticed her yet.

And then it happened.

Merle from accounting hobbled over to her. His balding pate was now coated in red blood and his thin wire-rimmed glasses were missing, the two beady eyes peering out of a face lathered in crimson. His tie was askew and his once white shirt was now a dark maroon, the inner pockets of his pants now hanging out, as if he was a poor man who wanted to show he had no cash.

As he moved up to Stacy, she saw the same maniacal expression on his features that had been on Mr. Masters and she was petrified. If this man attacked her and she tried to run, the others would see her and attack, too. One maniac had been bad enough, but now there was an entire floor filled with what appeared to be homicidal killers.

Merle moved up so he was inches from her face and sniffed her like a wild animal. Behind him, the others moved about, the ones not busy tearing into the prone bodies of co-workers looking for something to kill. Merle's nose was twitching as he moved up and down her and she realized this man was so far from the human he once was it was incalculable.

Somehow, he had been *changed* into something animalistic, with nothing but rage to fuel him onward. In his left hand he carried a severed arm and now he held it up to Stacy's nose, shoving it at her.

"*Here, you take it,*" he growled, but it was barely words, more just grunts and mumbles. It was as if he had lost the use of his language skills.

Stacy's mind was working overtime and her quick-witted skills at solving problems might be her only hope to save her life.

In an instant, she realized Merle thought she was one of them, that she was like him. Looking down at her arms and chest, she figured with all the blood coating her she must look like any of the other maniacs, and if so, then this charade may be her ticket to freedom.

Deciding she needed to take a more aggressive stance if she was to fool him, she twisted her face into one of anger and pushed him away.

"Fuck off, I don't want it," she snapped, standing her ground, adding a few growls for good measure.

Merle screamed at her, waving the arm in the air but Stacy swallowed the knot in her throat and didn't move. She knew, much like gorillas in the mist, to show fear would be the end of her.

"I said fuck off, Merle!" she yelled, her eyes going wide with a pure rage of her own. It wasn't hard, all the emotions she was feeling. Terror, grief, fear, all swirled inside her like a maelstrom. Merle stopped screaming and stared at her. Then he lowered his arms, turned around, and moved away, forgetting he had talked to her.

Stacy let out a silent sigh of relief, not believing it had actually worked. Deciding now or never, she took a step onto the main floor and began moving towards the elevator. She debated going to the stairs but she was twenty stories up and figured the elevator was as good as any other way to leave.

Besides, there were a lot more killers congregating by the stairwell door and she didn't want to run the gauntlet if she didn't have to. Stepping over a prone corpse of a secretary, the dead woman's eyes wide in death, the mouth hanging slack, Stacy continued to the elevator.

When she was a few feet away, another maniac stopped her. He wore a thousand dollar suit and his hair had once been maintained by a hundred dollar haircut, but now the man looked homeless. His once pristine suit jacket was wrinkled and covered in gobbets of flesh and his pants were soaked in blood, little drips falling off the cuffs as he walked. One of his five hundred dollar shoes was missing and the twenty dollar sock on that foot was now soaked in gore.

As he moved closer to Stacy, she turned to him and snarled like an animal. "Fuck off, asshole!"

The man growled back but he turned and moved away. Stacy reached the elevator and pressed the call button. As she waited, she turned around to watch the carnage unfold.

More than half the main floor was now dead and dismembered, the body parts scattered like decorations across the floor, while the rest hopped up and down and padded about, ripping what was left of the bodies into bloody chunks.

She watched a man and woman fight over a kidney, and she half expected one of them to shove the organ into their mouth, much like the zombies she had seen at the movies, but no such thing happened.

Evidently the blood lust was for killing, not feeding.

There was a pleasant *ding* and the door slid open and she was halted when she saw the car was occupied. But the passenger inside the elevator wouldn't be getting off on this floor or any other.

The man was slumped against the wall, his arms and legs spread out and he had a black hole the size of a quarter dead-center on his forehead. The back of his head and the inside of his skull were spread out behind him, the brains sliding down the stainless steel wall to leave slimy snail trails behind.

Telling herself the man was dead and couldn't hurt her; she stepped into the elevator and pressed the button for the lobby.

As the door swung closed and the elevator began to descend, she let out one more weary, yet relieved sigh, telling herself that whatever was happening was over and soon she would be free of the building and safe on the street.

Yes, she told herself, once she left the building everything would be fine.

Chapter 6

The elevator doors opened onto the first floor lobby and Stacy stepped out, expecting the security guard at the far desk to look up and run to her when he saw she needed help. After all, she was covered in blood from head to toe.

But that was the farthest thing to happen, she found out as she looked around the lobby.

The security guard wasn't behind his desk, but instead was standing in the middle of the lobby, his gun in his hand as he took potshots at people who were hiding behind planters and chairs,

Five bodies sprawled across the polished stone floor attested to the man's marksmanship and as Stacy stepped out, a bullet whined by her head, embedding itself in the wall of the elevator.

Screaming, she ducked down to the floor as another bullet missed her by inches and she looked back and forth like a scared rabbit.

When she turned to her right, she was greeted by the gaze of one of the building's cleaners. The short, Spanish man had wide eyes filled with rage and he growled like a rabid beast as he lunged for her.

Stacy, screaming, fell away from him, and as the man stood up to pounce on her, his head suddenly rocked to the side and half his head dissolved into bone and brain matter.

The body fell to the floor and landed on Stacy who kicked and screamed as she pushed the corpse off of her. More blood covered her face and neck thanks to the dead man's head wound and she spit copper as she rolled to her side, panting as her heart beat a steady staccato of fear in her chest.

The security guard was laughing as he shot an old woman in the chest.

The poor geriatric spread her hands wide as she tumbled over a chair, her face slack in death. More people ran at him, wanting to satiate their bloodlust, but the guard shot them dead, the bodies flinging back to land heavily on the floor as their life's blood pumped out of the wounds with each beat of their slowing hearts. The guard was yelling now, reveling in his power, the power of the gun, as he shot round after round at the shifting bodies.

But then the security guard's gun clicked dry, and before the man could attempt to reload, ten people came out of hiding and charged at him. Before the guard could do anything but cry out, he was knocked off his feet and promptly killed, his laughter, now mixed with screams, echoing off the stone columns.

Stacy could only watch in horror as the man's spleen and kidney were ripped out of the cavity to be tossed away like refuse.

She took in this information, though.

The guard had worn the same maniacal look of the other crazy people, but he had tried to shoot his fellow killers. In turn, they had reciprocated the gesture, attacking him once he ran out of bullets.

Stacy looked to her left to see a large, heavy set man who had to weigh more than three hundred pounds. He wore a suit jacket and corduroys, both looking like if she had them with her in the woods when she was camping, she could get a few wooden poles and use them as a tent.

The man was on the floor and he was crawling from planter to chair, to the next planter. As Stacy watched him, she could see the large man was normal, like her. Though his eyes were filled with fear, there was no rage lodged within the shifting orbs.

The man looked up and his eyes locked with hers and he halted for a second, realizing he had been spotted, but when Stacy didn't move or yell out or do anything aggressive to him, the man sighed, not knowing why Stacy was leaving him alone but grateful. Once again Stacy realized she looked like one of the killers, now covered in blood and gore, and she realized she could use that to her advantage to escape the lobby.

It was as she was about to take her first step towards the main glass doors leading to the street that the fat man was spotted by three killers. Before the man could do more than shriek in terror, the three killers were on top of him, tearing at his clothing to expose the flab beneath.

One man held a six inch hunting knife, and as the fat man squealed like a stuck pig, the killer slashed the large man's belly like he was gutting a freshly killed deer.

As the flesh parted, rolls of lumpy fat spilled out of the gash to splash onto the stone floor like curds of cottage cheese. There seemed to be gallons of it, for all purposes looking like liposuction gone bad.

The large man had a lot of body fat in him, and as the killer began to cut some more, his fellow attackers sank their hands into the large gash, now ripping it open like they were peeling the skin from an orange.

The fat man shrieked in pain as his insides were slowly torn apart, blood shooting into the air to splash warmly onto the killer's faces. The attackers opened their mouths and lapped the plasma up, like children playing at a water fountain in a school hallway, using their thumb to press on the spot and cause the water spray to shoot across the corridor.

Stacy felt her bowels go cold at the sight of the man being slaughtered, but she was acutely aware of her own welfare. She knew there was nothing she could do for the poor man and at the moment, she needed to only think of herself.

So with one last look at the dying fat man, she took another step away from the elevator and began walking through the lobby, while behind her, the fat man's screams for mercy fell on deaf ears.

Upon reaching the entrance doors, she glanced to her right to see the security guard. He was now in multiple pieces, his arms and legs spread out like a destroyed Ken doll after an unstable child was through with it.

His eyes were still open, but were now glazed in death as the killers working on him finished ripping him apart and then moved off to see who they may have missed hiding in the lobby. Stacy repressed the shudder she felt coursing through her as she pushed the doors open and stepped outside.

Whatever dream she had of things being okay once she left the lobby was quickly dashed as she gazed back and forth on the street.

It was complete chaos, with men and women running to and fro, many sprawled on the sidewalk or in the street with their attackers on top of them.

She watched a woman get run down as she ran for her life, and as the male attacker climbed onto her back, he grabbed her hair and began smashing her face into the pavement until there was nothing left of her features but a bloody pulp. He leaned back like he was riding a horse and howled to the sky, then climbed off her and charged after another runner.

Stacy looked to her right to see a man raping a woman on the hood of a car. The woman's skirt was high, covering her chest, and the man was on top of her, pumping for all he was worth. The woman's face was bloody from the pummeling she had received and as she was impaled again and again, her eyes looked back and forth for someone to help her. But there was no one to save her for each person not turned into a raving lunatic was now fair game.

Stacy stepped to the side of the door, staying out of reach of anyone running past her. Once again, none of the killers noticed her, each assuming she was one of them.

A large explosion filled the sky and Stacy turned and looked up and over the nearby rooftops.

The top floor of the Sears tower suddenly exploded as glass shards and bits of metal shot forth into the air to fall back to the earth where people were unaware of the danger plummeting down on them.

Many were impaled like shish-kabobs while others were flattened by rubble.

She saw a man, covered in gore, stop and look at her, as if he was going to attack her. But then a long, three foot piece of glass, impaled him, slicing into his head like a guillotine and exiting out his groin. The man stood immobile, staring at Stacy, and then his left and right halves fell away from one another to splatter onto the street. The man had been neatly sliced in twain, his internal organs sloshing to the sidewalk as his blood shot into the air as his heart beat its last few times.

Stacy looked up at the tower to see flames licking out of the windows and she wondered what had caused the explosion...not that it mattered.

A cab drove by with a screaming man hanging out the rear door with his coat caught in the jamb: he was running half in and half out of the cab. As the cab swerved down the street, bouncing off parked vehicles, the man lost his footing and fell, to then be dragged behind, pulled along like a leash when a dog escapes its master. He was scraped against the pavement like he was being pressed against a giant cheese grater, his skin shredding to red mush, leaving a red streak behind the screaming body.

By the time the cab passed her, Stacy was turning a far corner, and the man was nothing but a bloody mess of meat and bones, half his body scraped against the asphalt to the bone. In the bloody trail where he had been rubbed raw, she saw bits of red clothing mixed in with moist gobbets of flesh.

Stacy turned away, not wanting to look any more.

Sirens filled the day and she saw a police car approaching. The squad car honked its horn and blew its siren, and as Stacy watched, the squad car pulled up onto the sidewalk and two officers climbed out.

But if she thought they were going to help, she was sorely mistaken.

Like a well drilled team, both officers pulled their service revolvers, and with a yell of rage and anger, they began firing into the screaming, running crowd.

A man was struck in the back by one of the bullets, and as his chest exploded outward with bloody ribbons of flesh and bone, he pitched forward, his nose collapsing on impact with the street. He didn't move again.

A woman was running across the street, her arms waving in the air for help after seeing the two officers. She wore the uniform of a waitress and Stacy recognized her from the diner at the end of the block. The woman barely made it halfway to the two policemen before she was struck three times, one in the chest, one in the throat and one in the forehead. Any of the three bullets were kill shots but all three at the same time was devastating.

The waitress was stopped in mid-run and was thrown off her feet, her arms going limp before she hit the asphalt. Her head smacked the pavement so hard it cracked what was left of her skull, but her brains were already splattered behind her thanks to the shot to the forehead. Another woman wearing a light gray power suit tried to run to a nearby building, but she was shot in the back, the punch sending her flying forward and into traffic. A speeding car never bothered to swerve around her, and like she was a human speed bump, the driver ran over her. Stacy heard the audible crack as the woman's rib cage shattered into bone fragments. Stacy muffled a cry of anguish, knowing to show emotion other than rage would be noticed by the killers around her.

Then a bullet ricocheted a foot from her head and she ducked down, now realizing the cops might not care who they shot.

Deciding she needed to get off the street before she was shot, she stayed low and began to move down the sidewalk, using the cars at the parking meters for cover.

A windshield exploded behind her and she screamed in fear, now going so low she was almost crawling.

A man popped out from between two cars and snarled at her.

Not knowing what to do, she growled back. "Fuck off, asshole!" she screamed.

The man stared at her for another second and then turned and scuttled away. Stacy watched the man run into the street where he was shot in the shoulder. Blood spewed from the wound as a large chunk of flesh was taken away. The man grabbed his wound, picked himself up and hobbled away like he was stung by a bee and wasn't going to bleed out in a few minutes.

Stacy turned and moved away, her eyes trying to watch every direction at the same time.

The coffee shop at the end of the street was in flames, and as she peered through the smoke, she could see the prone bodies of the patrons strewn about the place.

It was while she stared into the smoke clouds that a form materialized out of the gray fog. With the smoke lowering the visibility,

Stacy couldn't see what was in the figure's hand, but as it moved closer and she saw it was a man, he stepped out of the shattered glass wall of the shop, and Stacy realized the man was carrying a woman's decapitated head, now using the hair like the strap on a purse.

As he walked, the head slapped his hip, bouncing and spinning like a ball at the end of a string.

The eyes in the head were wide open in death, the mouth hanging low, and as the man moved closer to her, Stacy saw the mouth of the head had no tongue, only a gaping hole surrounded by blood-red teeth. The once red lipstick was smeared across the lower chin and mascara dripped down the face from when the woman had cried tears as her life was taken from her.

Stacy knew she couldn't show emotion or the man would know she wasn't one of them, so gritting her jaw, she stood her ground, staring the man down as he stepped out of the coffee shop and passed her with barely a glance.

When he was gone, rounding the corner at the end of the street, she let out a sigh, but not too much of one for fear of being discovered.

Another car sped by with screeching tires, blaring its horn loudly, and when Stacy turned to see it, she saw five men and one woman hanging onto the roof and hood. One held a baseball bat which he whacked repeatedly on the roof, caving it in an inch at a time.

As for the driver, he was wide-eyed with terror as he tried to swerve the car to shake off his attackers. He sideswiped a Toyota and careened around the intersection, Stacy hearing the car bouncing off other stalled vehicles.

People ran past her, a few naked, their modestly now gone, along with their rationality, their newfound bloodlust now in control.

Stacy knew she needed to get off the street so she began moving down the sidewalk once more. Her eyes went up to the Sears Tower looming over the city and the smoke billowing from the upper floors was an ominous sign of what was to come.

A helicopter flew overhead and she glanced up, assuming it was a news copter but then, as she watched, the helicopter banked to the left and began to wobble like there was a drunk in the pilot's seat.

She was just thinking the helicopter looked like it was flying too low when it seemed to stall in the air and then the nose pointed straight down. It dropped like a rock and was lost from sight as it fell a few streets over from where she stood, but she heard the loud *bang* as the aircraft impacted with a building to then explode, shaking nearby windows in their frames.

A pillar of smoke rose into the sky and she knew the helicopter was destroyed. Turning away from the dark-black cloud, she began walking down the street.

As she had seen the other killers running, she decided that was what she would do, so she picked up her pace. It wasn't hard, her adrenalin was pumping and all she wanted to do was run, her instincts wanting her to run long and hard.

So with the city falling deeper into chaos, Stacy took off at a distance-eating jog. Reaching the next intersection, she averted her gaze to the five-car pileup with corpses hanging out the doors and shattered windows like they were old Halloween directions spilling out of a box in an attic.

With those images of dead faces now burned into her memory, she focused her gaze forward. With tears of horror and fright sneaking from the corners of her eyes, she ran, her blood-soaked body blending into the scenery until she was lost in the maelstrom of insane humanity.

Chapter 7

Chad's feet were killing him.

He'd been running for more than an hour and he felt like he was going to drop from exhaustion. Though not overweight, his job didn't require much physical exertion from him so he was like most Americans, lazy and slow. As he ran through his neighborhood and into the next town, he witnessed the same madness.

One house was on fire and at the front door were the remains of a middle-aged woman. Half her head was missing and her torso was ripped to shreds, reminding him of what someone looks like after being mauled by a mountain lion.

While he stared at the poor woman, a man had appeared in the doorway. If he cared that his house was on fire, he showed no emotion, and as Chad watched him, the man flipped him off, then pulled a long steak knife from his belt and knelt down by the corpse of the woman, quickly going to work hacking at what was still left intact. A wedding ring flashed on his left hand and Chad wondered if the corpse had been his wife, but then he moved on, not wanting to watch the grisly scene any longer.

Cars and trucks were few and far between, though more than once he came across accidents. Metal bumpers and fiberglass was entangled to the point that two vehicles became one, and more than half had either dead bodies sprawled in some horrible form of death across seats, car hoods or just had blood splatter on all the surfaces.

And children weren't spared whatever madness was engulfing the Chicago area.

Chad slowed when he came upon a daycare on what was once a quiet side street. The street seemed to have escaped most of the chaos he had seen in other parts of town and he wondered if he might find a place to hole up, even if it was just for a few hours.

The house was painted in a crisp blue with a decorated sign on the front lawn. Balloons were attached to the sign and the name of the daycare was painted in colorful colors.

Only he couldn't make out the name of the daycare now as the sign was covered over with the bright red words, ***KILL 'EM ALL***. They were painted in terrible penmanship, like a drunken artist had done the work.

He would have kept going, but he heard crying. It sounded like a child, and though he wanted to keep moving, not wanting to stick his nose where it wasn't needed, his conscience wouldn't let him continue onward with a child in need somewhere in the house. So, though he wasn't a hero, far from it actually, he decided he needed to investigate the house

With one more glimpse back and forth on the street, and satisfied that for the moment there was no one around to fear, though the sounds of sirens and screams could be heard in the distance, he turned and headed for the front door of the daycare, and the crying child within.

He didn't know what to expect when he entered the daycare facility, but what he found was something from his darkest nightmares.

Just inside the doorway was where the pool of blood began. An inch thick, it spread out from the center circle of corpses and followed the slight slant in the floor. The walls were splashed with crimson, splatter on the ceiling, resembling a giant Rorschach painting.

Chad gasped when he saw the bodies. The corpses were tiny, some no more than three feet tall with jagged bones sticking out of their torn flesh. He stared at the carnage and took in the charnel house smell for almost fifteen seconds, then he hunched over and emptied his stomach, the warm vomit splashing into the blood at his feet to make a disgusting slurry that had him vomiting until he could take it no more. After his stomach was clear and spasms finally resided, he raised himself to a standing position and stared once more at the small corpses.

These had been children. How in God's name could someone do this to such innocence?

There was the severed head of a small girl, no more than five, near the edge of the mangled bodies and butterfly clips still clung to the once red hair. The eyes were creased, as if the girl was just waking up from a nap, but as the head was severed from the body, Chad knew the little girl would never wake up from the deep sleep she'd been forced to enter.

A little boy no more than three lay sprawled across an armchair. The boy's shirt had been torn open, revealing horrible slash marks on every inch of skin. The boy's abdomen was sliced open, much like gutting a fish, and one thin coil of intestine protruded, looking like a large worm breaking free of the wet soil on a cool summer morning. The boys mouth was wide open in a silent scream, the eyelids closed for a change, but still Chad's stomach churned within him, and though there was nothing more to expel, his stomach did its best to try. Gagging, he leaned over and squeezed his eyes shut as the spasms wracked his body, the visceral scene of death too much for his fragile mind to take. When the dry heaves were finished, he went to the blood-soaked couch and pulled a wool blanket from its side, then tossed it over the boy, not able to look at the cherub-like face locked in a death mask of utter agony.

After that he kept his eyes looking away from the dismembered children, knowing he was on the verge of cracking. Once more he wondered if this was the onset of the disease or virus, or whatever was changing people into raving killers. But he forced the thoughts from his mind. There was nothing he could do about it if it was true so there really was no reason to focus on it. Chad's face had lost what color it had, the dash from his house and now the slaughtered children making him look like an old man, frail and weak.

Remembering why he came into the house to begin with, he stepped around another small corpse and moved deeper into the house. He was amazed at the sheer volume of flies already on the corpses, feeding on the blood and open wounds. Maggots could be seen squirming in the open cavities and Chad felt the need to retch once more but forced it down.

He was beginning to wonder if perhaps he had imagined the crying in the first place, as by the look of things in the house, nothing could possibly still be alive.

Walking to the opposite end of the room, he saw there was a long hallway.

The saying, *in for a penny, in for a pound*, came to him and he stepped lightly onto the thin runner on the floor.

The crying must have come from one of the doors that branched off the hallway on both sides. He paused, wondering if he should find himself a weapon, but as he looked around the sparse hallway he saw nothing he could use.

So deciding a child couldn't hurt him anyway, he moved on, slowing as he reached the first door. The door had a number 1 in the middle of it, about head height, and when he glanced at the other doors, he saw each one was also numbered.

His hand moved like it was underwater, rising to the doorknob ever so slowly. A large knot was in his throat and a small voice speaking in the back of his head, telling him to forget it, to get the hell out of there and keep running.

But he forced it down. He was no hero, that was true, but he couldn't just leave this place if a child was in danger or might need his help. His hand grasped the cool doorknob, the shaped glass making it easy to hold onto, despite his now sweaty palm.

Swallowing the knot in his throat, he counted to three in his head and then turned the knob, pushing the door open and standing perfectly still.

He didn't know what to expect as the door swung inward, and he breathed a sigh of relief to see the room was empty.

It was a small office. There was a wooden desk in the corner with a computer and a printer, and to the right was a file cabinet. There was a poster on the wall of a small kitten with big wide eyes. The kitten was hanging from a tree branch by its front paws. The words: **Hang in there, kid** was written in black script on the top of the poster. There was a coffee mug on the counter and the words, *I HATE MONDAYS* was scrawled on it. The mug had a chip on it.

Chad assumed this was where the owner of the daycare must have kept his or her office, though he assumed it was a woman. He tittered to himself, thinking about what he'd thought. He'd *assumed*, as in, he'd made an *ass* out of *you* and *me*.

He knew his giggle was from stress and everything he'd witnessed so far, but he also wondered if he wasn't slipping a little more into madness. Once more he wondered if maybe he was going to become another homicidal killer, but for some reason it was taking longer to affect him.

That made him wonder once again what had happened to everyone in the city.

Biological warfare, government testing; what could cause normal people to lose their minds like he'd seen?

With the office empty, he turned and moved down the hallway, and upon reaching the next door, he was slightly more relaxed. This was due to finding the office behind him empty.

Maybe the entire house was empty and he'd imagined the crying. Perhaps it was a symptom of what made people crazy and he was now in the first stages of going bonkers himself.

The blood covering him from head to toe itched where it was drying on his skin, but he ignored it, concentrating on the door in front of him.

It was like the others, the number 2 on this one.

Reaching for the doorknob, he wasn't as cautious as he should have been, partially due to the fact he was exhausted. So as the door swung open, Chad was entirely taken off guard when a woman no more than five feet tall with small hands and beady eyes came charging at him with a knife.

Later, when he was safe, Chad would wonder why the woman was hiding in what was obviously the kitchen, and why she hadn't come out when he'd entered the house, but for now he knew he needed to deal with her. Though not a brave man, the woman's small stature made her seem almost comical, despite the knife she wielded in her hand.

As she came at him, Chad stepped back so he was in the hallway again, and when the woman charged him, having to shift her hand with the knife in it to get through the doorway, Chad punched her as hard as he could in the chin.

It was like she'd run into a stone wall. Chad's blow wasn't very hard but his outstretched arm and the momentum of the woman was enough to rock her head back and shatter her jaw.

She went down hard, the knife arm falling under her, and she accidentally impaled herself, the blade sliding through her breast, ribcage and then into her heart, slicing the muscle in twain and killing her instantly.

Blood began to seep out from under the twitching corpse as Chad looked on, staring at his outstretched arm with his hand curled into a fist. In less than a minute, the body had stopped twitching and remained still. He felt powerful then, a feeling of strength filling him. He had defended himself and won.

Then he glanced at the small woman and came back to reality.

Huh, some tough guy, he beat up a woman barely five feet tall. He peered into the kitchen to make sure there were no other attackers and then he stepped inside the room.

It looked like a thousand kitchens across the country with the exception of the dead woman lying on the floor. There was a white refrigerator on his right, the front covered with drawings of houses and waving stick figures. On the top of the fridge were Saltines, cookies and paper towels, as well as a loaf of bread. There was a small sink on the left and it was filled with dirty cereal bowl dishes, residue of milk in a few as well as small bits of cornflakes. On the table, a large bowl of half eaten jell-o lay melting, a container of whip cream by its side. Across from the sink was the stove, and on it was a dirty pan, looking like it might have contained eggs at one time.

A knife set was sitting in a wooden holder to his right and he reached out and pulled one free. He glanced at the cabinets next, seeing the colorful paintings of watercolors and crayons from the children.

The same children who now lay dead in bloody pieces in the main room of the home. Then he heard a muffled sob and his eyes went to the large oak table in the far corner of the kitchen. Another sob came to him and he knelt down and peered under the tablecloth to see a frightened child hiding there.

As he moved closer, the child pulled a heavy chair closer to him and Chad realized the child hadn't been slaughtered like the rest due to the fact he was in a good hiding place and had managed to stay free as the woman had tried to get him.

The woman couldn't reach him with the chairs in the way, the child having a death grip on them, and the table was too heavy for the woman's small stature to move. So the child had survived, at least for a little while. Chad knew what would have happened if he hadn't shown up when he did.

Chad leaned down and smiled, not realizing with his face and clothing covered in gore he certainly didn't look very friendly.

"Hey, there, buddy, my name's Chad. I'm, not gonna hurt you," he said with as much charm as he could muster. Behind him on the floor, the woman's body cooled as blood meandered its way across the linoleum.

Seeing the knife in his hand and noticing the child staring at it, Chad set it down by his side, wanting to appear as friendly as he could in such a situation.

"Oh, sorry, 'bout that, here, see? It's gone now." He cupped a hand in a *come here*, gesture. "Come on out of there, I won't bite you."

The child sniffed a few times, wiped tears from his face, and then moved around the chair.

"That's it, come on, let's get you cleaned up," Chad said soothingly.

He was about to say more as he watched the child crawl out from under the table when Chad's eyes went wide in surprise as the child's face went from one of terror to one of rage.

Chad actually saw the change in the small boy. The eyes seemed to lose whatever intelligence was living there, snuffed out like a candle in a hurricane, and something far more sinister replaced it.

The boy was halfway out from under the table when he opened his mouth and snarled like a dog. He scampered on all fours at Chad who was taken aback by the little hellion. Chad fell onto his butt as the child scurried out from under the table, then the boy's eyes spotted the knife on the floor. Before Chad realized what the boy's intentions were, the child slid across the floor and picked up the knife, then turned back to Chad with malevolence glowing in his tiny blue orbs.

"No, son, put the knife down, please," Chad begged. Though the small boy wasn't too much of a threat, one good slash of the knife could cause Chad serious harm. With the way the city was acting, he could only imagine the chaos at the local hospitals. No, he wouldn't be seeking medical attention at a medical health facility anytime soon, which made the child all the more dangerous.

The boy snarled like a wolf this time and charged at Chad who jumped back, tripping over a chair behind him. He went flying backward and it was only dumb luck that prevented him from cracking his head on the hard floor.

The boy never slowed, and as Chad fell, the child jumped onto the chair and between Chad's now wide open legs. The boy was staring at the apex of Chad's crotch and Chad realized what the boy intended.

"Oh, shit," Chad gasped as the boy raised the knife over his head, a feral gleam in his eyes. Thinking fast, though panic filled him to his very soul, Chad pulled his left leg back and used it to kick the chair out from under the boy.

The child found his chair gone and he seemed to hover in the air like an old Looney Tunes cartoon, but then gravity took over and he dropped, his legs seeming to be running in mid-air for a brief second. But he was young and quick and he landed without harm, then slashed the knife at Chad's leg and charged again.

Shrieking in fear, Chad kicked out and his shoe caught the boy a glancing blow on his shoulder. The boy went flying to the right and landed a few inches from Chad's head.

The child turned his head and hissed at Chad who gulped and rolled away, coming to his feet in an instant. As did the boy.

Man and boy faced each other and Chad wracked his brain for what to do next.

This was a child, and though crazy, he still didn't want to hurt the little boy.

But the decision was taken from him when the boy came at him again, knife leading the way.

Chad danced back and yelped.

"Cut this shit out, kid, or so help me..." Chad threatened, though he could tell his warnings were falling on deaf ears.

The boy never hesitated; if anything he renewed his attack, wanting to see Chad's blood flow across the kitchen floor. Chad backed up as far as he could go and found himself cornered by the stove.

The boy laughed in victory, more of a giggle really, and with an evil gleam in his eyes prepared to lunge at Chad who had nothing but bare arms to protect himself with.

As the boy went for him, Chad reached behind his back, hands desperately searching for something to use as a weapon and his right hand found the handle to a frying pan with the residue of eggs in it.

Elation filled him as he wrapped his fingers around the handle and pulled the pan around, the arc following through to end up cracking the boy on the side of the head.

Like a small sack of potatoes, the boy fell to the side, dropping to the floor and sliding a foot to strike the refrigerator. Colorful magnets and pictures rained down on his head. The knife went clattering away and Chad let out a massive sigh of relief.

But no sooner did the boy come to a stop then he groaned and began to force himself to his feet again, only now with blood seeping from a jagged cut on his forehead. At one time, before the boy had *changed*, the cut would have elicited cries for his Mommy and wails of having a boo-boo, but now the boy ignored the throbbing wound.

Before Chad could move, the boy slid across the floor like a snake and found the knife again.

"Oh, come on," Chad gasped as the boy rolled onto his back, and with glazed eyes growled some more, the noise coming from low in his throat like a Doberman on guard duty who had found an intruder. The boy was dazed, perhaps having a concussion, but the adrenalin and rage fueling his mind overcame the blow to the head.

It was a frightful thing to witness first hand.

The boy sat up, his head swooning, but Chad could see in less than a minute they would be dancing again.

He had to make a decision. Should he run for it? Should he leave the house and keep running until he found someplace safer? No, this seemed to be a good place to hide for a while as everyone was already dead. He knew once the child was stopped he could rest, get something to eat, maybe even sleep for a few hours.

That decided it for him, and when the boy tried to get to his feet, Chad walked up to him and conked the boy over the head with the pan, a dull metallic *thwack* sounding as cast iron met the small skull.

The boy sat perfectly still for five seconds, his eyes rolling up into his head, then he slumped and fell over, out for good...at least for now.

Chad stared down at the small boy, a conundrum now affecting him. Just what exactly was he supposed to do with the child?

He shook his head, realizing he was too exhausted to care right now and he glanced around the kitchen, his eyes settling on a small pantry at the far end, the door slightly ajar.

Deciding this would work as good as anyplace else, he picked up the unconscious boy, carried him to the pantry, using his foot to open the door, and set the child on the floor, next to a ten pound bag of potatoes.

The shelves were lined with bottles of water, canned goods, boxes of cereal, snacks and crackers, so he grabbed a handful of each and then closed the pantry door, leaving the child locked inside.

For the moment that was the safest palace to keep the boy...for both of them.

With that problem solved, he went to the dead woman in the hallway and dragged her down into the main room filled with the tiny corpses, leaving her there. Chad wondered if it was the woman alone who had slaughtered all the children, and shook his head in sadness at the thought.

He snuck a peek out the front windows to see what the street looked like, and other than a few people running by with scared looks on their faces; no one was paying attention to the daycare. He was as safe as he could be for the moment. He could smell smoke as it seeped into the house and it had that acrid odor of a burning house. Insulation, vinyl siding, and furniture, that special smell that only came with a home going up in flames. But the fire wasn't nearby so he didn't give it any more thought.

Swatting at flies as he left the room, he went through the rest of the house quickly, praying he wouldn't find anymore children or crazed adults.

Ten minutes later he was finished, and with the last room inspected, he went back to the kitchen. He sat down at the heavy oak table, sighing heavily as he cracked open a can of peanuts and a bottle of water, devouring handfuls at a time.

His eyes went to the pantry once more but no sound came from within. The boy was still out cold.

After eating the entire can of peanuts and two boxes of snack crackers, washing it down with three bottles of water, he leaned back in the kitchen chair, bent forward, and set his head down on his arms which were crossed on the table.

He was so tired it hurt.

Though he didn't think he could sleep, his mind racing from the horrors he'd witnessed this day, he was out in seconds. Before he knew it, he was sleeping, lost in visions of madmen, while nightmares of slashed bodies and severed heads floated across his mind's eye like mist in the night.

Chapter 8

Stacy was five blocks away from her office building when she finally slowed down, too tired to run any longer. This part of the city was no different than where she'd been. All around her, people were going insane, turning into homicidal killers. A few married couples, still feeling an attachment, even after *changing*, were rutting on the hood of parked cars or in the middle of the street like dogs in heat.

Stacy slowed as she approached one particular couple.

The young woman was on the bottom, on the hood of a Buick, her man humping her like it was the end of all days.

He was biting one of her nipples, and as Stacy watched, the man's teeth clamped shut, severing the nipple from the breast. The woman moaned in pleasure and forced his head down more as she grinded beneath him like her life depended on it.

When Stacy passed them by, the woman glared at her, snarling, white teeth flashing in the sun.

"He's mine, fuck off, bitch!" she growled, the sentence barely intelligible.

Stacy blinked at the woman's words, not used to hearing any of the *changed* talking, but she quickly turned and continued on, while the woman screamed in ecstasy behind her.

She made it through another two blocks before deciding she needed to find a place to rest for a while. There was a pizza parlor across the street, so she headed for it. The large front window was shattered and there were bodies strewn about, looking like mannequins for a store window display haphazardly tossed to the floor in preparation for being set up. There was a sign blinking on the wall that bragged that this particular pizza parlor had the best deep dish pizza in the city.

As she stepped into the restaurant, her stomach rolled inside her as she stared at the corpses sprawled on the tables and chairs. The tile floor was awash with blood, beer, salt and pepper shakers, and pieces of pizza, the red sauce becoming lost amid the pools of congealing blood.

One particularly gruesome corpse was sprawled near the shattered window. The corpse had been an elderly woman, her arms and legs spread at odd angles, bones protruding from her wrinkled flesh like twigs and branches breaking through a plastic bag. She had taken three gunshots to the chest; the impacts of the rounds ripping open her torso like a shattered watermelon to expose the fractured ribcage and deflated lungs. One wrinkled breast sagged to the side, only strands of tattered skin to keep it in place. The old woman was wearing a printed dress with butterflies of different colors. Most of the design was now hidden under the collage of blood and gore covering her like a tapestry.

Stacy gasped at the rancid odor of blood and excrement, most of it coming off the old woman. She had expelled her bowels and bladder upon death and a fetid pool spread out from her dead body.

Flies buzzed everywhere, feeding on the old woman and the other corpses, and Stacy turned and decided there had to be somewhere else she could go to rest.

But then loud shouts, screams and gunshots came to her ears from just outside the pizza parlor and she realized it would be safer where she was.

Besides, they were just dead bodies. The corpses were nothing but rotting meat. They couldn't hurt her now.

Of course that was easier said than done. It was easy to imagine the bodies getting back up at the sounds she was making. She could see heads and dead eyes turning to stare at her as gnarled limbs snapped free from on-setting rigor mortis as the corpses climbed to their feet. Viscera and internal organs now exposed to the air would slide out of open orifices, as the newly awakened zombies rose to feed. Stacy saw flashes of bloody hands reaching for her as teeth made for tearing sank into her warm flesh and began to rip and bite.

Shaking the waking nightmare away, she closed her eyes and counted to ten. When she opened her eyes, the corpses were where they had been before, not having moved so much as an inch.

In control once more, she stepped deeper into the interior.

Booths with vinyl seats were on both sides of her, and she stared at a few of the frozen faces looking back at her, seeing their eyes locked in the pain of a hard and painful death. She had another vision of the corpses slowly blinking at her, then rising up to stumble towards her, their bloody insides seeping out of the openings in their torsos, their guts splashing onto the floor like fresh eels.

She felt herself losing it again and she closed her eyes once more, trying to think of clean beaches and crystal blue oceans. But the smell of death permeated her senses, and though she tried, her reality refused to let her leave, even for a moment.

Opening her eyes once again, she was relieved to see the bodies were exactly where they had been...still. Nothing had stirred and she knew she was letting her imagination get the better of her. Zombies didn't exist, it was all make believe.

But there were so many bodies in the pizza parlor.

She counted around twenty, but a few corpses were under others and it was hard to know for sure.

It was the small ones, the children, that got to her the most.

To her left was a family of four; mother, father, boy and girl, the children looking to be around nine or ten.

All four were still in their booth, but each had a slashed throat. The table looked as if it was painted red and the blood had dripped off the edges to add to the growing pool of congealing crimson. The little girl had pigtails, the small eyes now staring at the ceiling in death. Stacy had to look away or risk entirely losing her mind.

Her foot kicked a few glass jars, and glancing down, she saw it was parmesan cheese and hot pepper flake shakers. The pepper flakes made her remember her father who used to love to put them on everything he ate. He would often eat the peppers whole, and after biting the tips off, the hotness filling his insides like acid, he would grunt and groan from the sensation. Even now, she never understood why he liked them so much.

She wondered if her mom and dad were okay now, all the way back in Boston.

Was what was happening here in Chicago an isolated event? Or was it all across the country.

Before she reached the back of the pizza parlor, and the counter which would lead to the kitchen, she slowed and stared at the corpse of another woman.

The woman was sprawled across a table facedown, her head hanging off the edge, as thick rivulets of blood still dripped slowly from the tip of her nose. It was as Stacy was watching her that she saw the body move, right where the woman's back met the top of her ass crack. At first Stacy thought she might still be alive, but as she bent over to check for a pulse, the skin suddenly began to stretch.

It was like there was something inside fighting to get out, and a scene from the movie Alien came to mind. Then the skin split open, a tearing sound filling the enclosed space. As Stacy watched in horror, the gore-covered nose of a rat poked its head out of the jagged hole it had made, the whiskers twitching as the rat smelled the air. The rodent began to squirm until its body was free of its meat prison.

"Oh, God, oh my God," Stacy gasped as she stared at the scarlet rat.

It was now sitting on the dead woman's back; its front paws rubbing its snout as it patiently cleaned itself. Stacy figured out what was going on instantly. Like most large cities, rats were everywhere, always hidden just below the surface. But with so much dead meat now lying unattended across the city, and no humans to stop them, the filthy rodents were having a field day feeding on the cadavers. It didn't take long for the world to crumble, she was quickly realizing. She turned, picked up a glass shaker of parmesan cheese from the table behind her, and threw it at the rat.

"Get out of here, you little bastard!" she screamed as the glass shaker struck the rat a glancing blow. The rodent hissed and dashed away, leaving little bloody footprints behind.

Feeling more disgusted than a second ago, if that was possible; she turned and headed for the counter, wanting to check the kitchen for...what? She didn't really know what she was looking for exactly.

There was a piece of the counter that could be lifted up like a drawbridge so she could get to the back. She closed the counter behind her, careful not to let it slam, thus causing noise that might alert some *changed* person walking by that she was in the pizza parlor.

Stepping behind the counter, she let out a gasp of surprise and shock at the two bodies she found sprawled across the black rubber mats.

They were both the corpses of men. The first was wearing a stained apron and a small pizza cutter was lodged in his sliced-open neck, just below his chin. Much like the way you would roll the cutter across a pizza, someone had done that to the man. His head was hanging by a few tendons and strings of flesh, the pizza cutter now stuck in the few remaining sinews. The handle of the cutter was covered in gore and another pool of blood was on the floor, though the inch-high, rubber mats with quarter-sized holes in it helped to keep Stacy from stepping in it.

The other dead man wore a blood-spattered, three piece suit with a cell phone on his pants belt, the face of it now shattered. The corpse was lying next to the other man, who Stacy decided was the owner of the pizza shop thanks to the apron.

The man with the cell phone had a pen jammed into his right eye, only the small clicker still visible. It looked like the pizza owner hadn't gone down without a fight. Stepping over the bodies and waving flies out of her face, she moved deeper into the back.

Gazing back to the street, out the shattered front window, she watched people running to and fro. Many were covered in blood, but many more were just running, and when she got a look at the faces as they passed the pizza parlor, she saw fear and terror etched in their visages.

She saw a small crowd, maybe ten or so, dash past, each running for what seemed like their lives. Stacy considered going back out to the street, maybe trying to catch up to the crowd, thinking she would be safer with more people around her. As she turned to take a step toward the counter opening, another crowd began to run past the pizza parlor.

This crowd looked much different than the last one, as they were lathered in congealing blood and many were carrying severed limbs. All had weapons of some sort, whether it was knives, tire irons or pipes, whatever could be found in a major U.S. city on the fly. Realizing this crowd was filled with the *changed* people, the infected ones, Stacy stopped and ducked back down.

As the crowd went by, one man had been glancing her way and he slowed just as Stacy was ducking down. He barely glimpsed her and for a second he wondered if he had really seen her, but despite this, the man stopped, letting the rest of the crowd move on without him.

The man turned and moved towards the pizza parlor, his feet crunching on shattered glass, notifying Stacy that she had been discovered. The man wore a long sleeve white shirt, the tie still there but undone so he looked like a man who at the end of a long day had loosened his tie. He wore blue slacks and comfortable shoes which were now covered with maroon spots of blood from earlier kills. Even his shirt had many dark spots on it, looking like someone had taken the tip of a red pen and had poked him a hundred times. Blood spray was what it was...arterial blood spray.

The man stepped into the pizza parlor, his eyes searching back and forth as he stared at the corpses. His breath came in heavy gasps and there was a tent where his groin was located. His face was maniacal, the eyes bulging in rage and anger, his killer instinct stirred into a frenzy. All this man wanted to do was kill, kill, and then kill some more.

The man stepped over to one of the corpses, and as the body shifted on the table as it settled, the man thought it was alive and began hacking at it, screaming and yelling like a feral animal as he chopped and cut, turning the corpse into nothing but meat and entrails. When he was finished, he wiped his brow and continued deeper into the pizza parlor, licking his fingers clean of blood.

Stacy remained still, hearing the footsteps of the man as he slowly moved down the aisle between the tables, his breathing heavy and raspy.

The man halted at the table with the dead family and grabbed the little girl by a pigtail, yanking the body out of the booth. He had a small knife, no more than six inches long, and he used it now, gutting the corpse of the girl like she was a large fish. Cooled entrails spilled out onto the floor to splash like spilled cottage cheese and the man began tearing at the cavity, tossing organs across the pizza parlor like it was holiday garland. A small kidney splattered against the wall to roll down it like play jelly that would stick to the wall and then slowly crawl down.

When the man was through with the girl, he tossed the corpse aside like it was trash, then proceeded towards the rear counter, his eyes wide with anticipation of finding more prey.

Stacy was huddled into a small ball as she waited for the man to reach her. Her mind was racing as she tried to figure out what she could do to save herself from what was sure to be a certain death...a very painful death.

Then she remembered she was covered in blood and that to most of the *changed*, she looked like one of them.

Her eyes scanned the shelves under the counter, hoping to find something to use as a weapon, and she almost let out a yell of victory when she found something. It wasn't the best item to use as a weapon, but it was better than nothing.

It was a long knife used for slicing pizza into sections. It was arced, or curved, on one side with a handle on each end, and it was made to kind of roll across the pizza, so that the cutter would start at one side and then the person would push down while slicing the pizza in half, then the person would shift to make another section and then roll it again so the pizza was cut into eights.

She squeezed her eyes shut as she grasped the handle to the twelve inch long cutter, and tried to psych herself up for what would happen next.

Her limbs were shaking and her stomach was queasy, but she was strong enough to know if she didn't react to what was happening to her, she would be killed. All this flashed through her mind, as well as the urge to crawl into a corner and cry, in an instant.

The footsteps were louder now, crunching on the debris strewn across the floor, and Stacy knew it was now or never. So she scrunched her face up into the most feral, rage-filled look she could imagine and stood up, snarling at the man.

The man jumped backwards at the sight of her, his eyes creasing in suspicion as he stared at her. He didn't speak, but stared at her, his gaze roaming from her chest to her scalp and down again. With Stacy standing behind the counter, that was all the man could see of her.

He didn't move towards her and Stacy thought she was safe, that this *changed* man thought she was like him, when something about his mannerism changed.

Maybe it was because they were inside or just the fact that Stacy wasn't putting on a good enough show as before, but the man saw right through her disguise, and with a throaty yell, he charged at her, lunging over the counter like a robber looking for the cash from the register.

Stacy screamed, realizing the jig was up, and jumped away, her back coming up against a glass-faced refrigerator. The door was solid glass so the customers could see what they would want to purchase. Inside it, the shelves were full of bottles of spring water to soda cans, everything from Crush, to Coca Cola to Pepsi, not to mention a few Dr. Peppers near the bottom in case someone felt like a Pepper, too.

The man was over the counter and coming for her, his eyes full of rage and death, and just as he was about to grab her, she ducked and spun, the man actually going over her back. It was something Stacy had learned at self defense camp. She'd been pressured to take the course with her friend, Susan. At the time, she had thought it was silly, but now one of those moves just might save her life.

The man flew into the glass door of the refrigerator and there was a loud crash as his head shattered the glass pane.

As the man went head first into the middle shelf, Stacy jumped back and spun, her eyes wide with fear. She was ready to run away if necessary, but she didn't know if that was the proper course of action. If she stayed and fought, the man would assuredly kill her, but at least she wouldn't be taken down from behind, like he was the hunter and she was the prey. But the man wasn't pulling free of the door and Stacy realized his body was twitching. At first she stayed immobile, but after more than a minute she felt safe enough to inspect the man.

If he was dead, then she could stay in the pizza parlor as she didn't want to go back out on the street. It was when she was less than a foot from the man that he suddenly jerked up and out of the shattered door. But if Stacy thought he was going to attack her, she was stunned to see the man had other worries.

As he pulled free of the door, he spun on her, and she saw a large, six inch shard of glass lodged in his neck, just under his chin. There was a trickle of blood seeping out of the edges but the man was still alive.

But as Stacy watched in horror, the enraged man reached up and wrapped his right hand around the shard, then yanked like he was pulling out a splinter.

Immediately, hot blood shot out of the wound to bathe her from head to toe, the flow like a small geyser.

The man began to choke and he placed his hand to the wound, attempting to staunch it, but all that managed to do was cause the blood to spew out around his fingers. Staggering forward, the man reached for Stacy, but fell to his knees before taking two steps. Gasping for air, he slowly bled to death.

Stacy, now coated in thick blood once more, could only stare at the dying man. She watched his eyes as the rage filling them winked out, to be replaced by nothing...the emptiness of death as he succumbed to oblivion. Toppling forward, he crashed to the floor and Stacy felt her legs go weak. Her back was against the counter and she felt herself swoon so she slowly slid to the floor, her knees now up by her chin.

Not knowing what to do, her gaze glued to the dead man, his eyes still open, as if they were accusing her of killing him, she began to weep.

She wept for what had happened to the city, but most of all she wept selfishly, feeling pity for herself to the point of it spilling over, washing her away like the spreading pool of blood on the floor, where it was already congealing between the round holes in the rubber mats.

Chapter 9

The first half of the night was a restless one for Chad. He only managed to grab a few minutes of sleep at a time. Every time he would finally drift off, a scream would pierce the night, causing him to snap awake.

He huddled in the kitchen, waiting for a crowd of killers to break through the front door and tear him apart, but it didn't happen. Hiding under the kitchen table like the boy did the previous day; Chad wrapped his arms around his knees and prayed he would still be alive to see the sun rise.

And if that wasn't enough to frazzle his nerves, the child he tossed into the pantry had woken up sometime during the night. The banging on the pantry door had been light at first, as if the boy had been groggy and didn't know what was going on, but later, when the boy had regained his faculties, the banging had increased to the point Chad knew he had to do something about it.

But the question was: What should he do?

Yells and screams from outside made his decision for him. A group of ten people had slowed outside about two in the morning and Chad knew if he didn't stop the boy from banging, the group would hear him and come to investigate. He had already seen the group enter a home and drag a man kicking and screaming from his house. In the middle of the street they had taken him, and Chad had watched as they gutted the man like a deer on a hunt, disemboweling and finally decapitating the man. The shrieks of the man went on for what seemed like hours until finally his vocal cords were sliced and it ceased. But even when it was over, Chad could still hear the screams in his head, as if they were on a playback of a tape recorder.

And he would be next if he didn't silence the boy.

With no choice, he went to the kitchen counter and took a knife from the butcher's block, then quickly went to the pantry door.

Breathing quickly to get himself ready for what would come next, he grabbed the doorknob, unlocked the door, and pulled it open. The boy had his fists raised to pound on the door again and he seemed taken aback when the door was opened on him. But his disorientation didn't last for long. As soon as the door opened, the boy snarled at Chad and ran at him, teeth clicking like a rabid dog.

Though he had told himself he would have to use the knife on the boy, in the end Chad couldn't do it so he punched the child in the face. The nose of the boy collapsed and the body was thrown back, but in seconds the boy was on his feet, lunging at Chad yet again. Chad punched the boy again and this time the child went down and stayed down. But it wasn't for good and a minute later, though drowsy from the blows, the boy was coming at him again.

Chad was crying as he raised his fist to punch the boy one more time. Even with the feral look in the boy's eyes, he was still a cute kid. His hair was light brown and he had on a Naruto shirt, the two heroes of the Japanese TV show fighting in the sky.

This boy was a child, a little boy who needed Chad to protect him, but as the boy screamed in rage, Chad panicked and backed away, his resolve to kill slipping.

Chad stumbled backwards and tripped on his own feet as the boy came at him with spittle flying from his mouth. The boy never slowed as he jumped into the air like a wolf, coming down onto Chad's chest. But when Chad had fallen, the knife went to his stomach and it was now pointing straight up. The boy, heedless of the blade, fell on top of Chad to become impaled on the knife. The knife slid into his chest and pierced the small heart within, killing him instantly.

Chad, not understanding what was happening, stared up at the boy's face in the dark kitchen and gasped when a small amount of bubbling blood seeped from the boy's mouth. The boy released his bladder and Chad felt wetness touch his leg, then the child went slack, almost as if the child was his son and had been tuckered out after a long day at the park.

The boy wasn't dead, he was just sleeping, Chad thought to himself, and though he was in shock, he reached around the boy and hugged him, as if he was his father and wanted to comfort him.

He stayed that way for the rest of the night, while the group of killers on the street moved on. With the boy silenced, the home was just another dark house, no more interesting than a dozen others.

Chad didn't sleep any more that night; he just stared at the ceiling and cried, all the while hugging the small corpse to him like a safety blanket.

The next morning finally came and Chad prepared to leave the daycare. The body of the dead boy was now in the main room with the other corpses. After draping another blanket over the body, he said a silent prayer.

He wasn't hungry but he knew he should eat if he had access to food, so he forced down some dry cereal and another bottle of water. He grabbed a small, pink backpack, obviously one of the dead children's, and stuffed it with as much food and water as he could. Then he went to the front door, ready to get on his way. Of course, he didn't know where he was going, but he knew he couldn't stay in the charnel house of death.

It was as he opened the front door to step outside that he realized his mistake. In his apathy of dealing with everything, he didn't check the front window to make sure the street was empty of danger.

No sooner did he open the door and raise his foot to step outside, then he looked out onto a street filled with more than twenty men and women.

They all carried a weapon of some kind in their hands, be it a baseball bat, machete or knife, crowbar, or a simple block of wood, and as he stepped out onto the front porch, all eyes shifted to him, as if he was a President of a nation about to give a speech.

The crowd had been making low noises, more like grunts than actual speech, and all grew silent at the sight of Chad.

As for Chad, he let out a tiny squeak, his first step barely coming down before he took in the tableaux before him.

The crowd was disheveled, some wearing nothing but rags, every one of them was covered in blood, the condition either drying or still wet. It was obvious to him that the crowd of *changed* had had a busy night of killing and maiming innocents.

And like a fool, he had stepped out in front of them. If he'd set off fireworks, he could have been less subtle. The crowd would have passed the daycare in less than a minute, the timing beyond terrible for him.

For almost ten seconds, neither Chad, nor the crowd of killers moved; not so much as an eyebrow twitched.

Then, a man at the front of the crowd roared in anger and raised a machete. The man spun on his heels and charged at Chad, the others taking on the cheer and following. Chad still didn't move, immobile as a deer caught in the headlights of an oncoming truck, but then as the crowd screamed and shrieked in anger and madness, he snapped out of it.

He added his scream to the crowds' shrieks, spun around, and jumped back inside. He slammed the front door and dashed through the house, his destination the back door. Behind him, he heard glass shatter and then the sound of smashing wood as the windows facing the street and the front door was kicked in.

Just as he reached the back door, he glanced over his shoulder. What he saw chilled him to his very core. The crowd of killers was flooding through the shattered front door like a wave of death, their faces curled into visages of rage and madness.

Some were hacking at each other, all eager to get inside the house so they could reach him, wanting to cut him into bite-sized chunks. Chad stared into the void of his own mortality as he watched the people cascade into the main room.

Then he turned and opened the door, fleeing into the morning sun.

Behind him, the killers paused only briefly to examine the remains of the children. More than half continued through the house, still chasing Chad, but the rest hanged back and began tearing at the dead children, desecrating the corpses even more than what had already been done to them.

Chad swerved around a small jungle-gym, hurdled over Tonka trucks and kickballs, as he made his way to what he prayed was freedom. Coming up on his rear, he heard the crowd drawing closer.

There was a five foot fence lining the backyard of the daycare and Chad scaled it quickly, the pink backpack becoming a hindrance. If he had thought about it more, he would have tossed it aside, but in his blind panic to escape, he held onto it, his grip as strong as a vise.

The next yard was overgrown with shrubs, and he waded through it as he rounded the house and into the street. The crowd following began climbing the fence.

Chad stopped in the middle of the street, not knowing where to go. He had seconds before the first killer rounded the house and saw him, sounding the alarm for the others. At the end of the street was a traffic accident of a Honda Civic and a Dodge Ram. The Honda had lost the battle and the driver had gone through the windshield to lay sprawled on the hood like a ghastly hood ornament. The door to the Dodge was wide open and Chad made a run for it. If the keys were still in the ignition, he could drive it away. The damage the truck received from the Honda was minimal. The Honda's front end was caved in, but the Dodge had no more than a dented bumper. It was a very large dent that would need to be replaced, but nothing structural to the vehicle.

Sprinting as if his life depended on it, because it did, Chad reached the Dodge just as the first killer rounded the house.

Chad's hope of escape was shattered in an instant when he saw no keys. Whoever had been driving had taken them with them. But he needed to hide, so with no options, he dove under the Dodge, hiding behind the left rear tire. He spun around and peeked put onto the street as the first killer began to search for him. The man barely paid the accident any attention and ran off in the opposite direction. When the rest of the crowd rounded the house, they followed the first man, the herd mentality overruling any reasonable thought.

They waved their weapons in the air as they ran and screamed, looking for all purposes like a lynch mob.

Chad lay under the Dodge, shivering in fear, praying to every deity he could think of that they wouldn't think to double back and search the area.

He waited for a full two minutes, and when the last of the crowd was gone, he crawled out and began running again. He stuck to the middle of the street, but with roving bands of homicidal killers everywhere, he knew he needed to get to a safe hiding place...and fast.

As he studied the homes lining the street, he saw the same chaos everywhere. Doors and windows were shattered on each house he passed and more than one of them was on fire.

He found the home on the corner was smoldering, nothing but a blackened shell, and he assumed that was where the acrid smoke had come from the day before. He tittered to himself again, thinking he had used the word assume, and he fought it down, knowing he was a stone's throw away from cracking himself.

Turning the corner, his sneakers slapping the pavement, he paused when he came to a house with a man standing on the front porch. The man held a revolver in his right hand and was wearing a dirty gray bathrobe. Chad watched the man for all of ten seconds, and could see the crazed look he'd seen plastered to the killers' faces wasn't on this man. Chad turned and ran to him, waving his arms in the air.

"Help me, please! I'm not one of them!" Chad cried out. "I'm okay!"

The man swiveled his head like an owl, and as soon as he saw Chad, he raised the revolver and let off a round. Asphalt spit at Chad when the round ricocheted off the street a half yard from his feet and he halted, waving harder. "No, I'm not crazy! I'm like you!"

But the man with the gun ignored him and fired gain. This time the bullet went so close to Chad's head he heard the air as it whipped by. Ducking on instinct, he dove behind a parked car as another round was fired.

Chad placed his back to the car as the driver's side window blew out, safety glass raining down on him.

"What the fuck are you doing, you asshole! I said I'm not one of them!"

"Bullshit, that's bullshit!" the man screamed. "You're all one of them. You're all out to get me!"

Chad had no choice. He needed to reason with this man or risk being shot.

"I'm telling you that I'm not one of them! I can talk, right? Haven't you noticed that the infected ones don't talk?"

Another gunshot took out the front windshield.

"It's a trick! You're trying to trick me!"

Chad realized then that the man had lost it. Much as Chad had a tenuous hold on his sanity, this man had let go and was now completely mad. Though his insanity was a slightly different kind than the killers, it was still no less deadly.

Chad was about to reply when a group of five men and two women came running around the corner, four houses down, all of them galloping like they were in a marathon. They were yelling and whooping it up, their faces filled with rage.

The man on the porch immediately lost interest in Chad as he now had more important targets to shoot. And these targets weren't trying to hide.

Chad poked his head up to see the man begin firing at the approaching group.

The first bullet took one of the killers in the shoulder, knocking him to the street where he flailed about like a landed fish. He dropped his weapon and placed his hand to his wound, but fresh blood seeped from between his fingers. Chad watched as the man, who should have been down for good, crawled to his feet and began jogging again. He left a steady trail of blood splatter behind him, but he wasn't deterred by the gunshot in the least.

The man on the porch fired again and a bullet took a woman in the face, right between her eyes. Her head snapped back as the contents of her skull exploded onto the people following her. She fell back as if punched and dropped to the pavement, the others simply stepping over her. One of them bent down to take the metal pipe the woman was carrying, that particular killer now having a weapon in each hand.

The third bullet took a man in the abdomen, and other than a hole as big as a fist appearing, the man merely grunted as he bent over in pain, then he stood upright and continued on, only now a thin rope of intestines was sliding out of the wound.

The man fired one more shot before the remaining crowd was upon him. This bullet took a killer in the right ear, shearing off the ear and leaving a bloody exposed wound in its place. The killer could have cared less as the raging man charged forward, running over the lawn and up to the front porch.

The man with the gun fired one more shot, but this one went wild when a machete took off his arm at the elbow, exactly as he was firing the gun. The man with the gun dropped to the porch as blood shot out of the severed arm, spraying the side of the house and every attacker around him.

The man screamed one time when his arm was detached, a long, shrieking howl that anyone would be incapable of mimicking unless they were on the edge of death. Then the man was silenced as a pipe struck him in the throat, shattering his larynx and sending him to the paint chipped floorboards of the porch.

From across the street, Chad could only watch helplessly as the man was torn apart, piece by bloody piece. Like a pack of wild butcher's, the killers systematically sliced and chopped the man into chunks of unidentifiable gore, beginning with his remaining arm and then both legs.

Chad watched for a full three minutes, wondering when it might end, when he heard someone calling to him from a nearby house.

"Hey, psst, hey, you, over here," the voice called, trying to be heard over the screaming murderers yet at the same time trying not to be. Chad was pulled from the carnage to look around the street, then he spotted an arm waving from a front door two doors down. There was an overturned car on the lawn, but the vehicle was dead, no tires spinning, and Chad then saw a face peer out along with the arm. He saw immediately that the face was normal; it wasn't carved into a rictus of rage and hate, so he checked to see that the killers were still occupied on the porch and he took off at a run to the house.

As soon as he hit the front walkway, the door opened wide and Chad ran in, but just as he dove through the doorway, one of the killers on the porch chopping up the man with the gun spotted him, and with a war cry that shook the street, he spun around and charged off the porch, waving a bloody pipe in his hand.

The others quickly forgot about the mangled mess of human meat at their feet and took off behind the man with the pipe.

Meanwhile, Chad was falling into the foyer of the quaint home, unaware he had a group of raging killers hot on his trail.

Chapter 10

Stacy had lost all sense of time as she huddled in the back of the pizza parlor. When she was finished crying, she drifted off into a restless sleep, visions of her boss, Mr. Masters, coming for her with a bashed in head, thanks to her use of the fire extinguisher.

"You did this to me," the voice sounding as if it was filled with gravel. *"You killed me. Why, Stacy? I liked you so much?"*

"No, I didn't want to. I'm so sorry," she pleaded as she stepped away from the nightmarish ghoul.

"You need to pay for what you did, Stacy...in blood!"

She felt a hand clamp on her left ankle and she tried to fight, but Mr. Masters' grip was too strong. She screamed in her mind as he dragged her into a deep dark pit, one she somehow knew had no bottom. She would fall forever, lost in an endless night.

"No!" she screamed aloud, and when she opened her eyes, she found the waking world was far worse than her dreams.

For the man killed by the glass shard in his neck was somehow still alive! And he had her left ankle in a death grip as he tried to pull himself towards her on his knees. Before she could cry out, he fell on her, his crushing weight trapping her, his face inches from hers. By luck alone, she managed to place her hands on his throat and the fingers of her right hand sank into the ghastly wound up to the knuckles, causing blood to squirt between her fingers and drip onto her face. She spit out the coppery fluid and struggled to live past the next few seconds.

The man was trying to growl at her but his destroyed larynx wouldn't allow it. Instead, only a bubbly froth escaped past his blue lips. She could see he was close to death but the question was; would he die before killing her as well?

Adrenalin suffused her system and she used her left hand and raked her fingernails across his face, scratching deep, bloody grooves in his flesh. His mouth opened to scream at her but once more, only red bubbles came forth. His eyes were wide with desperation, rage and anger, all the emotions swirling and battling for dominance.

His foul breath washed over her, making her want to gag, but she fought the urge to vomit, instead scratching his face again, her index finger only a half inch from his eye. Perhaps if she had been more bloodthirsty herself, she would have realized that gouging out his eyes would probably save her life, but doing something so heinous was far beyond her. When she used the fire extinguisher on Mr. Masters, it had been on full instinct, she never rationalized what she had done before doing it.

His body still pressed down on her, his dead weight crushing, and she fought like a banshee to push him off. The man barely noticed as he leaned down and tried to bite her nose. His teeth clacked on empty air when she turned her head at the last moment. He was wiggling on her and she could feel his erection as he shifted his body on top of her. His hands were coming up then, quickly wrapping around her throat. The only reason she was still alive was the simple fact that the man was weak from blood loss. If he had been at full strength, Stacy would have already been dead and dissected as the man cut her up like a deer fresh from the hunt.

As his hands began to squeeze around her throat, she gasped for air, white spots flashing before her eyes. She could feel herself slipping into unconsciousness, a faint she knew she would never awaken from.

Her hands were flailing in front of her now, her fingernails scratching at his face again and again, but still he wouldn't stop choking her, and she knew she was about to die!

But then, just as suddenly as the attack began, there was a cessation of pressure on her throat and the man let out a heavy sigh as he slumped on top of her. From a distance, he resembled a man who had just orgasmed and was now lying on his mate as he rested and reveled in the feeling suffusing him, but then the tableau was lost when Stacy tossed the body off her, rolling to the side as she bucked her hips.

The man had finally died, the massive loss of blood finally taking its toll on him. Stacy could only imagine how the man had been able to attack her in the first place. Obviously, the rage the man felt for her was enough to make him move despite his mortal wound.

Once more she was drenched in blood, the man's bodily fluids covering her entire upper torso as well as her head. Her hair was sticking to her skull, making her look like *Carrie* after being doused with the bucket of pig's blood.

She had never wanted a shower more than right now. Shaking uncontrollably from her brush with death, she decided she needed to get away from the back of the pizza parlor so she stood up, and after a brief glance to the street to see no one was coming towards her, she headed deeper into the building.

At the back of the pizza parlor was a set of stairs, and with nowhere else to go, she climbed them, one step at a time. The stairwell was small, only wide enough for her, and if her shoulders had been larger they would have brushed the walls on both sides.

The stairs creaked as she made her way to the top and she paused at the old wooden door before her. Reaching out, she turned the doorknob and was pleased to see it was unlocked.

The door opened on creaking hinges and she held her breath in expectation of someone coming around a corner and attacking her. But when more than a minute passed and still nothing, she stepped into a small hallway and closed the door behind her. What she didn't know was that the door always needed a good shove to get it to latch closed, and as she walked deeper into the hallway, the door remained ajar, soon swinging open to stop when it tapped the far wall lightly.

But Stacy didn't see any of this as she slowly crept to the end of the hallway and found herself in a small, one bedroom apartment.

There were pictures on a worn mantle in need of a sanding and refinishing in the tiny living room and she saw the face of the pizza owner smiling as he held a fish in his hands. So he had lived up here, perhaps owning the entire building.

She figured this was as good a place as any to rest up and re-cover from everything she'd been through. There was a phone on the wall and she went to it, reaching for it like she was falling off a cliff and it was a rope ladder. She placed the receiver to ear and dialed 9-1-1.

"Hello? Hello, is anyone there? Hello?" But all she got for her trouble was dead air. She tried two more times and finally gave up. Whatever was going on had affected the phones. There was a television in the corner and she went and put it on, but of course, the cable was out. All she got on the screen was static, small snowy pixels dancing about until, disgusted, she turned it off.

With a long sigh of exhaustion, feeling safe for the first time since Mr. Masters had jumped over his desk and attacked her, she went to the bathroom in the rear of the apartment and prepared to wash up.

There was no shower, only a tub, which fit in perfectly with the old apartment, the dated fixtures showing the building's age. Deciding a bath would do just fine, she began to run the water, waiting forever for the cold water to turn warm. This simple task made her break out into tears, the simple idea of taking a bath–a task so mundane–after seeing and experiencing murder and death so close up, so *real*, seemed like a fairytale to her.

She turned and caught her reflection in the vanity mirror over the sink and jumped, frightening herself. What she saw was a madwoman, a killer who was covered in blood.

Small dots of what looked like toothpaste covered the entire mirror. It looked to her like the owner of the pizza parlor had been a messy brusher, spraying as he brushed his teeth each night.

She gazed into her eyes staring back at her, wondering if the person she had been just a day ago still existed. She frowned when she saw the blood-drenched complexion gazing back at her, her eyes like two shiny marbles amidst a sea of red. She could see why the other killers thought she was one of them. She looked like an extra in a horror movie.

Leaning against the sink, she closed her eyes and listened to her heart beat, the steady pulse calming her slightly. She still didn't know what she was going to do.

She had no plan, and if she didn't get one fast she knew sooner or later she would end up dead. She considered going to the closest police station, but after seeing the police out in the city killing innocents, she figured the authorities were as dangerous to confront as anyone else. Once again her mind went back to Mr. Masters, and how his eyes had changed from rational and kind to a homicidal maniac with rage fueling his actions.

Why? What had happened to him and everyone else? And why was she okay? Why were some infected while others appeared fine? Though those seemed to be the minority.

Why have some people *changed* while others became victims?

The tub was half full and she kicked off her shoes, figuring she would be able to think better once she was clean. Of course, then she would have to decide what she would do as she knew if she went out on the street not covered in blood and gore, she would be an easy target for the roving killers.

But she couldn't stand the feeling of the sticky, congealing blood on her skin any longer. She was slowly taking off her blouse when a soft creaking of loose floorboards came from the hallway outside the bathroom.

She didn't hear the noise however, as the tub was still filling, the water hiding any other sounds emanating from the apartment.

Unknown to Stacy, two men had entered the pizza parlor to investigate it, and when they reached the rear of the restaurant, they found the stairs leading to the apartment. Taking the stairs one at a time, they silently reached the door to the apartment; the one Stacy hadn't closed correctly. The two men stepped inside, each breathing heavily in hopes of finding something to kill. The first man was in his early twenties and was of medium height with dark red hair and freckles. He wore a pair of glasses but only one lens still remained, the other gone, the one still in the wire frames cracked, causing the man to see the world through a distortion. He wore a feral look, like a wolf, and his eyes darted back and forth constantly, his hands twitching like he was a junkie in need of a hit.

The second man was about thirty years senior to his partner, with thin gray hair and a nose that was too big for his face. His dark brown eyes were calmer, more calculating. He carried a large cleaver, while his younger companion carried a small hand axe.

Both men slowly moved down the hallway, drawn to the sound of the running water as the tub filled. As they got closer, they could see the light cascading onto the hallway floor and see the shadow of movement coming from within.

Someone was inside the bathroom.

With a smile to one another in anticipation of the slaughter to come, they raised their weapons and moved in for the kill.

Chapter 11

Chad tumbled into the foyer of the house as the door slammed closed behind him. The man who had called to Chad looked down on him.

"Hey, there, young fella, you okay?" the man asked. Chad saw he looked to be in his seventies, with stark-white hair and a wrinkled face. He had an oxygen tube under his nose and wore a small canister on his hip, like a purse. He wore an old blue bathrobe and slippers that had seen better days. As the bathrobe flapped slightly, Chad saw the man was wearing flannel pajamas.

"Yeah, I think so," Chad replied as he got his hands under him and went to his knees. "Thank you for helping me, I didn't know what I was gonna do when those people were through with that guy on the porch."

"Yeah, Phil was a little crazy even before all this mess happened. I'm Norman," the old man said as he helped Chad to his feet. "I've been holed up here since the neighborhood went to Hell. It's the damndest thing I ever saw and I was in W.W.2."

"Do you have a phone?"

"Sorry, son, the phone's out as well as the television," Norman said and was about to say more when the front door jumped in its frame. Chad spun around as Norman looked to the door, a perplexed look on his face.

"Damn it, I was afraid this would happen," Norman said as he went to the small leaded-glass window next to the door. It was four inches wide and was vertical of the door, the glass frosted. But

Norman was able to see out enough to frown deeply. The door shook on its hinges again, this time more violently.

"Some of them are out there, they must have seen you come in here," he told Chad as he spun and shuffled to the opposite end of the house.

Chad watched the man go, then looked back at the front door. The pounding was ferocious now, multiple fists and tools banging on the door and when the leaded glass window cracked, Chad knew it was bad. They couldn't stay in the house, not now that the killers knew they were inside.

Turning, he ran after the old man. They needed to gather what they could and get out the back way, to do the same thing Chad did when he ran from his house, cutting through backyards and praying he wasn't found.

When Chad reached the old man, he was making coffee of all things and Chad quickly filled him in on what he'd seen in the streets and what they should do next.

"No, no, son, I don't think I'll be running all over the city anytime soon," Norman said as he patted the canister on his hip. "Hell, I get winded just going upstairs to bed."

"But we can't stay here. Norman, they're gonna be in here any second, we need to get going, right now!"

Norman sighed. "Then you go, I guess I shouldn't have called out to you but I couldn't let you stay out there with those *people* so close. They would have gone after you next."

"And I can't thank you enough for doing that, but you need to leave with me now. I'll help you. Look, you can't stay here, they'll kill you!" Chad pleaded.

Norman went to a drawer and opened it slowly, then pulled out an old W.W.2 revolver. He handed it to Chad. "Here, son, take this. Maybe it'll help you out there. As for me, I'm ready to die. Even if all this shit hadn't happened, I have less than a month." He sighed deeply. "Cancer, you see, I've got one foot on death's door as it is."

"But..." Chad began but was cut short when the front door began to splinter under the attack of many weapons and fists.

Norman shuffled to Chad so he was just inches from him. Chad could smell the foul breath of the old man but he kept his face stoic, not wanting to insult the man who had saved him only to die because of the action.

"Just go, son, and don't let them get you. I'll hold them off so you can get a head start." The front door crashed inward and bodies began to spill inside, an animalistic yell of rage sounding from multiple attackers. They were fighting each other for who would be first through the doorway and it was slowing them down. Norman pushed Chad, his strength weak but still enough to knock Chad off balance.

"Go goddammit, they're in the house! Go, now!"

There was nothing to do or say, so Chad ran the few feet to the back door. He paused for a moment and Norman nodded, smiling slightly. Chad saw a man who was ready for death, though he couldn't understand how a person could ever get there. Then again, he wasn't afflicted with terminal cancer.

Chad opened the door and stepped outside just as the first of the killers gained the hallway and ran for Norman. Chad closed the door and jumped onto the yellow lawn of the backyard, not bothering with the four stairs. As he landed on the dead grass, he spun around and stopped. He could see Norman through the back window and he watched as the man began to half-walk, half-shuffle to another room just off the kitchen.

Norman got to the room just as the first killer reached him, but Norman was quick in his last seconds on the planet Earth. As the killer reached him, Norman grabbed a walking cane from where it was leaning against the wall and he used it on the killer, whacking the man on the side of the head. It wasn't enough to kill the man but it slowed him down. Norman didn't bother trying to keep the man down, however. As soon as the man was knocked away, Norman turned around and continued into the room. Chad was able to follow him as there was another window to the right, just off the kitchen door. He could see Norman in a room that looked like a den, including what appeared to be a mounted moose's head. Along one wall were backup oxygen canisters, each one lined up neatly on a shelf. But there was another canister there too, a large five foot one that was for when he was sitting in the den and not walking around. On the side, printed in white font, was the word *Flammable* and the chemical symbol for oxygen.

As the other killers piled into the room, Chad watched in awe as Norman lit a cigarette, taking a long pull and letting out the smoke as he held onto the disposable lighter. Just as he was surrounded, he raised the lighter to the large canister of oxygen and opened the valve, filling the den with pure oxygen. As the first and second killer grabbed him, one of them sliding a dull knife into his back, causing Norman to cry out in pain, the old man flicked the lighter, causing the flame to erupt.

Chad saw it all through the window. He saw the killers pile on top of Norman, saw the old man flick the lighter, saw the small flame become a massive one as the entire room was engulfed in bright flashes of oranges and reds. But the flames didn't stop there. They rolled through the house, consuming everything in its path, swallowing the killers and burning them alive.

Chad was thrown back onto the grass when the windows exploded and the first floor of the house became a raging inferno. Soon, the gas main was feeding the flames, sending an explosion that had the house jumping on its foundation. He was running away by now, but as the house exploded into a thousand pieces of flaming debris, he was thrown forward to land in the bushes of the neighboring backyard of the house behind Norman's.

He rolled out of the bushes and came to his knees as all around him severed body parts and debris rained down, a few coming so close he flinched.

He stared for more than a minute, the flames reflected in his eyes, as he tried to grasp what Norman had done for him. This man, who had been safe in his home, had called attention to himself to save a stranger. He then sacrificed himself so Chad could escape.

His ears were ringing from the blast but over the roaring of the fire he began to hear something else—voices, a lot of them. People were yelling and screaming, most of them sounding angry or feral. The blast had been a beacon and every raving killer in a half mile radius was now descending on the destroyed house.

Chad realized he needed to get as far away from this place as soon as possible before he was surrounded with no hope of escape. No sooner did he think this then two rage-filled faces popped up from the next yard. The two men were covered in blood and charged at Chad, screaming as they waved a three-foot chain and a lead pipe over their heads. Chad was caught off guard, but he remembered the gun in his hand.

Raising it up, he did his best not to let his hand shake, and as the men came at him with a thirst for blood in their eyes, he squeezed the trigger. The gun roared its statement of death and the first man was knocked off his feet, a large hole in his chest. He spit blood as he flopped about, but then stopped. His chest was still rising and falling but he was out of the fight.

That left one more.

Chad shifted his aim to the right, and just before the second man could brain him with the lead pipe, he fired point blank into the man's face. The revolver was big and the caliber of the round was so large that it destroyed the man's face and blew out the back of his head. As the man was shot, his head snapped back, but his body was moving so fast it continued forward. Chad found himself tackled and forced to the grass with a man with no face and half a head on top of him.

He screamed, revulsion filling him up to the point he knew he was going to vomit. Blood sprayed his face and upper chest as he tried to force the body off him. But the dead weight was too much and for a moment he wondered if he would be trapped forever under the corpse. Or until he was found by other killers and they began to do to him what they had done to the man on the porch.

That image gave him an adrenalin boost and he managed enough strength to shove the corpse off him. Blood still shot from the open face cavity and he tasted copper, warm and salty on his tongue. Spitting out what he could, he went to his knees and closed his eyes, waiting for the vomit to come, bile tickling the back of his throat. When it didn't, he stood up, once more staring at the burning house, the crackling of its interior reminding him of campfires with his father as the heat of the blaze warmed his face and dried the blood splashed on it.

Shaking himself from his stupor, he knew he needed to run.

So he turned and ran, keeping to the backyards and shadows where he could find them, while behind him, the house burned, the flames soon spreading as glowing embers went to other nearby homes.

In two hours time, half the neighborhood would be a raging conflagration that would consume half the town, but Chad knew nothing of this.

All Chad knew was he was still alive, and lately it seemed, that was enough.

Chapter 12

Stacy was sitting on the edge of the toilet seat, her head in her hands, as she tried to calm herself.

She was full of self doubt once more. What was going on? Why was this happening? Though she tried to rationalize her situation, the truth was that it couldn't be explained. She was absolutely in the dark as to why all of Chicago was going completely bonkers.

She wondered if she should get out of the city; try to make it to the suburbs. Maybe it's not as bad there or better yet, maybe what was happening was only restricted to the city.

The tub was about full so she put these thoughts away for now, wanting to get clean and feel normal, even if it was just for a little while.

She reached over and turned off the water, the splashing of the water cascading into the tub now ceasing. With the exception of a soft drip-drip, the bathroom was silent. And that was when she heard the floorboards creaking in the hallway just outside the bathroom door.

Her eyes went wide, realizing she wasn't alone in the apartment. She debated if she should call out to whoever it might be, to tell them she was sorry for invading the apartment, but then she remembered that the original resident was lying dead downstairs in a pool of blood.

She didn't have high hopes that whoever was stealthily creeping up on her was friendly.

She desperately looked around the bathroom, but there was no place to hide. There was a small, one-foot closet behind her and a laundry hamper on her right. Other than the sink and the tub, the small room was empty.

She spotted a blow dryer lying near the tub, the cord still plugged into the wall socket, and in the back of her mind the practical part of herself shook her head. That was very dangerous, having an electrical appliance so close to the tub. But then the thought was gone and survival took precedent.

The closet!

Maybe there was something in there she could use as a weapon.

Stepping the four feet to the closet, she opened it to see the standard bathroom equipment. Toothpaste, shampoo, some ointment for rashes, cotton balls, Q-tips, unopened plastic bottles of aspirin, and cold medicine were just some of the items she spotted. She was about to give up hope, the creaking floorboards growing closer, when she saw a can of gold hairspray lying on its side at the back of the middle shelf. She remembered seeing what the pizza parlor owner looked like and how short the man's hair was and he didn't seem like the type that would ever need the can of hairspray, but then, by the look of the design on the can, it may have been in the back of the closet for ten years or more.

Having no more time to decide her course of action, she grabbed the hairspray and a toothbrush sitting on the bottom shelf. She had no idea what she could do with these items, but it still felt good to hold *something* in her hands.

She spun around and darted for the bathroom door, sliding in behind it. She knew she couldn't stay hidden for long. When the owners of the footsteps in the hallway entered the bathroom, they would immediately see she was hiding behind the door.

To her left, the curved, chrome spicket still dripped tiny droplets of water into the tub, causing small rings to flow out like miniscule waves.

With a lump in her throat the size of a grapefruit, she tried to stop herself from hyperventilating and remain calm. She had to force herself not to scream when the creaking was right outside the bathroom door and a foot scuffed the hardwood of the floor. She couldn't be sure, but there had to be at least three people out there, maybe two. It was hard to tell from where she was. She could hear heavy breathing now, and as the first person took a step into the bathroom, she detected the redolence of unwashed bodies mixed with a coppery scent she'd smelled a lot lately.

Blood.

She held her breath as the first intruder entered the bathroom, followed by the second. She could hear the different tones of their breathing and she was fairly certain there were only two of them.

That made her want to laugh, or rather scream.

She had gotten to the point where only two men trying to kill her was not such a big deal. Gripping the toothbrush and the can of hairspray harder, she waited for the inevitable.

And it came seconds later when the first man spun around and his eyes went wide upon seeing her hiding behind the door. The man's mouth opened wide and issued a scream that made Stacy want to fall to the floor and cry in hysterics. The man had murder mixed with hatred in his eyes, there was no doubt about it, and though she had never been an aggressive person, she had learned in the past day that if she wanted to live, she needed to be strong, not squeamish like most of her fellow humans were even now being slaughtered. She needed to accept her new world for what it was and either embrace it or let it wash over and destroy her.

She chose the former.

As the man screamed long and loud and raised a small axe, Stacy was already on the attack.

What was her weapon?

The toothbrush of all items.

As the man raised the axe and prepared to bring it down on her head, cleaving it in twain, she darted at him and jammed the handle of the toothbrush into his left eye.

The toothbrush didn't slide in, however, as the bottom of the handle was round and dull. There was a reason prison inmates had to sharpen them before using them as weapons.

But the handle was still made of hard plastic and was tougher than the human eyeball, and when the handle made contact with the orb and pressed, the eyeball lost, seeming to explode like a hand had slapped a hardboiled egg. A clear white gel popped from the eye, some of it splattering her forehead, but she ignored it, pushing the toothbrush so deep into the man's skull that when she was done he had the bristles on the toothbrush for an eye.

The man jerked back and forth like he was being controlled by unknown strings as he fell back against the clothes hamper, his free hand reaching for his wounded eye. When he felt the toothbrush embedded in his eye socket, he shrieked even louder, this time in pain. He jerked and spasmed for a few seconds longer before his body went limp in death.

Stacy had no time to admire her handiwork, though, for no sooner did she jam the toothbrush deep into the man's head, then his partner screamed and punched her in the face. The blow was sloppy and only glanced her chin, otherwise she would have been on the floor, perhaps unconscious, but though her head was ringing with an imaginary, old-fashioned telephone, she recovered from the blow and turned to face her other attacker. This man was older and had a cleaver in his hand, a feral grin on his face as he prepared to sink the cleaver into her breastbone.

With nothing but a can of hairspray, Stacy brought it up and sprayed it into the man's eyes, eliciting screams of pain and anger as the man dropped the cleaver and stumbled forward, pushing her against the wall.

Stacy was also screaming as the man fell on top of her as she struggled to keep him away from her before his hand found her throat. She still had the marks on her neck from the last time she was strangled and didn't wish to repeat it again anytime soon.

They began a dance in the bathroom as the blinded man tried to grab her, and wipe his eyes clean at the same time. Stacy, having no clue what she should do next, fought and scratched as best she could.

Then, as they struggled in the small bathroom, the man fell over his prone partner, tumbling into the tub and sending waves of water cascading over the edge of the tub.

Stacy found herself free for a heartbeat, but as the man tumbled into the tub, he ducked his head under the water and his eyes were washed clear. He was now half-in and half-out of the tub, and though his eyes were beat red, he could see well enough to find Stacy amidst the tears. He was already roaring in rage as he tried to climb out of the tub.

Stacy, her eyes darting back and forth, knew she needed to run away, but the man would only be right behind her. Fight or flight filled her to the core and at the last second, before the man climbed free of the tub, she spotted the hair dryer again, now lying on the floor from the scuffle.

Before she knew what she was doing, she reached down and picked it up, flicked the button to turn it on, and tossed it into the tub as she jumped out of the bathroom to avoid the water on the floor.

The instant the hair dryer landed in the water, there was a sizzling sound and the lights in the bathroom and hallway dimmed as the man in the tub began to jerk and twitch like he was well....being electrocuted.

Stacy's gaze went to the electrical outlet the hair dryer was plugged into and she noticed fleetingly it wasn't one of the new special ones that were made to be around water. Oh, no, this was a good old-fashioned outlet, and that meant there was no trip to stop the fatal surge of electricity. Though the outlet began to smoke, it continued feeding killing volts of juice into the water.

As for the man, he was being cooked like a chicken in a kettle of boiling water. His blood-red eyes popped in their sockets, like overcooked eggs, and his skin shriveled on his bones as he was boiled alive. In less than ten seconds, he was very, very dead.

Other than a few sparks coming off his hair, all became silent in the bathroom, only the sounds of dripping water sluicing over the edge of the tub thanks to the man's body raising the water level.

Stacy stood silently in the hallway, watching the horror show, and as water seeped over the marble threshold separating the bathroom from the hallway to flow towards her, she jumped back, not knowing if the water was still filled with electricity.

With nothing else to do and not wanting to stay in the apartment a moment longer for fear there were more killers around, she turned and left.

So much for a bath; she was still covered from head to toe in blood, but at least she was still alive.

Which was more than could be said for her would-be killers.

Chapter 13

Chad slowed as he rounded a house on the west side of town. In the distance, Chicago was burning.

The Sears Tower looked like a massive candle in the falling dusk and he knew it would be a beacon to every killer for ten miles once night had completely fallen.

This was his second night roaming the streets since the world had gone mad and he still didn't have a real plan of what he should do. So far he'd merely been hiding where he could, then moving on when he thought he would be discovered.

The roving packs of homicidal killers had been growing as of late, and with the exception of a few people who looked normal here and there, it seemed the entire town was either crazy or dead, succumbing to the murderous crowd.

He was closer to Chicago now, and though he thought the suburbs might be safer, he also had seen zero police or military presence. He spotted a few military choppers flying to the city and he had a feeling if he wanted to get to help, he would have to go to Chicago where there must be some kind of help stations or camps set up for those in need.

But at the moment he wasn't going there, as he was on foot and there had been no vehicles worth taking. Every car or pickup he passed was either on fire or had flat tires and smashed windows. Senseless violence at its best, but that seemed to be what the liked to do.

He paused at the end of the street to see if it was safe to venture forth. He was at the last house on the corner and he would need to break cover to reach the next house adjacent to his position. He felt like a guerilla fighter in the jungles of some foreign country as he fought and crawled his way through bushes and shrubs. It was surreal. It was his town, backyards filled with pools and swing sets, but at the same time it was a battlefield.

He counted to five, waiting to see if the street would remain safe. If even one killer saw him, he knew he would be in deep trouble.

He'd been spotted two hours ago when attempting the same thing as now. He managed to make it halfway across the street before a woman hunched low in a parked car had sat up and shrieked like a banshee at him, her bloody fingers pointing at him accusingly.

Three seconds later, with the scream still echoing on the street, ten homicidal maniacs popped up from yards and inside homes. They flooded the street like locusts, all running directly at him. Chad had used the gun he'd received from Norman and had taken down four of the crazies before the weapon clicked dry. He threw it at one more, hitting the young, hate-filled man in the head and causing him to fall into the rushing crowd, but then Chad had to run or risk being swarmed like a hunting pack of lions was stalking him.

With his breath lodged in his throat, he made a mad dash into a nearby home, slamming the front door behind him. He ran through the house, ignoring the mangled corpses strewn on the floor of the living room, and by the time he was into the backyard and over the fence, the crazies were exploding out the rear door. Chad, thinking quickly, had crawled into a dog house, the collar and bowl sitting empty beside it. He huddled in fear as the heavy fall of footsteps trampled the grass only a few feet from his hiding place.

He sat perfectly still for almost an hour, too afraid to so much as breathe before venturing forth yet again, now minus the gun.

And so here he was again, ready to tackle an intersection and risk his life for the hundredth time.

When he thought it was as safe as it could get, he dashed into the street, and in seconds was on the opposite side. He went to his knees behind a parked car and gazed out over the street, praying he had made it.

He had.

No one was around this evening; all the killers were inside where they were chopping up the residents of the nearby houses. Chad heard a few distant screams and gunshots, but other than that it was quiet. Only the crackling of burning fires breaking the absolute silence.

Grinning to himself, thinking he was getting pretty good at this ducking and hiding stuff, he was shocked when he spun around and stood up, preparing to head into the next yard, to find himself facing a man with wild eyes and a necklace made of human ears. The man's clothing was nothing but rags, the once expensive shirt and tie now hanging off him in tatters that swayed back and forth in the wind. His blonde hair was matted to his scalp thanks to the generous covering of dried blood. The man held a thin knife, such as one would find at a steak house, the blade a dull maroon thanks to the coating of human blood coating it.

Chad barely had time to raise his arm in defense before the knife was coming down, directly at his chest, right over the spot where his heart was pumping in fear.

The killer screamed in rage and Chad replied with an outcry of his own, his arm blocking the knife by luck alone. Panicking, Chad shoved the man away and only blind luck saved him again when the man fell over backwards, off balance by his attack. But the man wanted another set of ears for his necklace and Chad's were perfect for the collection.

Rolling to his feet, the man came up in a crouch, prepared to slash at Chad's stomach when the loud report of a gun filled the street. Chad stared dumbstruck as the man's head disappeared in a brilliant fan of blood and bone matter, the neck stump shooting blood up and outward, bathing Chad in more blood. The warm fluid splashed into his eyes and caused him to go blind for a few terror-filled seconds. Blinking his eyes clear, he wiped them clean and turned to thank his savior.

But instead of being greeted by some warrior of the new world, another shot rang out and split the air an inch from his head. He heard the subsonic round crack the air and he ducked instinctively.

"No good crazies! I'll kill ya all!" a deep voice cried out. It was male; there was no doubt about that.

Chad followed the sound of the voice to see a man in his fifties with light brown hair and a flak vest on. The man held an assault rifle firmly in his hands, and as Chad watched, the man shifted the weapon to aim for Chad again, his finger already squeezing the trigger.

Chad dove to the left and waited to feel the impact of the round penetrating his chest. He imagined his ribs cracking, his heart imploding, as the round entered his body and then exited out his back, taking half his insides with it.

But the round missed him by a few inches and ricocheted off a mail box behind him. A fist-sized hole appeared in the blue facade of the mail box and Chad's eyes went wide.

"Jesus Christ!" he screamed.

Unknown to Chad, the shooter was using armor piercing bullets.

Chad sprawled on the ground and raised his head to stare at the man, knowing the next shot would surely hit him. But as if some divine fate was looking out for him once more, six killers appeared from backyards near the shooter and ran at him as if they were sprinting for the gold. The shooter spun and shot the first assailant in the chest, then took out two more before they were on him. The man continued squeezing the trigger of the weapon, the bullets flying off to God knows where as knives and teeth began tearing him apart.

Chad laid on the sidewalk, watching as the shooter was gutted, his intestines pulled out like a magician's hat trick. The killers tossed the organs aside and ripped and tore at the body. They were like wild animals only they weren't eating their prey, but merely wanted to kill it.

Chad picked himself up and began to walk backwards, wiping his eyes clear of the blood covering him as he watched the killers. One did look up and spotted him and Chad halted, frozen in fear. He expected the killer to cry out, to begin the chase, but the rage-filled man did no such thing. He stared at Chad, studying him from across the street, then turned back and began tearing at the shooter, pleased when he separated the shooter's left arm from the torso.

Chad, not understanding why the killer had dismissed him, turned and ran away, while the final screams of the shooter followed him, haunting him with each dying decibel of torture.

* * *

There was a church on the corner, its doors closed; the building looking like it was ready to open for Sunday Mass at any second.

The facade was whitewashed and the bushes trimmed. A large, fifteen foot cross stood tall on the foremost steeple, and people in the neighborhood would use the cross as a landmark when giving directions. They would say, "Go down to the end of the block and take a right at the cross."

For more than fifty years, the cross had stood tall, and Chad couldn't help but ride the wave of memories flooding his mind.

Though this wasn't his church of worship, he had visited it numerous times over the years when friends and family had gotten married or passed on into the next world and the funeral service had been held in the church.

He wondered about those same friends and family now. His father had died years ago but his mother was living in Maine. Was she safe? He could only hope she was and that when phone service was reinstated he could talk to her.

Scared and tired, the church was a beacon of hope to his frazzled soul, so he waited until it looked clear and darted across the street and up the stone steps, stopping at the large, oak, double doors. He knew to dally in the open could get him discovered so he prayed the doors were unlocked as he tugged on the left one, relieved when it opened.

With one last glance over his shoulder to see that the street was empty of killers, or anyone else for that matter, he stepped inside and locked the double doors using the small latch on each of the push bars. If there was someone else who needed to be let in, he would make sure to stay close to the doors so he could hear them, but he'd be damned if he would let them remain unlocked.

He didn't bother to think about the odds that the doors had been unlocked to begin with, and if he had, he might have hesitated before entering the church. But he wasn't thinking clearly with all he'd been through and his desperation overrode his fears as he sighed when the locks were secured.

He turned around to face the main stage of the interior.

He didn't know what he expected upon entering the house of worship, but as he stared out over the pews and the faces glaring back at him, their eyes filled with hate and rage, he realized he had miscalculated very, very badly.

Chapter 14

Stacy's feet slapped the pavement as she ran for her life. Behind her, a crowd of more than a dozen killers was chasing her. Each waved their arms over their heads as spittle went flying into the air from open mouths; more than half carried some kind of weapon.

She was exhausted, having run for almost an hour, but she knew if she stopped, she was dead.

As for the murderous crowd, they were indefatigable, their rage pulling them on for eternity. They were mindless killing machines now, and though they would tire eventually, it would be with their last ounce of strength. Like a trained horse, they would run until they could run no more, then tip over from exhaustion. Stacy felt if she could somehow manage to keep running, her pursuers would follow her until the end of time.

She was reaching the outskirts of Chicago now, figuring she should try to leave the city. Behind her, the Sears Tower continued to burn, the sunrise bathing the intense orange and reds of the flames with its own vibrant intensity.

All around her was utter chaos. Cars and trucks clogged the roads and nearby buildings were burning. Off in the distance, on the other side of the city, she could see plumes of smoke curling into the sky. The fire looked massive, as if it had been started intentionally, and as she thought about the murderous hordes roaming the streets, she believed that was probably what happened.

She was weaving her way through the streets lining the highway that cut through the center of Chicago, hoping she could lose herself in the dark alleys and storefronts, but each time she thought she made it, a blood-curdling shriek would cry out from behind and she knew she'd been seen.

The generous coating of blood and gore she once wore had rubbed off from countless times of falling to the ground or when she climbed over cars and wrecked vehicles. At first she didn't know her disguise was rubbing off as she managed to work her way through the streets with ease. Each time one of the *changed* had come up to her, she bared her teeth and growled. This had worked for half the day until she had to climb through a car wreck that had blocked the entire road. She tried not to look at the corpse of a business woman as the body hung out of the shattered driver's side window. The head was connected to the shoulders by a thin strand of flesh and would swing back and forth like a yo-yo with each passing breeze. Other bodies were wrapped in the mess of twisted metal and fiberglass, but all were very dead. Averting her eyes, she climbed through the wreckage and then down the other side. But as she did this, her arms and face continually rubbed the metal and tires, and when she was free, she didn't look quite so gore-covered.

So now she was running for her life, something she'd been doing for what seemed like forever, and as a pang of agony creased her side from the exertion of running, she knew she was on her last legs.

Her legs felt like spaghetti, and though she willed them to move faster, they were in fact slowing down. Her feet were throbbing from the abuse and she wished she had taken up jogging like her friend, Judy, had. She had wanted Stacy to join her every morning before work but Stacy had declined. Now, her lack of stamina would be her demise.

She rounded a corner and came upon a street lined with restaurants on both sides. Each one looked very closed and empty, some with shattered windows.

On the left side was a McDonalds, every glass window now shattered thanks to a large dump truck that had driven through the center of the building. On the right side, a Burger King fought for dominance of the fast food burger, and this burger joint fared no better than the competition. Two cars had plowed through the sides of the building and smoke drifted out in lazy clouds, but so far no flames.

It was as she was running past a quaint Italian restaurant, with a sign featuring a stereotypical Italian chef holding a pizza in one hand and a plate of spaghetti in the other, that she saw the double doors of the main entrance open and a man in an apron begin to wave at her.

She veered for the man immediately, knowing she might collapse at any moment from fatigue, while behind her, the crowd of killers also corrected their vector, each of them running faster.

Stacy ran around an overturned car and jumped over three corpses sprawled in the road before finally making it to the Italian restaurant. As she reached the doors, the man threw them open wider and Stacy ran full tilt inside. As she fell to the floor of a foyer with walls lined with pictures of Italian landmarks, the doors were slammed shut, and seconds later there came a pounding as the murderous crowd tried to get inside.

Stacy was on her stomach, her head in her arms as she sucked in breath after breath. Her heart was pounding a mile a minute and she didn't know if the banging in her ears was from her own pulse or if it was from the incredible beating the doors were receiving.

The man who had waved to her knelt by her side, placing a hand on her shoulder.

"There, there, you're safe now, they can't get in here," he said with a light Italian accent. Stacy rolled onto her side and gazed up at the middle-aged man who smiled down at her with a look that would melt most women into putty. "I'm Mario, welcome to my place," he said with a smirk.

Stacy sat up with the help of Mario, and as she did, she suddenly sensed there were others in the restaurant with her and Mario. As she looked behind her, she saw six more people staring at her. Some had what she thought was blood on their clothing, but when she looked closer; she realized it was pasta sauce. The red gravy was splashed on their clothing like blood splatter and Stacy figured they must have been patrons at one time before everybody went bonkers.

"Who are you people?" Stacy asked as she got to her feet with the help of Mario.

"Who are we?" a man asked from her left. "Who the fuck are you?"

"Knock it off, Brad, we don't need your bullshit right now," another man said to the first.

"Fuck you, Tim, if I wanted your opinion, I'd squeeze your fag head to get it."

"Real nice, Brad. Do you kiss your mother with that mouth?" Tim asked snidely.

"Fuck you," Brad said again.

"Jesus, it's like that's the only word he knows," Tim quipped to the others.

"Knock it off, both of you," Mario said, his smile now gone. He was a big man, well over six feet, and his arms were rippled with muscle from years of kneading dough and carrying sacks of flour and supplies for his restaurant. He glared at Tim first, then Brad, who took offense immediately.

"What're you looking at me for, Mario?"

"Because you started it," Mario replied.

"Please, everyone," a young woman with strawberry blonde hair said from Brad's left. "Can't we all just cooperate? There's people out there trying to kill us!"

"Jill's right," another woman said. "We need to work together if we want to get through this in one piece. The woman was in her late sixties with graying hair and a school-teacher look.

"Martha's tellin' the truth," the next patron said. "My wife's at home and I want to get to her as soon as possible." The man was in his thirties and the wedding ring on his finger looked new.

"And you'll get to her soon enough, Roger," Mario said to the worried man. "But it's not safe to go out there yet."

"Are you sure they can't get in here?" a young woman said lastly. She had brown hair and her voice was like the squeaks of a mouse. She was cute but petite to the point she had no figure. Stacy stared at her and wondered if the woman shopped in the kid's section at the Gap.

"We're fine, Tina," Mario said. "That door is solid maple. They're not getting in here that way."

"Thanks for letting me in here," Stacy said to Mario now that she'd caught her breath. "If you hadn't, I'd probably be dead by now."

Mario was about to reply when Brad spoke up. "Yeah, thanks so much Mario. So you could save a piece of pussy, now more of them know we're in here. Great job."

Mario looked at Brad but he didn't reply and Tim was going to give a rebuttal when Mario nodded for him not to. Stacy could see Brad was the asshole of the group and she wasn't looking forward to having to deal with him. Brad was the selfish prick who would throw everyone under a bus if it would save his own ass. She rolled her eyes, wondering if she had fallen into a bad book where the author had no imagination and fell back on old clichés.

Brad took a step towards Stacy and she shrank back. The man's breath smelled of cheap wine, and when he leaned closer, it washed over her. "Just stay the fuck away from me, sweetheart, and we'll be just fine. Maybe these other assholes drool over another piece of cooch, but not me."

Mario stepped between Brad and Stacy.

"Go get some more to drink, Brad, and leave us alone, all right?" Mario's voice was low, the meaning clear.

Brad waved his hand like he was brushing off Mario. "Fine, I was about to do that before all this shit happened. "Mark my words, she's gonna get us all killed, now that there's more of them out there." He didn't wait for a reply from anyone, least of all Mario. He spun around and entered the main dining room, grabbing a bottle of wine from a nearby table where a half dozen had been placed.

"Don't mind, Brad," Tim said as he stepped up to her, holding out his hand. "He's our prerequisite jerk. Every group has to have one, right?" Stacy shook his hand, smiling. "And I'm the prerequisite gay man. I'm Tim," he added.

"Stacy. I'm Stacy. Thanks, Tim."

"Are you hungry?" Mario asked. "Do you want to get cleaned up? You look almost as bad as the nutjobs outside."

Stacy nodded. "Actually I'm starving and I would love to wash up, thank you."

"Right this way then, you can meet everyone else after you've cleaned up." Mario looked at the others and shooed them away. "Okay, folks, the excitement's over for now. Go back to whatever you were doing before I let her in."

The others moved away, a few smiling at Stacy as they went. Some stayed together while others went their own way. She found it amusing to see the clicks of people. Even in such dire circumstances the dynamics of high school clicks came into play. It was just how people were wired, she supposed.

Mario led her through the dining room to the back of the restaurant. "The bathrooms are back there. But don't use the ladies room, we've had to use it for storage since everything went to Hell," Mario told her with a shy grin.

"Okay," Stacy said, not understanding. She walked off, moving through the tables and down a small hallway. There was a mirror on the wall next to a pay phone and she stopped, looking at herself once more. Her hair was matted to her scalp and dried flakes of blood covered her cheeks and forehead. There were dark circles under her eyes from lack of sleep and some new stress lines. She didn't think she had ever looked worse in her life.

When she shook herself away from her reflection and headed off to the bathroom, she forgot what Mario told her about not using the ladies room. Maybe if he had been more serious about it, made a stronger point that she should not go into the ladies room, she would have listened, but after the distraction of seeing herself and how awful she looked, his words had been forgotten.

Upon reaching the two, side by side bathroom doors, years of habit kicked in and she went for the women's bathroom.

The door opened inward, and as she stepped inside and flicked on the light, she was assaulted by an aroma of rotting meat so strong it was as if she had walked into an actual wall, the redolence causing her to stop moving.

As the door closed behind her, her mouth fell open at the sight before her.

Then she screamed.

Chapter 15

Chad stared at the people in the church, realizing immediately there was something very wrong with the tableaux before him.

From the looks of the church, it was decorated with the trappings of a wedding, complete with a red runner down the middle aisle. If that wasn't enough of an explanation, then the two dozen people, all wearing tuxedos, formal dresses and suits, would have sealed the deal.

But if this was truly a wedding, then it was one that belonged in Hell. Every single person still alive was covered in gore and at their feet, in multiple body parts, was the victims of the wedding party.

It looked to Chad that when whatever was turning people into homicidal killers had infected the people inside the church, those that hadn't immediately succumbed to madness, had been slaughtered by their family and friends, most using nothing but their bare hands and teeth.

Faces were splattered with blood, and the once, light-blue gowns of the bridesmaids were now a deep scarlet, thanks to the arterial spray they'd been doused in. The entire church was filled with a charnel house smell that clung to the back of Chad's throat and it was all he could do not to vomit right in front of everyone.

All eyes were on Chad now and he expected them to come for him at any moment, but for some reason they didn't, they merely stared at him.

Chad stood by the doors, covered in blood and gore and just blinked back at them, not wanting to speak for fear of breaking the spell that had befallen these killers.

On the one-foot, raised stage was a podium, as well as a waist-high table covered in white lace. This table would be where the wine was laid out as well as other trappings of the church. But now it was being used for something far more sinister.

Like a medieval altar, a body was laid out on the table, the form defiantly female. Chad stared in confusion at the odd scene that looked like something out of a dark fantasy novel.

The woman was secured by her hands and feet and she seemed to be unconscious. The bindings used to tie her down had the look of an ornate rope, such what is used with fine drapery. She was wearing a beautiful flowing white gown with intricate lace, and if Chad had to guess, he assumed this was supposed to be the bride of the wedding.

But it appeared now she looked more like a sacrifice than a blushing bride.

From the right of the stage, Chad watched a man walk out from the shadows. He was wearing all black, and the white collar told Chad he was a priest. But this priest seemed to have fallen from the path of God, the proof being the dagger in his right hand and the malevolent look on his face.

The dagger wasn't fancy, with gold trim or emeralds; it was a simple dagger anyone could pick up at an Army/Navy store for ten bucks.

The priest walked to the supine woman and raised his hands over his head, screaming at the top of his lungs. As he did this, the crowd of onlookers joined him, some shaking bloody, severed limbs in their hands.

The priest seemed as crazy as the rest in the church but at the same time seemed more in control, as if he had a handle on what had happened to him and was relishing the *change* that had taken over his personality.

Without hesitation or preamble, he stopped screaming and slammed the dagger into the chest of the woman, causing her to wake up and begin shrieking in agony. Her cries went up in pitch as the priest began sawing at her torso, cracking her ribcage and eviscerating her as all watched with hate in their eyes. He began to tear out her insides, tossing the glistening organs onto the stage where they splashed and slid across the polished wood floor.

The woman's screams abruptly ceased when the priest wrapped his blood-covered hand around her still beating heart, and with one yank, ripped it from her breast to hold aloft for all to see. Blood shot from the severed arteries as the remaining life in the organ spewed its contents onto the floor.

The crowd went wild, feet stomping on the floor as others pounded on the back of the pews, their bloodlust insatiable.

Chad stared in horror, wondering if it could get any worse, when the priest raised the heart to his lips and sank his teeth into it, tearing at the muscle as blood dripped down his chin. The crowd went wild, roaring their hate-filled voices to shake the very rafters of the church, the stained glass windows vibrating with their intensity. If God had once lived in this place, then there was no doubt in Chad's mind, He had moved out...or worse, He'd been evicted.

As the man chewed on the heart, the crowd cheering, the cloying stink of death filling Chad's sinus, he couldn't hold back and he vomited the contents of his stomach across the floor, the viscous fluid splashing near his feet. As he dry heaved in pain, all eyes turned to look at him again, and this time the priest was glaring at Chad, as well. The heart was still in his hand and he stopped chewing in mid bite, his attention only for Chad.

Chad didn't see this, his eyes closed as he upchucked his pitiful breakfast of water and crackers.

When he opened his eyes, he found the roaring of the church had faded and there was almost absolute silence. And to make matters worse, he now found he was the center of attention.

The priest dropped the heart into the exposed chest cavity of the woman and let out a roar of rage as he pointed a blood-soaked arm at Chad. Even though there were no actual words, Chad knew what the priest was saying. What he was telling his followers.

"Kill him! He's not one of us!"

If Chad hoped to find salvation inside the church, he fast realized he'd found the exact opposite. As the first of the crowd began climbing over the pews to get to the back of the church and at the imposter before them, Chad spun around, unlocked the door and prepared to escape.

But he wasn't fast enough and a screaming man came at him from his right, plowing into him and knocking him over. Chad felt like he'd been struck by a linebacker as the breath was knocked out of him. He hit the floor hard, but rolled to his side, punching out blindly at his foe. He got lucky and his fist connected with the killer's chin, and the head was forced away from him. But Chad hadn't made a correct fist and his thumb was in the wrong position. He yelled out in pain when his thumb began to throb and he rolled to his feet to dash for the door. Behind him, thunderous stomping could be heard as the cathedral walls bounced the sound back and forth. To Chad, it sounded like a thousand attackers were descending on him.

Struggling with his foe as the man reached out and grabbed his right leg, Chad kicked out as hard as he could. His sneaker connected with the killer's nose and sent a gusher of blood from the shattered sniffer. The man fell back, cradling his nose but a second later was trying for Chad again.

But Chad was gone, running for the double doors and throwing them open. He was about to take his first step through the doorway and what he prayed was freedom, when he found there would be no escape outside, as a dozen killers charged up the stone steps, every single one of them waving a weapon.

Chad was trapped, and he was about to give in and accept his fate, when he looked to his left to see a hallway that led off the main floor of the church.

And it was clear of people!

With nothing to lose, he ran off, just as the first group of killers came up behind him. He could feel their breath on his neck, though he was sure it was his imagination, conjuring up supernatural powers for these people. In truth, they were all too human, but they had numbers and Chad was alone.

There was a plain wood door at the end of the hallway and he used it, throwing it open so hard the doorknob put a dent in the plaster wall. His back hairs itched as he heard the killers following him. Their voices filled the church to the brim with rage as their feet pounded the floor continually, and Chad had to fight down the growing panic rising inside him. He knew if he let it take him over, he would never come back from the abyss.

With the door open, he ran through the opening, then spun around and pulled the door closed. There was a cheap lock on the inside and he used it now; a second later the door shook in its frame as bodies were thrown up against it. But Chad wasn't waiting to see if it would hold; he was already running down the stairs the door led to.

When he was halfway down the stairwell, a man popped up from the bottom landing. He growled once and then was running at Chad, taking the steps two at a time.

Chad was cornered with nowhere to go, and though he was terrified, he knew he would have to fight this man or be killed by him, the rage-filled face showing the man was one of *them*.

Chad waited for the man to get within a foot of him and then he kicked out with his left sneaker. He idly noticed how the sneaker was covered in blood, the white leather now hidden; the white laces now a dark red. Then his foot connected with the man's face and the killer was falling backwards, tumbling "ass over teakettle", as his mother used to say when he would fall down while playing as a boy.

Despite the pounding on the door behind him, Chad heard the audible crack of the killer's neck as the man rolled down the stairs. The dead man came to a stop four steps from the bottom.

Chad, knowing he couldn't stay where he was, began descending once more, pausing as he climbed over the body. The man's right eye was closed in death, but his left was wide open, and Chad stared at it, as if he expected the orb to jump in its socket when he was in the right position to be grabbed by the man. But the eye remained immobile, blood seeping from the cracked skull the killer received from his fall.

Chad breathed a soft sigh of relief when his feet touched down on the ground floor. He didn't know why. He was still in a dire situation and was only seconds from death.

Above him, he heard the door crack and splinter as hands and feet punched it. The sound of banging drums came to him as the steady staccato of fists continued their attack on the plain wooden door.

He was in the basement, but it was dark and he couldn't see. With only one path before him, he quickly ran down a short corridor. He began to hear a constant buzzing sound, like a thousand bees only more muted. It was as if there were a million little wings flitting about.

Reaching the end of the hallway, he stepped through the doorless opening, seeing there was no door but a place where hinges could go on the frame. The open basement stretched out before him, but he still couldn't see a thing, the entire room wreathed in darkness. There was a charnel house smell that had him gagging for clean air, but he covered his nose with his arm to prevent from vomiting yet again.

Feeling along the wall, he hoped there would be a light switch, and a second later he was greeted with exactly that. Behind him he could hear the beleaguered door taking a battering, but so far it was holding as he had yet to hear footsteps coming down the stairs.

He still had time to escape through the basement emergency exit.

His hand flicked the light switch and more humming filled the room as recessed phosphorescent lights flicked on in the ceiling.

The instant the basement became illuminated, Chad's eyes went wide and he leaned over and vomited, despite his best intentions not to. But nothing but a string of saliva seeped from his mouth, as his stomach twisted into pangs of agony. Leaning against the wall, he tried to suck in a breath of foul air.

Only seconds had passed before he was standing tall once more and staring out at the slaughterhouse that was the basement of the church. The room was as large and wide as the actual church above. Steel pylons, a foot thick, supported the ceiling and the church itself, and other than those, the room was one massive area. This, Chad knew, was where church socials and other financial drives were held. Craft shows and bake sales were just a few of the events to go on here.

But now, all that was gone. The folding tables and chairs were stacked neatly to the far wall and the open floor was now covered with the remnants of dead bodies.

Hearing the door giving way behind him, Chad stepped into the carnage, his sneakers squishing in the two-inch thick, pools of blood. There had to be an emergency exit he could use to escape the basement. If not then he was dead, as dead as these poor souls at his feet.

As he crossed the basement to the opposite side, he saw infants with their mothers, young children with fathers; all brutally mutilated to the point he could barely recognize what gender they were. The buzzing he heard, was of what looked to be a million flies, all feeding on the fast-bloating bodies of raw meat. He had to wave them away from his face and keep his lips sealed or else run the risk of having them fly inside his mouth and onto his tongue. They crawled into his ears and then back out, as there was more than enough blood covering him to make him interesting to the flies, and they quickly covered him from head to toe. Chad creased his eyes and continued.

Behind him and up the stairs, the door finally collapsed, and amid splintering wood, came the sound of many footsteps as the killers charged down the steps, seeking their prey.

Chad picked up his pace, knowing he was out of time, and as his right sneaker slipped in offal, he fell face first into the open stomach cavity of an elderly woman. When he fell, his face went five inches into a pile of intestines and the foul odor had him gagging once more.

He raised himself to his elbows, feeling like he wanted to die as the offal went into his nose and seeped into his ears. It was cold too; the bodies dead for more than two days and it reminded him of rancid tapioca pudding.

And then it was too late to move as the first of the killers charged into the basement.

Like a deer caught in a semi's headlights, Chad froze in shock, his head and body sinking back down into the meat under him. Playing possum was his only chance right now and he placed his head back into the intestines, the viscera seeping deeper into his ears and nostrils and muting the sounds of the killers as they ran into the basement. If he was lucky, his fallen body would look like just another corpse in a sea of them, and if he could last long enough and remain completely still, they might leave, figuring he had escaped the basement.

More offal slid between his lips as he tried to breathe and he felt his stomach preparing to heave as some slid down his throat, the rancid taste making him want to throw up with everything left within him, including his stomach lining if necessary. He had to admit that at this exact point in his life, death didn't seem such a scary thing. At least it would end his suffering.

All around him were the grunts, screams and frustrated yells of the *changed* as they ran around the room, searching for him. Folding table and chairs were overturned and closets and file cabinets were opened and destroyed, the contents dumped out carelessly.

One of the killers, too lazy to go around the pile of corpses, began to crawl through them to get to the other side, and he stepped on Chad's back, forcing his face deeper into the viscera. His face was now so deep into offal he couldn't breathe and he held his breath, knowing if he moved they would surely discover him.

It was like he was underwater, and if he attempted to breathe in, he would drown. But he couldn't, his life depended on it. He thanked God he stopped smoking years ago and hopefully his lungs were stronger now that he'd quit.

He couldn't hear anything, his ears clogged with viscous fluid that seeped around his ears and down onto his neck and under his shirt.

Muffled sounds penetrated his clogged ear canals and he began to feel faint. Spots of light danced across his closed eyes and the feeling of light-headedness grew until he knew if he didn't exhale and then breathe in, he was going to pass out. And when he did, he knew his body would twitch, alerting the killers that he wasn't a corpse.

He didn't know how long he laid there, face buried in gore. Three minutes, four? An eternity?

Finally, when he was on the verge of passing out and he knew he couldn't last a second longer, he pushed himself a few inches out of the muck and sucked in air. His chest heaved as his lungs began to work and he waited to feel hands on his arms and shoulders as the killers suddenly realized there was a moving body amidst the carcasses. But the fatal grip didn't come, and when Chad blinked his eyes clear, wiping them with his fingertips as he leaned on his elbows, he saw that the basement was empty, the harsh lights now illuminating nothing but corpses, the flies feeding once more.

Sucking in the gas of decomposing bodies, he began to hack and cough, and laugh at being safe. Though foul, the air never tasted so sweet, and he spit countless times to clear his mouth of the fluids of the rotting corpse beneath him. He was now absolutely covered in gore, and his face was hidden under a mask of viscera that made him look as insane and rage-filled as any of the murderers he'd seen thus far.

The killers were gone, and when he looked across the basement, he saw there was a door open on the far wall. It was an emergency door leading to the back alley of the church.

But still he didn't leave, knowing the second he stepped outside he would probably be spotted. So he stayed in the pile of muck, deciding another hour wouldn't matter. He was as dirty as a human being could get and if it meant staying alive then he would accept it as a necessary evil.

For an hour he lay in the corpses, as flies crawled over him, feeding on the blood coating his body, and as the sun finally went down, bathing the church in darkness with the exception of the harsh fluorescents, he finally climbed to his knees and crawled out of the bodies. His foot came down on the small arm of a little girl no more than three and he heard the audible crack of bones breaking. He barely flinched at the sound. It seemed the more he was exposed to the madness and carnage, the more hardened he was becoming to it.

Reaching the emergency exit, he peered out into the night, but saw no one. There were cracked stone stairs to climb before he was on street level once more, and as he stared into the darkness, he saw shapes moving about. But they were to his right. So moving left, he hugged the building and rounded the corner. He wanted to get to the next street over from the church, and beyond that, hopefully freedom.

He wiped his nose with the back of his hand, but it didn't help much. The odor coming off him was atrocious, the offal and gore covering him, the miasma like a heavy fog cloud surrounding him.

He began to laugh then. At first it was more of a titter, but soon he was laughing quite hard, though he was smart enough to quell his voice so he didn't call attention to himself. Still, he couldn't help it. He wondered if he was close to a breakdown, and had to believe it was true. And who could blame him? If he wasn't losing it after all he'd been through, then he hadn't been sane to begin with.

Crossing the street, he blended into the shadows, and with no destination in mind, he began to run; a loping gate that to any who saw him would automatically assume he was one of the *changed*.

Chad didn't know this, and if he did, he wouldn't have cared. All he wanted to do was run, and as he did, he couldn't help but wonder if he was truly insane and was even now wrapped up in a straitjacket and pumped full of drugs in an asylum somewhere.

And in reality, he was imagining all of it.

Chapter 16

Chad stared off at the horizon, seeing the outline of Chicago, the tops of the burning buildings looking like glowing stalagmites reaching up from the floor of some mythical cavern.

Only a few yards from him, sprawled on the ground like yard waste, lay the crumpled, mangled body of an elderly woman. Just behind the corpse was a house, and the door was hanging open, slowly moving back and forth in the gentle breeze.

It looked to Chad as if she'd been dragged out of her home and gutted right there on her front lawn.

He turned away, not wanting to look at the grisly sight, but wherever his eyes fell there was more carnage. Crashed vehicles, smoldering houses, bodies, whole or in pieces; it was like a battle-field.

Chad had been running all night, only slowing to hide here and there and try to grab some sleep. But there was a chill in the air and each time he drifted off, an hour later he would wake up shivering and would have to move on so he could stay warm.

Plus, the killers never slept it seemed; or not much anyway. Each time he drifted off, he would snap awake at the distant sound of shrieks of either pain or rage. A few errant gunshots echoed across the area, causing him to wince each time.

One time, late in the night, he'd heard the staccato of automatic weapons and he wondered if the military was out there, trying to bring back order. But just as fast as it began, it had stopped and he'd closed his eyes and fallen back to sleep.

When the coast was clear after five tense heartbeats, he crept to the next house, to then hide in the bushes. He was at the edge of town, only a half mile from where he could pick up the highway leading into Chicago. His plan was to find a working car and then drive there. He didn't know what the highway was like, but he figured he would drive for as long as he could and then walk the rest.

Leap-frogging from house to house, he found a bakery at the end of the street. It was a small, Mom and Pop one for sure, and the front glass windows were shattered, the glass shards lying on the sidewalk, twinkling like diamonds in the morning sun.

A bakery should have pastries and breads, Chad thought, as his stomach rumbled. God, he was starving. The backpack taken from the daycare was long gone and he gritted his teeth as his stomach grumbled some more. Knowing he had to eat, he checked the road and dashed for the bakery, running like a soldier on the frontlines of a foreign war. He made it to the bakery in seconds and jumped into the open window, sliding across the floor and hiding behind the counter. Then he peeked out into the street to see if he'd been seen.

He waited for a full five minutes, and when he was confident he'd made it safely, he spotted a small group of people come out from behind a house.

They were a straggly bunch, with torn clothes and filthy hair and faces. Dried blood covered each of them and more than one carried some kind of weapon. One carried something that looked like a purse, but the sun was behind the people and Chad couldn't see what it was.

The small group made their way down the street, and when they passed a house, the rooftop blocking the sun so he could see them better, Chad saw what he believed was a purse was in fact a human head, the straps of the imaginary purse the head's hair. By the length, Chad assumed the head was female, but other than that there was no true way to be sure. The face had no eyes, and the skin was peeled from the skull so that there was a permanent smile where the lips should be.

Chad closed his eyes at the sight, imagining what that poor woman had suffered, and then opened them again to watch the killers walk by the bakery.

When they were a good twenty feet from his position, one of the group began yelling, then took off at a run, the others following.

Chad figured the man who began screaming and running had spotted something worth attacking, and if it had been human, Chad wished the prey well for he knew how it felt.

He waited for another four minutes, and when nothing else stirred on the street, he turned and went deeper into the bakery, hoping there would be some remnants of food to be found.

Hey, who knew? Maybe even an apple or blueberry pie was still hiding somewhere, missed by whatever scavengers had already been through the place.

The back of the bakery was a charnel house of destroyed bodies. Heads were tossed to the sides like old kick balls and arms and legs had been draped over oven racks and counters. Chad stared at the back of the bakery in awe. Despite all the carnage he'd already witnessed, it still shocked him how violent the killers were.

A few of the torsos had aprons on and Chad figured they had once been the staff of the bakery. On the far wall to his right were framed awards, stating how the bakery had won **BEST IN COOKIES** or the **BEST PECAN PIE IN CHICAGO**.

An overturned sheet pan hid broken cookies and Chad began shoving them into his mouth, looking to anyone who might be watching like a kid set free in a candy shop. The cookies were colorful; blues, pinks and yellows, with bright candy sprinkles on top and made into flower-like swirls. He had a memory of going to the local bakery when he was kid with his father. As his father would get Italian bread and maybe a ricotta pie, the owner would always give Chad one cookie. It was a tradition, like getting a piece of cheese when you went to the corner deli while the clerk sliced your order.

By the time he was finished eating the pastries, his stomach was full and his mouth was bone dry. Going to a large, basin sink, he ignored the two severed heads staring up at him from the bottom of the sink and turned on the tap. As the water sputtered forth, he washed his face and hands and drank deeply.

As he stood up, he realized for the first time there was no power. Going to a wall switch, he flicked it on and off a few times but nothing happened. In the night, while he'd been on the run, the power had failed, at least in this part of town.

With his stomach full, he let out a loud sigh. It was amazing how things looked more positive when you weren't hungry. He decided to explore some more, wanting to either take some food with him when he left or perhaps even hiding out in the bakery for a while.

First he needed something to carry the remaining cookies and whatever else he could find. A sack, a bag, anything would do. He began searching the bakery, but all he found were plastic bags. He knew they wouldn't be strong enough to handle the abuse thrown at them. He needed something with resistance, such as a cloth sack or even a sheet that he could tie the ends together.

He went back to the front of the bakery and he spotted the cash register all alone on the end of the counter. It was an old one, dating back twenty years. It was so old it wasn't plugged in to an electrical outlet.

Going to it, he pressed a few buttons and it popped open. Sitting in the drawer were five's, tens and ones. When he lifted the drawer up, he saw a few twenties lying unmolested. That made him laugh for some reason. Out of all the death and carnage, out of all the violence that had taken place in the bakery, none of it had been about money. If so, then the cash register would have been cleaned out.

All the things money represented were now null and void and the currency of blood had replaced it.

Pushing the cash register closed, he continued searching. Outside on the street, a few gunshots rang out but so far the bakery appeared safe. None of the nearby buildings were on fire and the wind was blowing the wrong way to blow embers on the bakery. Once or twice Chad heard footsteps slapping the pavement, but they soon passed without incident.

Returning to the back of the bakery, he renewed his hunt for anything of use. He found a decent sized paring knife and shoved it into his belt in case he needed it to defend himself, then he renewed his hunt for a bag.

Near the back door, he came upon a walk-in freezer. By the items lying on the floor by the door, it looked to him like this was where the cookie dough and other perishable foodstuffs were kept until needed. Though the power was out, he knew as long as the door remained closed—which it was—then whatever was inside would still be fine. Deciding there should be plenty of edibles inside, he unlocked the freezer with the pin that slid through the latch and yanked on the handle. It was set up like an old refrigerator handle, one good pull and it was open.

As the door began to open and cold air issued forth between the gap, Chad was already thinking about the frozen treats waiting within. He was so wrapped up in this vision, he was taken entirely off guard when the door was shoved open hard and a partially frozen man with a large cleaver came billowing forth like an ice demon, the man's stature seeming to dwarf Chad's by almost a foot.

The second Chad saw the man's blue complexion from the low temperature and rage-filled eyes, he knew he was dealing with another *changed* person; one who wanted his blood.

With a guttural scream of hatred, the man came at Chad, the weapon already raised to come down and cleave him in two. Chad, panicking, fell back, tripping over his feet in his desperation to escape certain death. His butt came down on the floor and the man loomed over him, looking like a frost giant from a Robert E Howard story, thanks to the cold air from the freezer resembling fog. Chad looked around frantically for something to use as a weapon and his hand came down on a sheet pan that had been knocked from a table. Grabbing it, he thrust it up like a shield an instant before the cleaver came at his head. There was a loud *clang* and Chad saw the tip of the cleaver penetrate the sheet pan an inch from his forehead. Then the sheet pan was ripped from his hands as the man pulled back, wanting to try again.

Chad let the pan go as he searched for something more offensive. Remembering the knife he'd found, he pulled it out and stabbed the man in the left thigh, but the frozen giant only roared in anger and kicked Chad away from him.

His heart was beating fast and he was scared to death, the decision of fight or flight came to him, but he knew flight was out of the question and was able to stay sane enough to fight.

That was the difference between Chad and all the others who had been slaughtered throughout the city. Though not a violent man, he had come to accept his fate in a mad world and wasn't afraid to kill to survive, unlike all the other *civilized* people who had been taken down in seconds.

His eyes darting back and forth, he spotted a rolling pin no more than two feet away. As the giant attacker came for him, sweeping the cleaver horizontally to take off his head, Chad rolled to the side, more luck than skill saving him from a beheading.

He reached out desperately, frantically wrapping shaking fingers around the handle of the rolling pin as the cleaver came for his arm. He pulled the rolling pin to him an instant before the cleaver bounced off the floor tiles, a few sparks jumping to be lost in the scattered layer of flour dusting every flat surface.

The cleaver came down again, and Chad rolled to the left, the cleaver missing his right shoulder by an inch. As the frozen killer became off balance, Chad used the rolling pin and whacked the man's right knee.

There was an audible *crack* in the bakery as wood met bone and bone lost. The man roared in pain and stumbled backwards, crashing into a shelf full of baking pans. As the pans crashed to the floor in a cacophony of gong-like sounds, Chad jumped to his feet. He wanted to run then, run away as fast as he could, but he didn't know if the giant man would follow him. He would need to put the guy out of action just enough so he could make his escape.

The man was kicking and knocking pans off the shelf as he struggled to right himself and Chad swallowed the knot of fear in his throat and lunged forward with the rolling pin, this time going for the left knee cap. Now that Chad was standing, he had more leverage and he used all his upper body strength to bring the rolling pin down on the man's exposed knee.

This time the crack was meatier, as the knee cap shattered and the man's leg went limp. The cleaver fell from his hand as the man began to tumble forward. The killer fell like a tree taken down by lightning in the middle of a storm, and Chad didn't wait for the man to complete his journey to the floor. When the man's head was two feet from the floor, Chad raised the rolling pin and brought it down on the back of his head, the force of the blow helping the head to reach the stone tiles faster.

The man's face was suddenly flattened when his nose struck the floor, followed by the rest of his features. His eyes imploded by the force of the blow and his teeth were sent into his brain, as well as cartilage from his pulverized nose.

The body began to twitch as blood poured out of the head wound and face of the man, the legs jerking spastically in the death throes that seemed to go on for a very long time.

Heaving with the exertion of battle, Chad lowered the bloody rolling pin and watched the man die. When he couldn't stand it any longer, he went to a pile of ten pound flour bags and sat down. He watched the growing pool of blood meander across the floor like he was watching a snail make its way across a stone walkway.

He sat there for a full hour before screams from the street pulled him back to reality.

Standing, he gripped the rolling pin tighter and snuck up to the front of the bakery. There was a group of *changed* making their way down the street. He saw some young ones in this group, some no more than ten years old and they were all growling and snapping at one another. A pack of wild dogs was the image Chad thought of, only this pack walked on two legs.

He watched them reach the end of the street and disappear around the corner.

Deciding the danger was passed, he went back to the rear of the bakery, careful not to step in the dead man's blood. He returned to what he'd been doing before opening the freezer again, and when there was no suitable bag to use, he cut open a bag of flour and poured the contents onto the floor, then he used the sack for a storage bag. He ignored the way the blood soaked into the flour, making a red paste that bubbled like vinegar and baking soda.

With the freezer still open, he grabbed a few plastic wrapped hunks of cookie dough and a couple loaves of bread from a metal rack. The loaves were already cooked so at least he wouldn't have to eat raw bread dough. As for the cookie dough, hell, he loved eating raw cookie dough.

Returning to the main section of the bakery, he stuffed the remaining cookies into it, and then with one last look at the destroyed bakery and the dead man, who was already drawing flies, he snuck out the back door.

He needed to find a car or a truck, something that he could use to get him to Chicago where the National Guard or State police were set up.

Surely the city had to be better able to handle what was going on than the suburbs.

And if he was wrong, then he would probably die, killed by a crowd of the *changed*, but though he had been fighting for his life for almost three days, he knew sooner or later his luck would run out.

Because simply, the odds were so highly stacked against him.

Chapter 17

As soon as Stacy screamed, the bathroom door was knocked inward and Mario was standing there. Behind him was Roger and Tim, all with concerned looks on their faces.

"Stacy, are you all right?" Mario asked as he grabbed her by the shoulders. "What are you doing in here? I told you to use the men's room."

"I...I didn't think, I forgot what you said," she stammered as she stared at the pile of corpses sprawled on the bathroom floor.

There had to be a dozen or so, maybe up to twenty. All were covered in blood and a few were missing limbs. Flies and maggots were everywhere, crawling over open eyes and in festering wounds. Though it was only days since the people had died, already the bodies were decaying. Bloated stomachs were the norm and fetid gases hung in the air in a miasma of death.

"Come on, let me get you out of here," Mario said as he led her out, closing the door behind him. Mario looked to Tim and Roger. "You two, get something to block access to that room. No one needs to go in there anyway. We don't want this happening again," he told them as he led Stacy away from the door and into the main dining room.

"All those people," she said. "What happened to them?"

Brad walked up to her and Mario, smoking a cigarette and holding a wine bottle. He blew smoke towards Mario as he frowned. "That's what's left of Mario's lunch guests from the other day," he joked, or tried to. No one was laughing. "When everyone went fucking crazy and tried to kill one another, most of us that were fine fought back. We were stronger than them and we took them out." He shrugged, thinking back to the other day. "It was a fucking massacre."

Mario pushed Brad aside. "Shut up, Brad, no one asked you. Go have another drink."

"Why, Mario, she deserves to know the truth," Brad replied. He looked at Stacy. "Even after we killed the ones that went crazy, a few hours later some of us that were fine then went nuts and tried to go on a killing spree. We had to kill them, too."

"We didn't have a choice," Mario said as the others gathered around. So far no one spoke, only listening. "It's not like we could have kicked them out, Brad," Mario said. "Even then there was a crowd outside trying to get in."

"Oh, you mean like the crowd that's out there now? The one you called right to us when you let this bitch in? Until then, no one was bothering us; they'd finally left us alone."

Tim spoke up. "Yeah, they left us 'cause they spotted something outside that was easier pickings."

"Shut up, fagboy, no one asked for you're your opinion," Brad snapped back.

Tim gave Brad the finger but he did quiet down. Stacy watched the two men and saw that whatever was between the two men had been going on for days. The way Tim flipped Brad off was so casual, as if he'd done it countless times before.

"He's a jerk, but he's right," Mario said to Stacy. "I was in the back, cooking with the other chefs and everyone here was eating lunch. Nothing spectacular, right? Everyone has lunch at a restaurant now and then. But then I heard these screams. I thought maybe someone was choking or something so I ran out to the dining room, but when I get there, I see some guy killing his wife. A bunch of us drag him off and hold him down, but then one of the guys holding him down goes crazy. He grabs a fork and stabs the first guy in the eye, popping the eye out like it was a white tomato. I almost thought the guy was gonna eat it but he tossed it away. Then the dining room went crazy as others began attacking each other. It was madness. Eventually those of us that weren't crazy stopped the others and the only way was to kill them. The others in here with us, well, I called out to them too when I saw them outside; just like you."

"It's all true," Martha said as she stepped up next to Mario. She brushed her gray hair out of her eyes. "My husband tried to kill me and if Tim didn't stop him I'd be dead now."

Stacy nodded. "Yeah, something like that happened to me, too. I was taking a letter from my boss when he went crazy and jumped his desk. He tried to kill me but I got lucky and got away."

Roger spoke up. "So how is it out there? Are the cops getting things under control or what?"

Stacy shook her head. "No, it's crazy out there, too. I saw a few policemen, but they weren't any better than the crazy ones. Whatever's happening is affecting just about everyone."

Mario nodded. "Yeah, we talked about that some. It seems we're immune to whatever's going on."

Brad chuckled. "Or we're gonna flip out at any second and try to kill each other." He looked at Tim. "I got dibs on fagboy over there."

Tim crossed his arms and scowled. "God, Brad, how can you be such an asshole? Doesn't it hurt you? Even a little?"

Brad smiled so wide it looked like the smile was going to fall off his face. "I love who I am, Timmy my boy. Sounds to me like someone might not, though? What's the matter, having second thoughts about sucking dick?"

Mario stepped between Brad and Tim. "Knock it off, you two, Christ, every five minutes." Mario turned to face Tim. "Why do you let him get to you? He's an asshole, we all know it. Just let him be and he'll stop bugging you. He only does it 'cause he knows it gets to you."

"Easy for you to say, he never gives you any lip," Tim replied to Mario.

Roger shifted next to Tim. "I think Brad is a closet homosexual. Maybe he has the hots for you, Tim, and he doesn't want to admit it."

Tim smiled then, and it was genuine. He liked Roger, the two becoming fast friends in the short time they'd known each other.

"No way, Roger, it's never gonna happen. I wouldn't do him with your dick."

Roger laughed and slapped Tim on the shoulder and the two moved away. Martha decided she'd said what she wanted and she wandered away to join Jill and Tina who were in a corner booth. Tina sat quietly, barely looking up let alone speaking.

Mario patted Stacy on the shoulder and pointed to the men's room. "If you're okay now, you can try the bathroom again. This time use the men's room, okay?"

She smiled wanly, the gesture forced. "Don't worry, I won't make that mistake again." She jumped when a particularly loud bang came from the front doors. The steady beating of fists and hand weapons had continued since she'd arrived, but after a while it became background noise. Mario saw her jump and patted her arm.

"Don't worry, like I said, they can't get in here."

Stacy glanced to the windows lining the front of the restaurant. The shades were drawn but she could see they were glass. Mario saw where she was looking and he nodded, knowing her next question.

"Those windows are made of a thick, tempered glass. You could toss a brick at one of them and it wouldn't break."

"But it's still only glass. If enough of them tried, is it possible they could break in?" she asked.

Mario nodded. "Sure, it's possible, I won't lie to you, I've thought about it, too. But so far they haven't been able to organize like that. They saw you go in the door and that's all they can think about. If things go like last time, eventually they'll get bored, see something on the street that's better pickings, and take off. Then I guess they forget about us. I don't think those people out there have a long memory. Must be a side effect to whatever's infected them. Now go get cleaned up, and while you're doing that I'll make you something to eat. Nothing fried, though as my fryers are electric. The power went out this morning and so far it hasn't returned. But at least I still have the stoves which are gas."

Stacy began to walk back to the bathrooms. "Anything's fine, Mario, really. Thank you for that." She stopped and turned, looking him directly in the eyes. They were a deep blue and she found him very handsome. "And thank you again for saving me. I don't want to think about what might have happened if I was still out there all alone."

He waved his hand at her, brushing off her thanks. "It's nothing, really. I would have done it for anyone. That's why I brought in the others, too. This time it just happened to be you."

She nodded, the gesture quick, then turned and went back to the bathrooms, already looking forward to getting cleaned up.

* * *

Fifteen minutes later, Stacy exited the bathroom feeling like a new woman. The second she stepped into the main dining room, she could hear the pounding of the killers outside. They wouldn't give up, she knew, and she felt a chill go down her back at the thought of all the people out there who wanted nothing more than to tear her apart.

As she entered the main dining room, she immediately heard raised voices. Two voices actually, both male. Walking towards the group of people, she pushed past Roger and Jill to see Brad and Tim standing chest to chest.

"I don't have to apologize," Brad was saying. "I can say whatever the fuck I want and I say you're a buttmuncher."

"Jesus Christ, Brad, what the hell is your problem with me?" Tim asked, his face red with anger. "Ever since I met you, you've been riding my ass."

"Yeah, and not in the way he'd like it," Roger said under his breath so only Stacy and Jill could hear. Jill slapped his arm to make him stop.

"What's wrong with me? Nothing's wrong with me. I just hate fags, is all. Everyone in this damn country thinks they have to kiss your people's asses, that 'cause you like to suck dick you think you're somehow special. Well, it's a load of bullshit and I won't do it. So fuck off or so help me..."

"So help you what?" Tim growled, throwing down the gauntlet.

"So help me I'll kick your fag ass all over this place."

"Like hell you will," Tim said and pushed Brad away from him. "You're just a loud mouth, that if made to put up or shut up, will shut the hell up every time!"

"Why you little fuckin' pansy," Brad snarled and lunged at Tim, knocking him over a table as Brad fell on top of him.

Brad began punching Tim in the face as the others began to yell at them to stop. Tim wasn't taking it lying down though and he bucked his hips and pushed Brad away from him. Rolling to his feet, he charged at Brad, the two knocking over a table and chairs in a crash that overrode the pounding on the front doors.

"We have to make them stop!" Martha cried as she watched the two men rolling across the floor.

Roger shrugged as if he was watching a wrestling match. "Why? The two of them have been at each other's throat since day one. Let them fight it out, then maybe they'll leave each other alone."

"But one of them might get hurt," Jill added.

Roger shrugged again. "So? We got a first aid kit, I say let 'em duke it out."

Stacy said nothing. Being new to the group, she didn't think she had a right to give her input, so she watched the two men go at it, secretly rooting for Tim. She didn't know either man very well, but Brad had already come off as a selfish blowhard while Tim seemed nice. In the end, she hoped Tim was the victor.

Brad yelled in pain as he was kicked off his feet and he fell back into a table, knocking the silverware and plates piled on it to the floor. Tim was on him in an instant, sending blow after blow into Brad's side. Stacy could see Tim might have been a gay man, but he knew how to fight; perhaps he was a boxer in school or had taken a self defense class. Brad on the other hand, fought like he was a kid in a school yard, throwing punches out blindly, although sometimes he managed to land one.

Tim blocked a punch to his face and sent an uppercut into Brad's chin. He followed this by a punch to Brad's kidneys. Brad doubled over in pain and Tim used his knee to send Brad's head flying backwards. The wounded man fell onto the floor like a sack of potatoes and he seemed stunned for a moment.

"Stay down, Brad, and this can be over," Tim said gasping from the exertion of the fight.

"Fu...fu...fuck you," Brad gasped as he wiped blood from his lips. Before Tim knew what Brad was going to do, Brad reached out, picked up a fork lying nearby in the midst of others, and jabbed it into Tim's left leg just above the knee.

Tim howled in pain and jumped back, the fork sticking out of his leg.

Brad laughed, a throaty chuckle filled with blood as he went to his elbows. "Take that, you fuckin' fag."

Tim reached down and pulled the fork from his leg, wincing when it came free. Blood flowed down his leg and into his shoe as he raised the fork to his eyes. "You no good bastard," Tim hissed. "You'll pay for that."

Tim tossed the fork to the side and picked up a steak knife from another table. With the knife held in a thrusting grip, he advanced on Brad.

"What the hell is going on in my restaurant?" Mario bellowed from the swinging doors that led into the kitchen. He was holding a plate of cold pasta and a basket of bread for Stacy. In the back, as he was preparing food, he hadn't heard what was going on. His eyes were wide and his jaw was taut and he wasn't pleased with what he'd seen. Mario had become the defacto leader of their little group, more because of his will and stature than because he owned the restaurant.

Tim stopped in mid-stride and Brad turned to look at Mario.

"He started it, Mario," Brad said from the floor.

"Like hell I did," Tim rebutted. "I've been taking this asshole's shit since we got stuck in here and I'm sick of it."

Mario set the food on a table and walked over to the two men. He looked at Tim's leg and gave him a questioning look.

"It's fine, it didn't go in too deep," Tim said as he looked at the blood on his pants leg. "He did it," Tim said and pointed to Brad. "The son-of-a-bitch actually stabbed me with a fork."

"Is this true?" Mario asked Brad as he loomed over him.

"What if it was? You're not the fucking cops. What're you gonna do about it?"

Mario knelt down next to Brad and let out a long breath. "I can toss you outside and let the crazies deal with you, that's what I can do."

Brad's face blanched. "What? No way, you wouldn't do it. Everyone would stop you."

"Oh, yeah? You think so?" Mario asked as he looked at the others. "So, anyone object to me throwing Brad outside and letting the nutjobs deal with him?"

No one said anything and each of them began to wander away, as if they had important business elsewhere in the restaurant. Brad looked at Roger who was still watching. As the only other male, he hoped Roger would support him.

Roger shrugged as he returned Brad's gaze. "Sorry, buddy, you dug the shit pit yourself, now you can try and climb out of it all by yourself." He turned and walked away, casting a quick smile to Stacy.

Brad's confidence faltered and he swallowed the knot in his throat. "You wouldn't dare," he said without much resolve.

"Try me, Brad. I'm sick of your shit. You'll get along with these people or you can leave, it's as simple as that." He helped Brad up, lifting the prone man like he was a child. Brad felt the strong grip on his arm and knew Mario could break him in half if he wanted to. Brad was a loud mouth, but he wasn't a stupid man and he saw the way the wind was blowing very quickly. With a lowering of his head, he nodded assent. "Fine, Mario, I'll behave."

"Good, Brad, that's real good. We all need to work together in here if we're gonna get through this. Surely you understand that. Black, white, gay or straight, we're all human beings. That has to count for something, doesn't it?"

"Yeah, I guess so," Brad replied.

"Good, then go get yourself cleaned up and the next time Tim does something you don't like you remember it might be him that saves your life if those nutjobs get inside here."

"Fine," Brad said, now sounding like an impatient child having to listen to a scolding by his parents.

"Go on, now, I'm through with you," Mario said, dismissing him.

Brad looked up, his eyes locking with Stacy's for a second. Before he turned away, she could have sworn he sneered at her, as if everything Mario had said had gone in one ear and out the other. But she may have imagined it.

Mario went to her and smiled sincerely. "Sorry 'bout that, cabin fever and all. You drop a bunch of strangers in a restaurant and have them try to survive a city full of killers and what do you get?"

Stacy shrugged. "The next big reality show on TV?"

Mario chuckled. "Yeah, you may have a point there." He gestured to the table holding the food he'd carried out. "Come on, don't let that stuff bother you. I made you something nice to eat. Here, I'll sit with you and we can talk."

She let him lead her to the table, and when she glanced over her shoulder, she saw Tim getting patched up by Jill and Martha, and Brad skulking to the men's bathroom.

It looked like it was over, at least for now. So she sat down and began to eat, suddenly realizing how truly hungry she was.

Chapter 18

It was late morning when Chad left the bakery to continue his search for help, for someone who wasn't a stark-raving homicidal killer.

Once more he leap-frogged from house to house, slowly making his way to the onramp to the highway that would take him into Chicago.

He had a little more than a mile to go when he came to his first potential vehicle, but when he got closer, he saw the battery was dead, the ignition left on for too long. And if that hadn't made the vehicle unwanted, then the dead man with a shattered skull in the driver's seat would have. The dead man's head now resembled a Halloween pumpkin after it had been tossed from a high roof. Gray matter splashed the sides of the vehicle as well as the windshield, and it looked like dozens of gray worms were crawling about. But Chad knew they weren't worms, they were the man's brains.

From sitting in the sun for almost three days, the inside of the car was atrocious and Chad knew if he tried to use the vehicle, he would have ended up vomiting the entire time. The stench of rancid meat mixed with the aroma of bile was so strong even the most seasoned garbage man would have been hard-pressed to maintain his composure.

So Chad continued on, wondering how the dead man's head had become a shattered wreckage of bone and brain matter. If he had to guess, he would have figured it was by a gun, perhaps a shotgun. He imagined the man running to his car, jumping in and turning on the ignition. But just before he turned the key past electrical, someone had run up to him, placed the shotgun to his temple, and squeezed the trigger, sending the contents of his head across the dashboard.

Chad halted when he saw movement at the end of the street, and he jumped into the nearby hedges of the closest home, peering through the small leaves as he watched one man, then others appear over the low rise of the street.

Like before, there was a crowd, mixed with men and women, a few children thrown in for good measure. Each was covered in blood and gore, and like a well drilled marching unit, they stomped past Chad's hiding place until they were lost around the bend of the next intersection.

Chad waited for another two minutes after they had passed by him, then he came out of hiding. He let out the breath he'd been holding, fighting off the chill going down his back.

If they had seen him before he'd hidden, he would be running for his life right now.

But it was he who had spotted them first and so he was still safe and alive for another five minutes.

He turned and continued on.

Chad found another car worth trying to salvage a half hour later. He'd passed countless others, but there was always one reason or another why he couldn't use them, such as no keys, had been of fire, flat tires, ect. The list went on and on.

But as he slowed at an old Datsun parked inconspicuously at the curb, he had high hopes it might be okay. The tires were fine and there were no bullet holes in it that he could see. He'd found a car ten minutes ago that had been shot in the radiator, thus leaking out all the coolant. Worthless.

The Datsun car had an occupant, too, as most did that he'd found. When everyone had gone crazy, most had tried to run for help, but had only been caught out in the open.

Making his way to the Datsun, he continually searched the area around him for danger. Houses stood alone, doors and windows open or broken, a few smoking or still on fire. The ones on fire were a few streets over and the neighborhood surrounding him seemed mostly intact. In the distance, he could see the skyline of Chicago and the thick plumes of smoke. It looked like someone had gone to the far edge of the city and had set it on fire, as insane as that seemed. Maybe a tanker truck had exploded or something, but still, the entire skyline on the rear of Chicago was nothing but a black, sooty cloud. The flames were massive and would soon consume the entire city if no one so much as attempted to put them out.

But despite seeing this, Chad was still confident going to Chicago was the right decision. With the fires, the army or National Guard would be gathering on the opposite side of the city as they helped people to flee to safety. If anything, the fire should help Chad find others who went crazy as they would be running from the flames and not hunting prey.

But first he needed a car and one was sitting right in front of him.

Opening the driver's door, he was pleased to see the overhead dome light come on. That meant the battery was fine. But there was still the body behind the wheel to deal with and he needed to get it out. It was a woman, in her early twenties by the looks of her face. She was pretty, or had been, with a sharp nose and high forehead. She had golden blonde hair that even in death was beautiful. Her eyes were closed, thankfully, and if it hadn't been for the flies and the smell, Chad might have thought she was just sleeping.

Chad couldn't see what had killed her, at least not yet. Cringing in disgust, he grabbed her by the shoulders and pulled her gently from the seat. As he did this, he heard a peeling sound, such as when Velcro is separated. When he had her out of the car, he laid her on the road. He felt guilty about leaving her in the street like trash, but what was he supposed to do, bury her?

Once the body was gone, he found out what had killed her immediately. It looked like she had been shot by a small caliber weapon. The bullet had entered her stomach, leaving very little mess but there had been a larger hole, though not by much, in her back. Blood had seeped onto the seat and had literally glued her to the fake leather. Maggots crawled everywhere, wriggling and feasting on the dried, congealed blood as flies flitted about incessantly.

There was a towel in the backseat, looking like it was leftover from a gym workout, and he grabbed it and used it to wipe the squirming white maggots off the seat as best he could. Some didn't go so easily and they rubbed between towel and seat, breaking open into squishy white globules of flesh. Chad controlled his stomach from heaving and continued until the seat was cleaned as well as possible given the current circumstances.

No sooner did he finish wiping the seat clean, then a hash bark of a scream sounded from a few houses down. Looking up, Chad saw the same group of people he'd seen before when he was hiding in the hedges. They must have claimed this neighborhood as their own and would do a circuit as they searched for something to kill. Chad could see almost the entire group was covered in fresh splashes of blood, which meant they had found some poor soul hiding somewhere and had slaughtered him or her.

And now it was Chad's turn.

Like they were storming the Alamo, the group raised their blood-splattered weapons into the air and began yelling as loud as humanly possible. Then they sprinted at him, their faces curled into a rictus of rage that would only be satiated with Chad's blood.

Panicking, he dropped the towel on the street and jumped into the Datsun, ignoring the flies that settled on his face and exposed arms. After all he'd seen and been through, a few maggots and flies were nothing to fear. He realized he was forgetting his bag full of supplies so he reached out and grabbed it, dragging it to him and then tossing it onto the passenger side floorboard as he slammed the driver's door shut.

With the door closed, he set the locks, hoping in a matter of seconds he'd be home free. He turned the key in the ignition, stepped on the clutch, and pumped the gas. The engine sputtered but didn't catch and he felt his stomach tightening to the size of a golf ball. Glancing into the rearview mirror, he saw that the group of killers was only moments away from him. Trying to stay calm, though he wanted to scream at the car for not starting, he turned the ignition again, this time the engine almost catching before droning over.

"No, no, this can't be happening!" he screamed as he pumped the gas again; ready to try for the third time. He was panicking despite his best efforts not to. His foot wanted to slam on the gas pedal, but he knew he needed to be gentle. The Datsun was over fifteen years old and probably had all kinds of idiosyncrasies only its owner had known about. It was possible he had to pump the pedal twice, wait a second and then pump again, or something like that. It would have been a ritual for the woman, one she would have had to explain to anyone she let use the car.

But he was alone and if he didn't figure out how to get the old clunker moving, he was dead.

Then rational thought was gone as the first of the *changed* reached the Datsun. The man carried an aluminum bat and he used it on the rear window. There was a crunch of glass and then the window was exploding inward, small bits of safety glass flying into the car to pelt Chad in the back of the head. A few pieces went down the back of his shirt but he ignored them. The flies in the car escaped out the opening where the back window once was.

"Come on!" Chad screamed as he tried to start the Datsun again, the droning of the starter lost in the screams and shrieks of the *changed*. The passenger side window shattered thanks to a lead pipe, and a second later, hands were reaching inside trying to grab him. He punched them away as he valiantly tried to start the engine.

He looked to his left to see a gore-covered woman with a crowbar glaring at him, and he knew if she brought that weapon down on his driver's side window, it would shatter. And then, as if the woman was reading his thoughts, she did just that.

But she wasn't using all her strength and she was jostled by others trying to get at Chad so her blow was off. Instead of striking the window head on, it glanced off the glass. Still, Chad saw a small crack in the glass, an imperfection that told him the next blow, no matter how mild, would shatter the window.

And then an elbow did just that as a raving man used his arm as a club. Chad heard two things at the same time. He heard the window shatter and he heard the crack of breaking bone from the man, who yelled in pain but still tried to wrap Chad with his other working arm, the hand trying to grasp whatever it could find.

Chad screamed as hands began crawling along his face, pulling his hair and tearing his shirt.

Desperate and knowing this was his last chance, he pumped the gas pedal and turned the ignition key.

He didn't hear the engine begin to idle, thanks to the yelling raging crowd of killers, but when he stepped on the gas pedal he could feel the motor rev.

It was running!

Chad didn't hesitate; he pushed in the clutch and slammed the transmission into first gear, then stepped on the gas, expecting to shoot out of the mass of bodies and freedom.

But that didn't happen. The car wasn't very big even for a compact and there were too many people holding it in place. The window to Chad's right shattered and a screaming man tried to crawl in the passenger side so Chad reached out and punched him, shoving him away. The man fell back out, but was replaced by a woman with dark-red hair and freckles. Even in her madness she was beautiful and Chad felt a hint of pity for her. But that was gone when she reached out and scratched his right arm. He punched her in the face and she fell back.

The engine was sputtering and he gave it some gas, feeling it idle out. It wasn't easy as the killers pounded on the roof and side panels, raining dents and dips in the metal.

He stepped on the gas again, trying to break free of his prison of human bodies and he could feel the car rocking. But still it wouldn't move. A man reached in through the driver's window and grabbed Chad's left ear, and as he cried out in pain, Chad punched the man in the face. Blood poured out of the broken nose and the man fell back, only to be replaced by yet another. The only reason Chad hadn't been pulled from the car was the simple fact that the killers wouldn't work together. No sooner did one try to grab Chad, then he was pushed away by another killer who wanted in.

Their lack of cooperation was Chad's salvation, and when a few bodies fell off the car, tripped up by their fellow attackers, the Datsun broke free and it began to move. The Datsun's front end rose a few inches into the air and a high-pitched scream rent the air. Chad realized he'd run over a body, crushing a woman's ribcage into kindling. As the Datsun dropped back down, the screaming ceased, but then the back tires were rolling over the woman and the screams began anew. But then they ceased abruptly, as the woman died from internal hemorrhaging that no doctor could ever hope to staunch.

Chad knew none of this as he tried to force his way through the crowd.

A hand shot through the opening of the missing driver's side window and wrapped around Chad's throat, biting in with a steely strength only found in the insane. As the fingers dug deep into his flesh, Chad began to see white spots flood his vision and he fought with his left arm to get the attacker off him.

Swerving toward a mailbox, there was dull clang and scraping of metal, and then the hand was gone. Glancing in his rearview mirror, as his side mirror was now gone, he saw the attacker laying supine in the road. He wasn't moving.

The small left rear window behind him shattered but it was too late for anyone to get inside with him. Chad swerved to the left and right, knocking people over like tenpins at the bowling alley. Glancing in his rearview mirror, he saw a half dozen people lying in the street, their ankles or legs shattered from when he ran over them.

The rest were chasing him now, waving their arms and weapons overhead. Two ran faster than the others and they leaped for the trunk of the Datsun, grabbing the lip of the rear window. There was a sudden *thump* as the bodies landed on the car.

They were now lying on the trunk, their legs hanging off as they tried to pull themselves into the vehicle. One carried an axe, the other a wooden club made from a two-by-four which he was using to pound on the back of the car, to no effect but simply wanting to create violence.

Already they were trying to climb into the Datsun and Chad knew if they did, he was done for.

Thinking drastically, he had no choice but to try something desperate, and as he swerved around a corner, leaving the rest of the killers behind, he began sideswiping parked cars wherever he could find them. The sound of tearing metal was cacophonous, but still he continued, knowing he needed to shake his two unwanted passengers.

It worked and the man with the axe fell off, rolling a few times and leaving a fair chunk of scraped flesh on the pavement thanks to his tumble. But there was still one more, and no matter how erratically Chad drove, the man wouldn't let go.

The road was clogged with stalled vehicles and Chad had to swerve around them or risk crashing. He struck one car, upside on its roof, a glancing blow and the car began to spin like a top; the roof metal scraping the pavement an unsettling sound, like crunching rocks.

Chad glanced in his rearview mirror to see the man with the club was now crawling through the opening, heedless of the safety glass becoming embedded in his palms. With each inch he took, he left bloody handprints behind.

Chad swerved and struck a bread truck stalled half-on, half-off the sidewalk, but the killer managed to hold on. Then he was inside the vehicle enough to fall onto the back seat. Chad swerved to the right, knocking the man over so he was upside down, but Chad knew in a second the man would right himself and then it would be done.

Game over, finished, check please!

As the man groaned in rage, Chad knew he had one chance to stop the man from killing him; even now the club was being raised to crack him on the side of the head.

Chad stepped on the gas, the little Datsun jumping forward as he shifted the transmission into fifth gear, the little car going up to forty so fast the owner would have been proud.

Chad reached down and put on his seatbelt, fumbling with the clasp with only one hand and having a hard time of it; the other hand steering the car.

The wooden club was up and was going back, the man about to use Chad's head as a baseball. Chad stepped on the gas pedal so hard he thought he would put his foot through the floorboard, and the Datsun jumped forward again, going so fast the wind whipped like a cyclone into the interior thanks to the now shattered and missing windows.

At the last second before hitting the tree, Chad managed to click his seatbelt, then he was thrown forward and the belt was biting into his chest and upper shoulder as the front of the Datsun wrapped around the trunk of the tree.

The man in the backseat was thrown forward like he'd been blown out of a cannon. His head went into the front windshield and then through it, the shattering of the glass lost in the chaos of car meeting tree, metal kissing wood.

Chad might have blacked out for a second, because when he came to, it felt like time had passed. Glancing around, the sun was in the same place in the sky and there was no one on the street yet.

Though his mind was foggy from the crash, he knew he needed to leave immediately before the crash attracted more people. The accident would put out a call to every *changed* in the area.

Steam hissed out from the fractured radiator, bathing the area around the car in a sticky fog that tasted sweet on the tongue if breathed in. His door wouldn't open so he undid his seatbelt and crawled through it, falling onto the small median of grass lining the sidewalk and street. He looked up at the sun and tried to get his thoughts organized, but no matter how hard he tried, they just floated out of reach. Closing his eyes, he breathed in; his chest was sore but intact. He was lucky and no ribs had been broken in the accident.

Looking up, and seeing the man sprawled on the wrinkled hood of the Datsun, his neck at an odd angle, Chad didn't want to think what would have happened if he hadn't gotten his seatbelt clasped in time.

Another ear-piercing scream came to his ears and he knew his time was up. The killers had heard the crash and were even now coming. With shaking arms and legs, he pulled himself to his feet. The club the man was holding was inside the Datsun on the front seat and Chad reached in and took it. He grabbed his sack of supplies taken from the bakery and turned to go, but before he did, he glanced at the dead killer and said, "Should have buckled up, asshole. Don't you know that speed kills?"

He hobbled away and was into a backyard of a two-story Victorian when the first of the murderous arrivals appeared to investigate the crash.

He needed to find another car fast or he would be spending another night in the suburbs.

Chapter 19

"That was great, Mario, thank you so much," Stacy said as she pushed her plate aside. She'd eaten every last morsel and was stuffed.

"Not at all, it's always nice to see someone appreciate my cooking."

"Have you owned this place long?" she asked while sipping water from a wine glass. He had offered her wine, but she'd declined.

Mario nodded as he leaned back in his chair. "You bet. It was my parents' place before they died a few years back. I inherited it from them. Dad died of a heart attack and then Mom died of a broken heart. They say it was a stroke that took her, too, but I know it was from grief because she missed Dad so much. They had a great marriage, never fought. They were the best of friends."

"That's nice and sad at the same time," she said, setting her glass down. If it wasn't for the banging on the doors of the restaurant, she could have pretended she was on a date with Mario.

"Yeah, it is," he replied.

The table she was sitting at was right near the kitchen doors and she glanced over her shoulder into the dining room. She could see everyone sitting and talking together. All except Brad who was sitting alone, smoking. A thick fog hung over him like a thunder cloud and she wanted to go over and tell him to cut it out. They had enough to deal with without having to suck in his lung-clogging garbage. But then she realized how petty she was being and she let it go. Secondhand smoke was the last thing she should be worried about at the moment. The doors were still vibrating from the abuse tossed on them but it had abated in time. Either the murderous crowd was getting bored or some of them had moved on, the pounding sporadic at best.

Roger was sitting with Jill, the two chatting quietly, while Tim and Martha were together. Tina sat alone, like a wallflower at a party. She jumped each time a bang came from the doors, making her look more and more like a mouse. Brad watched her, smiling each time she was startled. He seemed to feed off her discomfort. Stacy had already made up her mind that she disliked Brad…a lot.

"What did you say?" Stacy asked, realizing she had drifted off and Mario was asking her a question.

"I said, is there a husband or boyfriend out there you're worried about?"

She smiled bashfully, her cheeks going red. Luckily, with the shades pulled down and the power out, it was dark in the dining room. Candles had been lit on the tables, and Stacy's blushed cheeks were hidden from Mario.

"No, 'fraid not. I was in a relationship recently but we broke it off. He had some issues I couldn't get past."

"Oh? What kind?" he asked.

"He liked to sleep with other women and I didn't want him to."

Mario nodded again, understanding completely. "Ah, I see. Well, on behalf of men everywhere, I apologize for our gender."

She chuckled as she picked up her wine glass. "Apology accepted," she grinned and raised her glass to him. With Mario doing the same with his glass, the two toasted one another.

"Oh, please, get a fucking room, will you two?" Brad called out from his booth.

Stacy blushed deeper and Mario turned a shade of red that was more from anger than embarrassment. He was about to get up and go have a few words with Brad when Stacy placed her hand on his arm.

"No, don't, let him be. If we ignore him he'll let it go. He reminds me of a school yard bully. If you don't give him the attention he wants, he gets bored and moves on."

Mario lowered himself back into his chair. "Fine, I'll do it for you."

"Thank you," she said. "So," she added, wanting to take his mind off Brad. "Is there a Mrs. Mario?"

"Huh? Oh, no, I've dated here and there but never met anyone who wanted to work with me here. You see, this place is my life. If a woman wants me, she needs to accept the restaurant, too. That means long hours, dealing with all the crap of ordering supplies and taxes. Plus the staff, hiring, firing, scheduling. It's a lot of work and most women don't want to be bothered with it. They want to work nine to five and then clock out and have every weekend off. That's not gonna happen with me."

Stacy leaned forward, listening intently. As she listened, she didn't think a life with Mario and making meatballs and pasta late into the night sounded so bad. In fact, it sounded pretty damn good.

Suddenly, a loud gong-like sound filled the restaurant and everyone looked up from what they were doing to stare at the front windows. With the shades drawn, no one could see what was happening, but the vibration that went along with the gong sound didn't bode well for them and they knew it. Mario was the first to jump up and dash to the windows. He peered out the side of a window shade to see a man covered in dried blood with a bat in his hand. As Mario watched, the man used the bat like a club and whacked the glass on the next window, the gong sound the rebounding of wood on glass.

"What's going on?" Stacy asked as she came up behind him, followed by the others. Roger was near her, as was Tim. Brad was hanging back, as if when the window shattered he would be the first to run for it.

"One of the nutjobs has got a bat and he's trying to break the window," Mario said, the note of worry in his voice apparent to all.

"Yeah, but you said the glass is strong, right?" Roger asked. "You said they couldn't get inside by breaking them."

Mario shook his head. "Look, that's not entirely true. Sure, the glass is strong, it's stronger than your average window on a house, but if that guy keeps pounding on it with the bat, sooner or later either the window is gonna crack or others of his kind are gonna get the same idea. And when that happens, we're screwed."

"We need to run for it before that happens," Tim suggested.

"And how do we do that?" Martha asked.

"The backdoor that leads into the alley," Roger said. "We can sneak out and be gone before they know it."

Mario waved the idea away. "No way, Roger, you forget there's a few of them back there. If so much as one of them gets off a warning then the entire crowd will be on us in a flash."

"Maybe they left the alley since the last time you checked; you know, got bored," Jill said, hoping she was right.

Mario frowned, then let the shade fall back to the window. "Its possible, it can't hurt to check. We need to do something before that guy gets lucky and the window cracks, 'cause it will happen, people."

"So let's go look," Stacy said, understanding immediately what was going on. She was one of the group now and wasn't about to sit idly by while others made decisions. Not like Tina who never said a word to anyone.

Mario, Roger, Tim and Stacy all ran out of the dining room, into the kitchen and to the back of the restaurant. On the rear wall was a metal fire door that was locked, a small glass window with mesh inlay about head height was inset in the door. Mario went to the mesh window and peered out into the alley. The sun was high, and though the neighboring buildings cast the alley in shadows, there was still more than enough illumination to see by.

"I don't see anyone out there," he said hopefully as he pressed his cheek to the glass and tried to see to the right, which led to the street behind his restaurant. When he had looked long enough, he switched cheeks to look to the left. "Maybe we *can* sneak out this way, like Jill said."

It was as he said the last word that a bloody, rage-filled face slammed up against the window. The mouth was dripping red saliva and three of the front teeth were missing, looking as if the man had been punched by a steel fist. The mouth opened and closed like a fish as red mucous lathered the window. Then the face was pushed away by another, a female face this time. The woman banged her head against the glass like a retarded child on the special bus, bruising her forehead in the process.

Mario jumped back with a muffled cry when the first face slapped against the window. He stared at it with revulsion, his hands coiled into fists. Stacy could see he wanted nothing more than to go outside and knock some heads together, but he had to think about the others first. Besides, it would be suicide to try and fight the crazies one on one.

"Damn it, they're still there. Sometimes they're not as dumb as they look," Mario said.

"It may just be coincidence, too," Roger replied. "They just want in and there's a door there. They saw you when you opened it before and still remember."

"Yeah, maybe, but the end result is we still need to do something about the ones out front," Mario added. As if to illustrate his point, Martha ran through the kitchen doors and called out to them. "Hey, the man with the bat is still going. I swear I saw a crack in the window."

"Shit, we don't have much time," Mario snapped, not knowing what they could do.

But Roger's face lit up with an idea. "I've got an idea. Mario, doesn't your place have a roof access door? A way to get onto the roof?"

Mario nodded. "Sure it does, it's over there by the walk-ins, why?"

Roger grinned as he looked around the kitchen. "And the stoves, they still work, right?"

Mario nodded again. "Yup, they're gas, don't need electricity, why, what are you thinking about?"

"We treat this place like a castle and those people out there are the raiders trying to storm it. We heat cooking oil up to boiling and then bring it up to the roof. Then we dump it on their heads. That ought to get rid of them for a bit, at least distract them for a while."

Tim spoke up then, not liking the idea. "But there's so many out there," he commented.

Roger waved the objection away. "Don't matter. We just need to keep them away from the windows, the rest can bang on the doors and sides of the building all they want."

Mario rubbed his jaw, while behind him, the two crazies pounded on the fire door. Made of metal, they wouldn't be getting in anytime soon, if ever.

"Damn, Roger, that's a great idea. It could work, too. I have gallons of fryer oil and there's a few tins of shortening, too. It would be easy to heat it and get it up there using some of the pasta pans I have. They'll hold ten gallons easy."

Roger shook his head. "They can't be too full, though, we don't want to risk spilling it on ourselves. Plus, how *do* you get up to the roof?"

Mario's eyes widened with understanding. "Oh, I see. It's a pull down ladder that leads to a small platform. From there, there's another small ladder. It would be a pain trying to climb up there while carrying a pan of hot oil."

"Exactly," Roger said.

"There, I see a crack!" Martha yelled and Brad ran to the kitchen doors separating the dining room and glared at Mario and the others. "What the fuck are you idiots doing in here? That window is gonna go any second!"

"We have an idea," Mario said. "Brad, get Martha, Jill and Tina in here. If it works, then in a few minutes that guy won't be interested in that window anymore, believe me.

"Fuck, Mario, I don't think you got a few minutes," Brad gasped.

Mario thought fast and then his eyes brightened as he came up with something to distract the man with the bat. "Then we'll just have to distract him long enough for Roger's plan to work."

No one knew what Mario was thinking, but when he looked at Stacy with a wide grin, she had a feeling she might not like his answer.

Chapter 20

"This is so embarrassing," Stacy said as she danced topless in front of one of the windows.

"Tell me about it, but it's working so it's worth it," Jill replied from the booth next to her. Her breasts swayed back and forth as she wiggled her hips in a pretend striptease.

Outside on the street, the murderous crowd was hooting and slapping the windows, wanting to get at the half-naked women, but none were using weapons on the glass. Even the man who had been using the bat had been pushed aside so that the others could get a better view of the female flesh on display.

"I feel like a hooker in Amsterdam," Stacy said as she gyrated her hips.

"Yeah, just give me a red light for the window and I'll be good to go," Jill quipped.

"I can't believe we let Mario talk us into doing this," Stacy said as she jumped back a few inches when a manic face slapped the window. Though muted from the glass, the screams and shrieks of rage and murder still filtered into the restaurant.

"Well, it's not like we had a choice. It's either do this or die when they break those windows," Jill added as she tried not to look directly into the hungry faces staring at her. Whenever she did, she became queasy. A few of the males in the raging crowd had taken out their penises and were even now stroking them with fervor. It was a frightening thought to think about what would happen if that crowd got a hold of her.

Back in the kitchen, the others were working hard on heating as much oil as possible in a short time. Brad came out of the kitchen and grinned widely as he watched Jill and Stacy shaking their bodies.

"Damn, I wish I had a few dollars to stick in your g-strings," he joked as he lit a cigarette, blowing the smoke toward the ceiling.

Stacy tried to cover herself so Brad wouldn't see, but Jill didn't seem to care.

"Take a good look, asshole, 'cause it's all you're ever gonna get," Jill snapped as she slowed her gyrating to stare at Brad. "They're breasts. Every woman has them. They're as natural as breathing, so get your mind out of the gutter and do something to keep us all from dying."

He chuckled, his eyes darting to the crowd of killers outside. He could see some of the males masturbating and he barked out, "Looks like you got some fans out there. Maybe you can get a job as an exotic dancer when this shit blows over."

Jill flipped him off. "Fuck you, asshole," she said simply then went back to dancing. Stacy had slowed her gyrating, realizing she really didn't need to move at all. All she had to do was stand there and the crowd watched her as if hypnotized. And she wondered if it was even necessary that she and Jill had removed their tops at all. But as she watched the men masturbating, she figured yeah, it did matter. They were so worked up that any thoughts of breaking the windows were forgotten in the excitement of the two dancing women. Stacy also saw women in the crowd and they were as worked up as the males, though Stacy figured the females probably just wanted to kill Jill and herself. Not a comforting thought.

Martha poked her head out of the kitchen to find Brad. "Brad, what are you doing? We need your help back here," she told him.

Brad turned and took one last hit from his cigarette, then dropped it on the commercial carpet, stepping on it with his left foot. He grinned slyly as he stared at Martha.

"Thank God you're not up there, Martha. One look at those withered tits and the crowd would have gone fucking crazy in a bad way. Hell, they probably would have torn the place down just so they could get you to stop."

"Very funny, Brad, you're a laugh riot." She became melancholy then and was about to tear up when she stopped herself. She had been thinking of her husband, now dead. "You're lucky my husband isn't with us or he'd teach you some manners."

Brad turned and with a grin at Jill, walked over to Martha, the woman not moving so he could go by her. "Yeah, well, he's not here, is he? He's dead, like thousands of other people by the looks of it. Fuck, maybe millions. For all we know, the entire country has gone fucking nuts and this isn't localized to just Chicago. So, excuse me if I don't pity your poor, dead husband."

She stared at him, her jaw trembling. She was so angry it looked like only her force of will was stopping her from slapping Brad.

"I pity you, young man. You're so full of anger and self-loathing, you refuse to let anyone in. You're just like those animals outside, except at least they seem to be admitting what they've become. You're still in denial."

Brad pushed her aside. "And fuck you, too, you old bat, get out of my way. Like you said, they need my help in back."

Martha was shoved aside and she stood in the doorway, tears welling up in her eyes.

"You okay?" Jill called from the window.

Martha shook herself off and smiled wanly. "As much as any of us can be in these troubling times, dear. Thank you again for what you're doing, the both of you."

Stacy shrugged. "It's not the end of the world. Like Jill said, breasts are natural; it's everyone else who has hang-ups over them." She jumped when a face slapped the closest window, leaving bloody streaks on the glass. In most places, the glass was so smudged you could barely see through it. Mucous, blood, and snot were some of the viscous fluids coating the windows.

"Were almost ready to bring the oil up," Martha said.

"How will we know when we can stop?" Jill asked.

Martha actually let a wicked smile cross her lips then. "Oh, I have a feeling you'll know. There's no doubt about that." Then she went back into the kitchen and the doors swung closed.

Jill looked at Stacy. "What was that about?"

Stacy shrugged. "I guess we'll find out when it's time." Turning, she began shaking her hips a little more, as the crowd of murderous killers hooted and hollered like college boys at a frat party.

* * *

"Okay, you ready, guys?" Mario asked Roger and Tim as the two men stood next to him on the roof of the restaurant. In each of their potholder-covered hands they held a large pot of boiling oil. Roger could detect the odor of French fries and onion rings as the aroma wafted up to his nose before being lost in the wind.

"Ready when you are, Mario," Roger said as he gazed down at the crowd below. The front windows of the restaurant were directly below them, and so was the crowd of killers. The building was only one-story high and the people seemed so close that Roger could just lean over and touch them. And he would, but not with his hands, but with boiling hot oil.

"Okay then, on three," Mario said, looking at Tim who nodded that, he too, was ready. Tim had a burn on his left arm—now bandaged–from where oil had spilled out of the pan when he'd carried it up to the roof. He knew from personal experience how painful the burn was, and though he knew it had to be done, he still felt some guilt for what they were going to do in a second. After all, those were *people* down there, *human beings* with feelings and families...or they once had those things.

"Two," Mario said and Tim realized he'd drifted off and hadn't been listening. "Three!" Mario yelled and dumped his pan of oil, while Roger and Tim did the same with theirs.

Tim watched the oil arc over the edge of the roof and slowly fall to the earth. For a brief few seconds, nothing happened when the oil landed on the heads and shoulders of the crowd. But then, a crescendo of shrieks and screams filled the street as the *changed* began to boil alive in their skin; to have their flesh literally melted off their bones.

On the roof, Mario, Roger and Tim turned around and picked up the other pans of scalding oil. Without hesitation, Mario tossed his over the edge and dropped the pan on a man's head for good measure. Even over the screams of anguish, Tim heard the gong-like sound when the pan bounced off the man's head. The man dropped to the sidewalk where he was promptly pummeled by feet, his body flattened into what basically would become a meat-carpet mixed with bones.

Tim poured his second batch of oil and watched it land on a trio of women, one of them still wearing her housecoat from before she'd gone insane. She looked up at him just before the oil landed on her face and Tim watched in horror as her eyes bubbled and melted in her head, the woman raising scarred hands to her dissolving eyes as she fell to her knees, screaming.

Roger dumped his second batch on a group of men and two children. It broke his heart to do so, but both children wielded knives and he knew if the kids had a chance, they would gut him like a fish. The oil splashed onto their heads and ran into their ears; sizzling and scouring out their ear drums like drain cleaner to a clog. One of the kids opened his mouth to yell in anger and pain and oil dripped into his mouth, scalding his tongue and cooking it like a clam in a steamer. The kid dropped his knife and ran away, howling in utter agony.

The scene was the same everywhere oil was dropped, the crowd of killers now the victims. More than half were now covered in third degree burns and the other half had burns of some sort from the scalding oil. A few now blinded, lashed out with weapons at anyone who came too close to them. A man gutted a woman from head to toe, not knowing she was like him. A woman, carrying a skillet, was swatting left and right like she was chasing imaginary flies. Each time the skillet flew, a head was flattened to wet mulch and brains splattered the sidewalk.

Up on the roof, Mario gazed down at his handiwork. "Damn, Roger, if that didn't work out great. Just look at the bastards twitch."

Roger wasn't listening, however, as he looked out to the end of the street. He pointed and said, "Looks like all the noise is attracting more of them."

Mario looked where he was pointing and his smile fell into a frown. "Oh, shit, you've got to be kidding me," he said in shock.

From around the corner and out of nearby alleyways, more of the *changed* were appearing. They heard the screams of pain and suffering and it was like a dinner bell to their rage-fueled minds.

"Shit, what the hell is happening?" Tim asked as he stared at the approaching horde.

"I don't know, this might be a good thing or a bad one," Mario said. "Look," he pointed to the crowd below who were writhing on the ground in agony. "They're not trying to break the windows anymore. And the new arrivals won't have a clue. So it looks like we did what we set out to do. Let's get downstairs and join the women."

"By the women, do you mean Brad, too?" Tim joked.

Mario chuckled a little but it was more for show. Truth was, the growing crowd scared him...a lot.

"Yeah, I guess so. He is kind of a woman, isn't he?" Mario mused.

"Huh, and he calls me gay. That guy makes me look like Rambo," Tim added as they turned to leave.

"Well, we're stuck with him for the time being so you might as well get used to him," Roger said as he kicked a pan off the roof. It soared out a few feet and then fell to the sidewalk. It missed hitting anyone and bounced off the cement with a dull clang, the cooling oil splashing anyone within a few feet of it.

"Don't remind me," Tim said as he headed for the roof access hatch. It was while the three were walking across the gravel roof that the very building seemed to shake and a loud hum filled the sky, making their teeth hurt.

"What the hell is doing that?" Roger asked as he looked off the roof to the surrounding buildings.

"Don't know, but it can't be good," Mario added as, he too, searched for the origin of the sound. The three men stood silently on the roof, looking around to no avail when Tim let out a gasp and slapped each of the others on the shoulder.

"There, look over there, holy Christ, is that plane too low or what?" Tim asked.

Roger and Mario followed Tim's outstretched arm and both saw, a few miles outside the city, right over the suburbs, what was obviously a passenger jet. It was tilting at an odd angle and the engines whined louder with each passing second.

"Good God, that bastard is gonna crash," Mario said as he stared in shock. Though it was miles away, it seemed like it was just hovering out of his reach and he could stretch his arm out and touch it, perhaps lift it back into the sky to save all those people.

The engines whined higher and the vibration grew. Mario wondered how bad it felt to be right under it. All those people hiding out in their homes; unaware that what was basically a giant bomb was falling out of the sky directly onto their heads. It broke his heart to watch, knowing he was helpless, but what else could he do but bear witness to such carnage?

"It's gonna get hot any second," Roger said as he took a step closer to the edge of the roof, as if he wanted to get the best seat possible.

All three men stared with mouths open as the whining of the turbines reached a crescendo, then the plane's right wing clipped the roof of a house and the chain reaction began. The plane titled more and was then cart-wheeling across the neighborhood. The fuselage cracked in half and the jet fuel ignited, washing the land in a golden glow of oranges and reds.

Even from such a distance, in time the three men felt the hot blast of the shockwave roll across them, the hot breeze stinging their cheeks and tinting their skin red, as if they had been at the beach in the sun for too long.

"Jesus Christ, will you look at that?" Mario gasped as the ferocious blast consumed everything for blocks, the conflagration reminding him of a picture he'd seen in Sunday school. He thought of the Devil himself rising from Hell in the midst of the growing fireball, the demon preparing to rain fire and brimstone onto the world. The sound of the crash was deafening and the very ground shook when the plane impacted, the roof feeling like an earthquake was about to cave it in, reducing the restaurant to wreckage.

And then, another blast began to erupt, reminding Mario of bombs detonating in succession, and section after section exploded.

"Holy shit, the plane crash must have ruptured the natural gas lines buried in the ground," Roger said as he watched the successive explosions. The entire sky in the distance was black and gray roiling smoke, the clouds so thick they blocked out the sun.

"You think anyone survived that?" Roger asked as he stared like he was hypnotized.

"No fucking way," Tim stated matter-of-factly. "Anyone caught in that is nothing but charcoal."

"Jesus Christ," Roger said, dragging the words out as he tried to imagine the size of the flames rolling across the suburbs. But there were no suburbs west of the city, now there was only devastation.

Eventually the explosion slowed and the gas mains must have stopped erupting. But the flames still continued, looking like the world itself was burning and would soon consume everything in its fiery wake.

"You think we need to worry about that?" Tim asked. "If it keeps going like that, we could find ourselves running from the fire."

Mario shook his head. "Nah, there's too much highway between us and that. Even if the fire burned for days, it wouldn't have enough fuel to reach the city."

"I hope you're right," Roger said. "We got enough to worry about as it is without roasting to death." He pointed to the opposite side of the city where the black clouds of more fires could be seen. "It looks like a good section of the city past *The Loop* is burning already. If we have to worry about that one, too, we could end up caught in the middle with nowhere to go."

Mario pulled his gaze from the fire to look at Roger, and then Tim. "One thing at a time, guys, okay? For now, let's worry about the crazies, then we can worry about the fires. Besides, if the fire gets too close, at least it should take care of the nutjobs."

Roger sniffed and shrugged as he thought of Mario's reasoning. "Oh, sure, as I die of smoke inhalation, I can have peace of mind of knowing the crazies died first. That's real comforting, Mario."

"Hey, I'm not your priest, I don't do comfort, I do facts. Now, come on, let's get back down to the women. I bet they're freaked out by what's happened. They probably think it's an earthquake or something."

Roger and Tim headed for the roof hatch, both men glancing one last time to the conflagration in the distance. Suddenly their predicament didn't seem as bad as it was before. After all, at least they weren't surrounded on all sides by a raging inferno, or worse still, at least they weren't dead yet, nothing but a charred corpse that no one would ever know was there. Just one more casualty in a city with nothing but.

Mario was the last down, and as he snuck one last look at the distant flames, he felt a chill slide down his back—which was odd. With the heat of the crash, a chill should be the last thing he'd feel.

He hoped it wasn't a premonition of things to come.

Chapter 21

A few hours before the plane crash, Chad was crossing a devastated street as he searched for another car to get him to Chicago. His luck had been bad so far, with nothing of use to be found.

But then he spotted a gray Volvo with the driver's door hanging open as well as the trunk. When he was sure the street was clear, he darted to the Volvo and came up with his back against the passenger door, then crouched down low. He resembled an urban guerilla soldier as he pressed tight against the cool metal, hoping he hadn't been seen.

When he was confident he was fine, he tried the passenger door, but it was locked. So he snuck around to the open driver's door. In a flash his eyes took in the scene before him.

No blood, no signs of an attack, just the keys hanging in the ignition, as if the owner had forgotten something and had run back inside the house for a second.

Relief filling him, he was about to climb inside when a lone killer came out of nowhere. The man darted from between two parked cars and Chad never saw him until he felt a hand grasp his shoulder and try to pull him out of the car.

If the man had held a weapon, perhaps a knife, Chad would have been dead before he knew what was happening, but by luck or design, this man had nothing but teeth and hands to try and kill him with.

Chad let out a yelp of surprise as he was yanked out of the Volvo, both he and his assailant falling to the pavement in a flurry of arms and legs.

The man was on top of him and trying to strangle him in no time, and as the man leaned in close, growling like a wild dog, Chad stared into the eyes of his approaching death.

With desperation filling the blow, Chad punched the man in the face, feeling the force of the punch down his arm and into his shoulder. The man's head rocked to the side and he spit blood, but he shook it off and continued to squeeze Chad's throat.

Chad pummeled the man's chest with his fists but the killer was filled with manic rage, and no matter what he did, the man wouldn't let go. Chad was losing consciousness fast as white spots danced in his vision.

The killer's eyes seemed to almost glow with intensity as they widened in manic glee at the kill. And Chad, seeing those eyes looking down on him, unprotected, knew he had one chance at salvation.

Reaching up with his hands to the man's face, he then placed the fingers of each hand on the side of the man's head so that his thumbs were hovering over the killer's eyes.

Then he pressed down with all his might feeling the soft eyes give almost immediately as his thumbs popped the orbs like rotten grapes and continued into the sockets. The man screamed as he was blinded and pinkish ooze slid from around Chad's thumbs to drip onto his chest. The man immediately let go of Chad's throat and tried to escape, but Chad was in the driver's seat now and he wasn't going to stop until this man was dead.

This man, this *killer*, represented everything he'd been running from, scared of, the last three days. With hatred fueling his actions, Chad got on top of the killer and pressed down, now using his body weight to emphasize the plunging of thumbs into yielding meat.

The killer's screams reached a crescendo and his hands went to Chad's arms, trying to force them away, but Chad held tight. And he would have killed the man right there and then if not for an errant fist the killer sent into his side, causing him to lose his concentration enough for the man to knock him off.

But the killer was blind now and he rolled around on the street as he pressed his hands to his eyes. Chad jumped to his feet like a street fighter and glanced behind him to see shadowy forms coming out from houses and backyards.

They knew he was here thanks to the screaming and were coming to investigate.

Deciding he needed to leave, he went back to the Volvo, wiping his thumbs clean on his pants as he went.

Getting in, he closed the driver's door and turned the ignition key. It was a well-maintained vehicle and it started on the first try.

By now the new arrivals were only twenty feet away, and the blind killer had rolled in front of the Volvo, his hands touching the gaping holes where his missing eyes had been as red tears slid down his filthy cheeks.

Placing the transmission into drive, Chad stepped on the gas and felt the car surge forward with power. He didn't bother to turn to avoid the screaming blind man, in fact, he adjusted his course just a hair to make sure his front left tire was lined up with the man's legs.

There was an audible *crack* that filled the street as the Volvo drove over both of the man's legs, shattering them into a dozen pieces. When the back tire came down to the pavement, he glanced in the rearview mirror to see the bent and twisted bloody body of the killer writhing in the road.

A feeling of satisfaction filled him then and he wondered once more if he was finally slipping into madness. That he wasn't immune after all, but was just taking more time to change. After all, he knew it was sadistic to want to dish out pain, but after receiving so much of it himself, something inside him wanted to be the one with the upper hand for once.

The beginning of the murderous crowd had reached the screaming blind man and they barely slowed upon seeing him. They knew he was one of them so he wasn't worth killing, and they weren't about to be administering medical help.

They ran past the man and charged after the Volvo, but Chad simply stepped on the gas pedal, avoided a few car wrecks in the road, and turned the corner, leaving the running crowd behind.

By the time he was ready to turn the next corner and head for the onramp to the highway, he could see the crowd was slowing, something in their rage-filled minds knowing they couldn't possibly catch him.

Chad grinned then, wiped his right thumb clean on his shirt when he spotted some extra ooze he'd missed on the knuckle, and he drove on.

* * *

Ten minutes later brought Chad to the next neighborhood. As he drove slowly to avoid an accident, he saw that this part of the town resembled a Third world country, houses were on fire, cars in the streets, trash and debris strewn everywhere from knocked over trash cans. It looked like when things went crazy, it had been trash day in the neighborhood.

He saw a few people with rage in their eyes here and there, but none bothered to go after him. He continued on, the highway a quarter mile away.

As he passed an elementary school on his right, he saw there was a mass of activity there. Looking on the roof of the school, he saw a group of people on it and from the way they moved, they didn't seem to be infected. A middle-aged man and a woman in her sixties could be seen as well as a man in his twenties with blonde hair. The entire school was surrounded by crazies, the men and women screaming and waving their fists in what seemed to be frustration. Chad slowed down slightly, wanting to take in as much as he could in the limited time he had as he drove by.

He shook his head at the foolhardy people on the roof. Up there, they were trapped, and unless help came in the form of the National Guard or Army, he didn't see how they would every escape.

He continued on, hoping the poor souls made it, but in the end knowing he needed to worry about himself. It was easy to do this as there was nothing he could have done for them anyway.

There was a gas station just before the highway and he slowed at the entrance to the paved lot, wanting to fill up if it was possible.

He thought he had just enough gas to get him to the city, but he didn't want to take any chances.

What was funny was the gas station seemed untouched and there was a man actually fueling his car at one of the pumps. Chad was about to join him when five killers came from behind the gas station and attacked the man with clubs and sticks.

The man was thrown to the ground where he was kicked and pummeled. Chad could only stare helplessly, realizing that if he had arrived a little earlier, it might have been him now being killed.

One of the killers reached for the gas nozzle, taking it out of the car's spout and raised it into the air. Gas spewed out to splash on the ground and some of the attackers, two of them, screamed in pain as the gas seeped into their eyes, burning their retinas.

The killer holding the gushing nozzle bent over and slammed the tip into the victim's mouth, the gas filling his stomach as the man's legs twitched in utter agony.

Meanwhile, he was being sliced and diced as blades appeared to cut his clothes away and peel him like a fish.

One of the killers raised his knife high in the air and brought it down on the struggling man, whose stomach was now stuffed with gasoline. The blade came down and missed the man's flailing arm, but the blade rebounded off the cement, causing sparks to ignite the fumes of gas now clogging the air.

Chad couldn't believe it when the entire crowd went up in a blazing fireball, and then the victim exploded like a Molotov cocktail, the gas in his stomach one giant incendiary bomb.

The ground shook as debris flew into the air and a tire came down on the hood of Chad's car, bouncing away and leaving a large dent. More debris rained down, pieces of the car, the gas pumps, and body parts. A severed, burnt arm landed on the hood of the Volvo to then roll off, leaving a bloody streak behind like a wounded snail had been there.

Chad stared in horror as flaming bodies rolled about the ground after being thrown for thirty feet or more.

He realized right then that he didn't need gas that bad and swung around the burning gas station, going as wide as he could.

He could feel the heat as he passed and he sped up, heading for the highway.

If he ran out of gas, so be it, but at least he was still alive.

* * *

The highway was choked with cars and trucks, but so far he'd always been able to get through, sometimes by rubbing the Volvo against other vehicles to the point his teeth would hurt from the sound of scraping metal.

It had been over an hour since he left the burning gas station, the traveling slow going thanks to the wrecked and abandoned vehicles on both sides of the road.

It was when he was only a few minutes to the city limits that he first felt the ground begin to shake. It reminded him of the sensation one gets when a train is coming, the very earth vibrating, but he knew from experience there were no train tracks nearby.

A loud whine quickly filled the air and he stopped the Volvo and got out, needing to know what was happening.

He looked up into the sky to see a plane listing dangerously at an odd angle, one of the wings practically facing downward. And then, as he watched in shock, he saw the plane dip and crash into the neighborhood where he'd been only a few hours ago.

At first there was nothing, only the noise of the plane connecting with the homes and structures it plowed into. But then there was a thunderous explosion that knocked Chad off his feet, the shockwave massive as the planes fuel ignited, sending a roaring fireball that consumed everything behind him.

Picking himself up and leaning against the Volvo, he stared in horror as orange and red tongues of the conflagration reached heavenward, incinerating everything for more than a mile. Chad's eyes reflected the flames as his mouth hung open in amazement, the devastation was more than he'd ever thought to witness in his life. And then the natural gas mains went, successive explosions that felt like concussion waves and everything behind him seemed to evaporate into fire.

Shaking his head, he couldn't believe what he was seeing was real, it had to be a fever induced dream or maybe he was in a coma, trapped between the real world and that of nightmares.

But as he felt the warmth of the air wash over him, he knew if he was sleeping, then this was the most real nightmare he'd ever had.

Backing up to the Volvo, he climbed in and began driving again. He tried not to think what would have happen to him if he'd stayed close to home, if he hadn't decide to try for Chicago.

With his mind wrapped in knots, he drove on, his eyes avoiding his rearview mirror and the orange flames that filled it; as if the very fires of Hell were on his tail.

Chapter 22

With black ash coating every surface, Chad had finally reached the city limits and his car showed how hard it had truly been. Both sides of the Volvo were scratched to the point only metal showed through, and the fenders were so dented the best body shop in Chicago would have thrown up their hands in defeat; all of it solid proof of just how congested with wrecked vehicles the highway was.

He took the first off ramp into the city, wanting to take the surface streets. As he approached the bottom of the ramp, he didn't bother to slow own. Why would he? There was no traffic, the roads deserted. It was a four-way intersection, and when he reached the middle of it, another car screeched out of the street to his right and plowed into him with devastating force.

The airbag went off and knocked him back into the seat as the Volvo flipped onto its side, sliding fifteen feet before rolling onto its hood. The horn went off, filling the air with its shrill scream as the world turned upside down.

Chad lay in and out of consciousness as the Volvo settled on its roof, the tires still spinning as the engine died, not able to run with the fuel system upside down.

As he lay there in a daze, he peered through the cracked windshield at the thin layer of soot that was falling onto the Volvo. Like black snow, it covered every flat surface, looking like a volcano was spewing ash from a few streets over.

He didn't know how long he lay there, upside down, blood rushing to his head, but eventually he came to his senses enough to crawl out of the wreck. He hadn't worn his seatbelt and the airbag had given him a one-two punch to the face that was so bad, his head pounded like a jackhammer was inside trying to break out of the back of his skull.

Crawling on hands and knees out of the car, he looked around at the crash site to see a Lincoln Continental with a pushed in front end sitting in the middle of the intersection, steam drifting from under the hood of a fractured radiator.

Chad pulled himself to his feet by using the Volvo for support and he could see there was something on the hood of the Lincoln. When the waves of dizziness went away, he stumbled towards the car, his feet pushing the soot to the side as he moved.

When he was closer, he saw the shape on the hood was a female body, the head now bent at an odd angle with part of her skull seeping pink brains onto the warm hood; both arms twisted behind the woman's back like she was a rag doll.

Chad got closer still, and as he leaned forward to inspect the woman's face, he saw nothing in those eyes but glazed death. Whether the woman had been infected or normal like him he would never know. Now that he was closer, he could see her abdomen had been sliced open in the crash when she went through the front windshield and her intestines were spread out on the hood of the car like summer sausage for a buffet. Turning away, Chad went to the driver's door of the Lincoln, hoping it would still run.

Shouting and screaming in the distance alerted Chad he was going to have company, the horn of the Volvo calling out to all in the area there was human prey about. With a glance over his shoulder to see how close the attackers were, he slipped behind the wheel of the Lincoln. The ignition was on and he turned the key, the engine making a clattering sound as the fan rubbed the radiator. Three times he did this until the engine began to sputter, then caught. The fan made an awful racket but the motor was running. Putting the transmission into drive, he swung the wheel and stepped on the gas. It jerked forward, and as it did, he stepped on the brake. The dead woman on the hood slid off like ice on the roof of a warming car, her arms and legs flopping around like they were made of straw. Chad ignored the corpse, seeing people running towards him from the street on his left. Swinging the wheel again, he pressed the gas pedal. The Lincoln chugged forward, the fan clattering like a locomotive, steam seeping out from under the hood.

Chad ignored it all, just wanting to escape.

As he turned onto the next surface street that would bring him directly into the city, the fan stopped clattering. Whatever it had been hitting had broken free. Making less noise, Chad sighed with relief, not wanting to alert any more killers to his presence than needed. He glanced in the rearview mirror again to see a dozen people surrounding the Volvo. One reached inside and pulled out the airbag, and finding nothing human, tossed it to the pavement in frustration.

Chad allowed himself a sly grin. He had escaped again, but he wasn't stupid, he knew if he wasn't careful, his luck would run out. He saw in the rearview mirror that he had a cut on his forehead, his blood covering his face in a thin sheet that had splashed onto his chest and shoulders. He knew head wounds were notorious for bleeding, and as he inspected it gingerly with his fingers, he could see the wound was already clotting. Looking back at his eyes as they peered through a face covered in blood, he thought he looked like one of the *changed*.

For the time being, he ignored the blood, not bothering to wipe it off. In the past few days he had grown comfortable with blood, whether his or another's, and he could get cleaned up when he found a safe haven.

With the steam from the damaged radiator still drifting into the air, and black ash falling around him like new-fallen snow, he drove deeper into the city.

* * *

Four blocks later, the Lincoln was on the verge of overheating as Chad slowed at the end of the street to see an Italian restaurant. Above a set of double doors, there was a sign on the facade of a chef holding a pizza in one hand and a plate of spaghetti in the other. While the other restaurants on the street all had shattered windows and open doors, this one was still intact, though it had a raucous crowd of people around it. Some were lying on the sidewalk and road outside the building, looking like they had been dipped in a deep fat fryer, while others had deep wounds and burns on their bodies. It looked to Chad like a battle had been fought and the *changed* had lost. Still, there were others that looked fine and these were the ones making the most noise.

Wondering why this restaurant was still intact and of interest to the *changed*, he soon found out when he spotted a face peering out from behind a drawn window shade. The face was gone in a flash, but in that glimpse, Chad saw a frightened visage, not one filled with rage.

So that was why the *changed* were there, they wanted in.

And he wanted in, too. He now knew coming to the city was a mistake and at least with others like himself, who were still normal, he could help them and they could help him. Plus, he was starving and that was a restaurant.

But he needed a way to get the murderous crowd away from the building, at least for a few minutes, so he could reach the front doors and get inside.

He watched the crowd for the next fifteen minutes, trying to come up with a way to get them away from the restaurant when finally something came to him. It was so simple; he didn't know why he hadn't come up with it before.

Now with a plan, he got to work, and he needed to hurry before the Lincoln overheated.

It didn't take him long to jury-rig his distraction, for all he needed was some rope and a heavy brick, which he found lying on the sidewalk from a damaged section of a nearby building. The rope was also found lying in the street; he ignored the blood covering it.

First he tied the steering wheel so that the front wheels of the Lincoln would stay immobile and keep the car in a relatively straight line, then he got ready to use the brick to keep the gas pedal down.

When he was ready, he put the transmission into *drive* and jammed the brick onto the gas pedal, wedging it between the brake pedal and the floorboard so it would hold the gas pedal down. The Lincoln surged forward so fast Chad was almost dragged with it. He barely managed to fall out of the car as it shot forward, the engine sputtering as the coolant drained and the temperature rose.

The car shot into the street where it rebounded off a stalled car, then it continued on for another five car lengths. From there it bounced off the curb and then continued down the street. It ran into trash cans, other parked cars and sideswiped a postal truck, but it kept going, never hitting anything head on. By the time the road curved to the left, the car was still going straight and it plowed into the front windows of a bridal store, smashing the glass and knocking over the mannequins adorned with white dresses for spring weddings.

The sound of the crash was quite loud on the street and almost every man and woman in the insane crowd in front of the restaurant turned as one to see the Lincoln smash into the store front. The back end popped up a few inches and the rear tires continued to spin, as glass fell from the upper window frame to shatter on the hood and roof of the vehicle.

Chad watched the crowd turn and run after the crash, their arms waving over their heads. Only the mortally wounded ones stayed behind as they crawled about like soldiers wounded on the battlefield.

He waited for the right moment and charged across the street. He jumped over prone bodies and swerved around reaching hands. One man with a melted face and upper chest, managed to get his fingers on Chad's pants, but he kicked out and was free again.

He was running so hard he crashed into the front doors of the restaurant, not able to stop in time. He bounced off them and fell onto his butt, shaking his head in a daze.

But he was up in a second, and with a frightened glance over his shoulder to see that the crowd was still occupied, he began banging on the door.

"Let me in! Let me in! For the love of God, hurry up! They'll be back in a second!"

A five-year-old boy with a butcher's knife came at him and Chad dodged the blade and kicked out, pushing the boy to the pavement. But the boy was on his feet in an instant and coming at him again. Chad ducked back as the knife swiped where his abdomen was a second ago and then did what he had to. He punched the boy in the jaw so hard his knuckles hurt from the blow. The boy's head rocked to the side and the small body crumpled to the sidewalk, unconscious. Chad spun around and began banging on the doors again. "What the fuck? Open the goddamn door! I'm not one of them! Let me in before they come back!"

He shot a glance over his shoulder to see that was exactly what they were doing. The crowd, having seen the crash had nothing to kill in it, had left it and was now returning to the restaurant. Behind Chad, a woman with a peeled face and no eyes, drawn by the sound of his voice, had crawled up to him and wrapped her right hand around his ankle. He looked down, cried out in revulsion and fear, and kicked the woman away from him. Her head snapped back and blood shot from her mouth as she bit off the tip of her tongue. She writhed on the ground, suffering unbelievable pain, but didn't bother him again.

Chad turned back to the front doors and began to pound on them frantically. "What the hell is wrong with you people? I saw one of you in the window! I know you're in there! Open up, dammit! They're gonna kill me!"

But pound as he might, the doors remained closed. Chad spun around and placed his back against the left side door, realizing he was out of time. The crowd of murderous killers was only twenty feet away and closing fast. He'd waited too long before deciding he needed to leave, that the people inside the restaurant wouldn't let him in.

He used his right fist to uselessly hit the door over his shoulder as his back slid down it, crumpling to the ground in defeat. "Open up, dammit, I'm not crazy, I'm normal," he pleaded but as the shadows of the *changed* loomed over him, he knew his desperate word were not enough to save him.

Chapter 23

Inside the restaurant, everyone gathered by the front doors, as they tried to decide what to do about the man banging and pleading to be let in.

"We can't let him in. Did you see him? He's covered in blood, he's one of them," Roger said after looking out the window to see the man frantically banging on the doors.

"Roger's right," Tim agreed. "He looks like any one of them nutjobs. It's a trick to get us to open the doors."

"That's crap, Tim," Stacy said. "Look, I've been out there, remember? And besides, other than some guttural growls, those people don't talk. That guy is yelling for us to let him in. He's not one of them."

"But we can't take that chance, Stacy," Mario added. "If he is one of them then the second we let him in, he can try to keep the doors open so that the others will get in. We'd be committing suicide.

Martha was by one of the front windows, watching outside, and she spoke up now. "Whatever you decide, you need to do it fast. The crowd that left is coming back again."

"Don't do it, Mario, the guys just another crazy," Roger added.

"I can't believe I'm saying this," Brad said, "but I have to agree with Roger and the fag. Don't let him in. It's not worth the chance."

Tim turned to Brad with a dark glare, but he held his tongue. He knew Brad was only agreeing out of selfishness, and for no other reason. But at the moment, one more vote was good enough, no matter how that vote came to be.

"Don't let him in," Jill said when Mario looked at her for her opinion. Tina was in a booth, curled up, not caring what the decision was.

Martha was by the window still and couldn't give her opinion. "It's now or never," she said. If you don't do it now that guy's dead," she commented as she watched the murderous crowd running toward the restaurant.

Mario bit his upper lip, looking at each face, not knowing what to do.

"What if that was you out there?" Stacy asked. "Wouldn't you want to be let in? Would you want to know as you're being killed that people were only a few feet away and they did nothing to help you?"

Mario weighed her words carefully, but couldn't make up his mind. If the man wasn't normal, the risk was too great. Stacy looked into Mario's eyes and saw the man couldn't decide, then saw the resolve on the others faces.

"Fuck it," she whispered as she turned and dashed to the front doors as the others realized what she was doing and cried out.

"Stacy, no, don't do it!" Roger yelled as Tim lunged for her. He just missed her shirt, his fingers brushing the material, but coming up empty.

Mario ran after her, but even as he darted down the small hallway leading to the doors, he knew he would be too late. Behind him, the footfalls of Roger and Tim came to his ears.

Stacy reached the doors, unlocked the left one, then opened it. As she did, a blood-covered man fell inside, but as he did, so too did three of the murderous crowd that had been about to kill the first man.

Mario ran up to Stacy and punched one of the other killers in the face, then grabbed him by his shirt and yanked him aside so he could close the door. He used his shoulder and forced the door closed as a hand tried to get in-between the frame and the door, wanting to keep it open.

The door was heavy, and with Mario shoving it closed, the fingers were caught in the middle. Like a scythe, the door took the fingers off, and as blood shot out, the door slammed closed, the fingers twitching as they dropped to the floor. There was more pounding on the doors now as the crowd attempted to get in once more, but Mario heard none of it. Spinning around, he saw Roger and Tim battling with two armed assailants while Stacy tried to drag the bloodied man she'd let in out of the way. The man Mario had punched was getting to his feet and the cleaver he held in his right hand gleamed in the shadows of the foyer.

Knowing it would do no good to try and reason with the man with the cleaver, Mario lunged at him, his right fist connecting with the man's already fractured nose thanks to his last punch. The killer rocked back and bounced off the wall, but with a growl of rage, was rebounding off it immediately to lunge at Mario.

Mario dove out of the way as the cleaver missed his face by an inch.

"Brad! Get the fuck over here and help us!" Roger yelled as he and Tim struggled with the other two killers. One was female, the other a male teenager, and both had sharp weapons. One held a piece of glass, the bottom slicing into her palm and the other held a stake, such as what you use when setting up a camping tent. The woman held the glass shard in a vise-like grip, and she sliced at Tim, who dodged out of the way, but not before receiving a shallow cut to his left arm. Meanwhile, the teenage boy was trying to impale Roger like he was Dracula. Roger had nothing to use for defense other than his hands, and each time he tried to block the stake, he got a deep scratch on one of his arms for his trouble.

Mario had got in close and was grappling with his foe like they were wrestling, trapping the crazed man against the wall. Mario had both his hands wrapped around the man's wrists, and as the killer growled from deep in his throat, Mario did the same, letting his hatred of what the killer stood for override his rational side. With a yell to rival any of the killers, Mario used the hand holding the cleaver to bring it around until it was between the man's legs. He grinned broadly as he spit into the killer's face, then with a quick jerk, pulled up on the wrist, thus bringing the cleaver up between the man's legs. The killer screamed, the tone going high into a falsetto, as the cleaver sliced into his groin and then into his pelvis. Mario felt warm blood gush over his arm as the man twitched and jerked between him and the wall. Then the eyes glazed over and the body went limp.

Mario stepped away just as the body went slack, letting it crumple to the floor. He was covered in blood from the waist down, and it was sticky, like going swimming with your clothes on. But there were two more killers to deal with.

He reached down, picked up the cleaver from the dead man's hand, and tried to see if he could help Roger and Tim.

Roger wasn't doing too well, his hands covered in cuts and bruises, the boy faster than him. But the boy wasn't a rational fighter, the virus filling inside him making him only want to kill and rend apart bare flesh. With a throaty yell, he charged at Brad and the old man spun around, missing the stake like he was the bull and the boy the bullfighter. As the boy went by him, he used his elbow and cracked the boy behind the neck, the blow so hard it pushed the small killer to the floor where he twitched and drooled. Unknown to Roger, he'd broken the boy's spine with the blow.

Tim wasn't fairing too well either and was on the floor with the woman on top of him. From a distance, it looked like they were having sex, she on top of his groin as she writhed about. But she wasn't moving with passion, but with rage. Tim tried to push her off, but the woman was about his size and weight, and as Tim's hands were knocked away, the woman raised the glass shard now held in both hands and was about to bring it down and slam it into Tim's chest.

Tim could only stare in horror, helplessly, as the glass shard began its downward arc to impale him.

Just as the shard was halfway down, though, Tim watched in amazement as the woman's head was split in two, a bloody cleaver now even with her chin. He looked up and behind her to see a blood-covered Mario standing behind the woman, the cleaver handle in his right hand. Mario wiggled the cleaver a bit to loosen it and pulled it back, the sickening squish of meat filling the foyer. The two sides of the woman's head slowly separated as blood shot out of the exposed veins and arteries of her brain. Like a flower opening on a summer morning, the bifurcated head fell onto both shoulders. Tim bucked his hips and the body fell off to land heavily on the carpet, blood spitting out to coat the floor in red.

Mario helped Tim up. "You okay?" he asked him.

"I'll live, thanks to you. Christ, I never saw anything like that before," he gasped in awe as he gazed down at the still twitching female body. An eye that was on a slice of head glared back at him.

Mario shrugged as he hefted the cleaver. "I was a butcher for a few years, too. I know how to wield one of these babies."

Roger walked over to them and nodded to the boy. "I think he's paralyzed, he hasn't moved since I clocked him one. What do we do with him?"

Mario shook his head. "One thing at a time, for now let's see to the guy Stacy let in and almost got us all killed."

The three men turned as one and went to Stacy who was crouched beside the blood-covered man. Mario held the cleaver in front of him, ready to use it if the man so much as looked at him the wrong way.

The man looked up at Mario, Roger and Tim, and blinked his eyes through the blood. Mario could see the man had a gash on his forehead that looked as if it had been bleeding, though it seemed to have stopped now. He could also see the man's eyes were clear, and though frightened, they weren't filled with a rage to kill and rend.

"I...I'm okay, I'm not one of them," the man said in a shaky voice. "I...I don't know how to thank you," he said to Mario.

"Forget about it," Mario stated. "It's done. Nothing personal, but I wouldn't have let you in if it was my choice. But you're in now and you're fine, so let's move on. You got a name?"

The man nodded. "I'm Chad, I came from the suburbs, thought it might be safer in the city what with the National Guard and the police and all. Guess I was wrong, huh?"

Mario chuckled slightly. "Yeah, you could say that."

"How'd you survive the explosions from that plane crash?" Roger asked as he knelt down next to the man. "We saw it from the roof and I can't believe anything's left alive in that burn zone."

Chad shook his head. "I was already on the highway when the plane hit. I still can't believe it, the entire area's been wiped out...it's awful."

"Why'd you want to get in here so badly, anyway?" Tim asked as he wiped his brow with his sleeve.

Chad shrugged. "Don't know, really. I figured it would be better to be with other people, and this is a restaurant, I'm starving and I didn't know where else to go."

Mario helped the man to his feet as Stacy stood beside him. "Well, friend, that saying about the grass being always greener? It's a load of shit. We're trapped in here like rats and sooner or later those nutjobs are gonna figure out they can smash the windows to get at us. They tried once before, but we stopped them. They don't have long memories from what we've seen."

"So what're you saying?" Chad asked as he leaned on the wall for support.

Mario lowered the cleaver, unaware it was still raised in a defensive gesture. "What I'm saying is that unless we figure out a way out of here before they come in here, all you did was delay the inevitable.

As if on cue, the pounding on the door grew in pitch and all eyes went to it, each knowing how dire the situation was.

"Well, at least I can feed you, come on, let's get you cleaned up and get some food in your belly," Mario said.

Chad nodded, and the men turned and walked back into the main dining room of the restaurant. Stacy and Chad walked side by side and Chad turned his head so he was looking at Stacy. "So you let me in, huh? They didn't want to?"

She nodded. "That's right. I couldn't let you get killed, not like that, not when we were standing inside listening to you."

"Then I owe you my life," he said. "Does my savior have a name?"

She grinned and lowered her eyes bashfully. "Stacy, I'm Stacy."

"Well then, thank you Stacy, I owe you one."

"Help us get out of here alive and we'll call it even, okay?"

"Okay," he said and the two limped into the dining room so Chad could meet the others.

Chapter 24

The next few days went by slowly for Chad, Stacy and the others. Chad was accepted into group the same as Stacy and he fell into the same boredom as the rest.

For some unknown reason, Brad and Chad hit it off. No one understood this, but everyone was glad there was now at least one person in the group that Brad would listen to if there was a problem.

Jill and Chad had also hit it off and had become fast friends. Stacy and Chad had also become friends, but with Jill, Chad found he was attracted to her in a sexual way, where Stacy was more like his sister. Not that she wasn't beautiful, also; it's just the way it was sometimes with men and women.

Mario and Stacy grew closer, the two often sneaking off to a dark corner to talk and perhaps do more. No one asked and they didn't tell.

Martha kept busy by folding napkins, as if any day now things would be better and the restaurant would be ready to open for business again. Tina said nothing, just sat in a corner booth and played with her hair or stared at the wall.

The pounding on the doors continued unabated, but on the dawn of the third day, something happened within the murderous crowd that put everyone in the restaurant in danger.

Like before, one of the *changed* figured out the glass of the windows, though strong, was an easy access point to enter the restaurant. The entire group of survivors was sleeping in the early morning when the first crack of a bat against glass caused them all to snap awake, each looking about in panic.

"What was that?" Roger asked, his voice groggy from sleep.

"It sounded like one of them is hitting the window again," Tim replied as the others got up. Brad went to a window shade and pulled it back a bit, peering out into the false dawn. It was still dark, though the coming sunrise could be seen lightening the horizon. The fires at the opposite end of the city also caused the sky to glow a pale orange, and the light was suffuse thanks to the smoke drifting across the city.

"Shit, one of those assholes has a bat and..." Mario didn't need to finish when the bat connected with the window, a gong-like sound filling the interior of the restaurant.

"Dammit, I knew this would happen," Mario snapped as he ran to another window. "And it looks like there's more out there that have the same idea!"

Chad ran to another window and looked outside. He saw a crowd of dark forms, and in the shadows a few came close to the windows, each holding some kind of weapon. A tire iron, a car jack and pieces of pipe were just a few of the assortment of blunt objects. Chad was knocked backwards when a madman came at the window and smacked it with a tire iron, causing a piece of the window to spiderweb from the crystallized center of the impact.

"Shit!" Chad cried out as he fell away.

'They're gonna get in, we're so fucked!" Brad yelled as the others looked about.

Stacy ran to Mario, and wrapped her arms around him.

"What are we going to do?" she asked.

Mario's face was serious as he looked at Stacy, the others, then back to the windows. "I knew this was gonna happen, I just didn't want to say anything. I jury-rigged something in the kitchen yesterday just in case, but it's a last resort."

Brad stepped up to Mario. "Last resort? Are you fucking kidding me? There's gotta be two hundred of those bastards outside. There is nothing but a last resort left."

"What's the plan, Mario?" Roger asked. Jill was next to Chad, the two hugging one another.

"We need to get to the roof. From there we can try to get to one of the neighboring buildings," Mario said.

"That's the fucking plan?" Brad snapped. "That's crazy? We'll still be surrounded by hundreds of those people. We'll be slaughtered!"

Mario grabbed Brad by the shirt and shook him violently. "If you got another idea, asshole, we're all ears!"

"Well, I don't, shit, let me go, you big ox!"

Jill stepped up and shoved Mario away from Brad. "What's wrong with you two? There gonna get in here any second, we need to work together."

"Fuck you, *work together*, fuck all of you!" Brad shouted. It's every man for himself as far as I'm concerned." No sooner did he finish his statement, then one of the windows shattered, the shade moving inward as the wind outside pushed it back. Then another window was shattered, the crashing of glass filling the restaurant.

Before anyone could do anything to try and stop it, the window shades were ripped from their moorings as the murderous crowd began to pour into the dining room.

"Shit, we need to stop them or we're all dead!" Mario yelled as he ran to the first screaming man and kicked him in the head. The man's head snapped back and the body slumped forward, thanks to a broken neck.

Roger followed Mario's lead and picked up a steak knife from a table and darted in, slicing a woman's throat from ear to ear. Blood shot out and bathed Roger in red, but he was already moving on to the next attacker.

"There's weapons on the last table, get them!" Mario yelled, and Chad, Stacy, Tim and Martha each went to the table Mario had indicated. On the table were knives taken from the kitchen, two shish-ka-bob skewers, and a rolling pin, as well as an assortment of pots and frying pans.

Chad and Stacy each picked up a knife and dove into the fray, swinging the blades back and forth like they were playing ninja.

Stacy's knife caught a woman in the jugular and she was splattered with blood from head to toe. She shoved the woman aside and slashed at a man as he crawled through the window frame. Chad was beside her, and as a middle-aged man with wide eyes and a yell on his lips came at him, Chad used the knife like a spear and stabbed the man in the chest. Chad felt the blade slide in, feeling the resistance as steel carved flesh, and it made his skin crawl. When he removed the blade, blood shot out of the wound to bathe him in crimson gore.

Tina was still in a booth, catatonic with fear. She never so much as screamed as the killers descended on her, hacking and slashing her until she was very, very dead. Stacy saw this out of the corner of her eye and realized Tina had never said one word, with the exception of when Stacy had first met her.

And now the woman was dead.

Chad looked up to see Roger and Tim fighting side by side and Martha behind them. Stacy was fighting with Jill as Mario did battle by himself, using a tire iron he took from one of the killers after breaking the killer's neck with his bare hands. He crushed heads and knocked attackers over as he waded into the carnage like a modern day Viking. There were more than ten killers in the restaurant now with more pouring in every second and Roger called out, "There's too many, Mario, we need to fall back!"

At first Mario didn't hear Roger, as he was lost in a berserker's rage, but slowly he came to his senses and realized what Roger was saying.

"We need to go!" Roger yelled again.

Mario kicked a man in the balls and slapped a woman with red hair away from him, then began to back up, grabbing Tim by the collar. "Roger's right, we need to go, everyone to the kitchen, then to the roof!

"But won't they just follow us?" Chad shouted as he dodged a baseball bat and stabbed a man in the thigh. The killers were uncoordinated and charged in without care for their personal safety. That was the only reason the survivors had lived through the initial rush of killers.

"Don't worry about that, just get to the damn kitchen!" Mario yelled as he began to back up, Roger and Tim with him. Martha had already turned to flee, and Jill and Stacy now began a slow withdrawal. Chad found he was alone, and he quickly began to backup. The windows were now filled with bodies, the killers swarming in like raiders sacking a village.

Mario almost fell into the kitchen, but Martha was there to hold him up. Her eyes were wide with fear and blood covered her face. "Don't worry, I have a plan to see you guys to safety," Mario said to her, his breath coming in heavy gasps.

"But how...?" Martha asked but Mario cut her off.

"It doesn't matter, just do what I say and you'll be fine."

The rest of the survivors staggered into the kitchen until finally Chad ran through the swinging doors, coming in last. Mario was there waiting and he closed the doors, sliding a wooden bar across them. The wood was left over from when Mario had done some light jobs around the restaurant, such as fixing some ceiling tiles and replacing some sheetrock at the back of the kitchen.

"This won't hold them for long, so all of you, get to the roof!" Mario turned and ran to the pair of stoves against the wall, then went and pulled out five, twenty pound cylinders of propane. "We use these for BBQs in the summer, but I got a better use for them now." He looked over his shoulder to see the others standing there, watching him. The swinging doors began to bend inward as the first of the killers reached it. Seconds remained before the doors were kicked in.

"What're you people standing there for? I told you to get to the roof! Now move!"

"You heard the man," Roger said. "Let's get going."

"Hey, where's Brad?" Jill asked as she looked around the kitchen.

Tim went to the stairs leading to the roof and he looked up to see the hatch was already open. "The son-of-a-bitch has already flown the coop," Tim said angrily.

"Doesn't surprise me in the least," Mario said. "Now get going and follow him," he said as he continued to open the valves on the propane. There was a hiss as the flammable gas filled the kitchen.

Martha and Jill headed out and Tim and Roger paused for a second. "Aren't you coming, too?" Roger asked Mario.

Mario nodded, but didn't look up as he was busy working. "Sure am, just give me a second or two." He shook Roger's hand, then Tim's. "You guys are good men; it's been an honor to know you."

"What the hell does that mean?" Tim asked, confused.

"It means to get the fuck out of here, dammit!" Mario yelled and glanced at the swinging doors which were bowing inward each time they were hit by bodies. He shoved Roger and Tim away from him. "Go!" He looked to Chad and Stacy. "You two, get moving, what the fuck are you standing there for?"

Chad looked at Mario, seeing the propane tanks, and the stoves that were on with no flames to light them; he could smell the gas and he nodded, understanding coming to him instantly.

"Thank you," Chad said simply and shook Mario's hand.

"Hey, someone's gotta do it and this is my place, so…"

Chad patted Mario on the back, then he turned and headed for the stairs leading to the roof. Stacy held back for a second with tears in her eyes, which created thin channels through the blood covering her face.

"You need to come with me, you can't do this," she said, figuring it out, too.

He turned and grabbed her by the shoulders. His eyes were filled with emotion but he held it in check.

"I have to, baby. Someone has to slow these fuckers down or else they'll just follow you. Take the chance I'm giving you and use it."

"But you can't, we were becoming…I mean, we were getting…"

He shook her violently to snap her out of her reverie. "No, Stacy, that was all a dream. This is real, this is the world we live in and I want you to keep living in it." His eyes softened and he moved in close to her, hugging her tight. "If it matters, I believe we could have been happy together."

Chad ran back in, after getting worried when Stacy wasn't following him. Mario shoved her into Chad's arms. "Take care of her, Chad, see she gets off the roof safely," he said as he turned away, as if he was ignoring her.

"Mario, no," she said but Chad was dragging her away. At first she fought him, but then she succumbed, Chad pushing her in front of him to the stairs. She stopped at the edge of the kitchen, and turned to look at Mario, who was working to open the valves on the last of the propane tanks.

"Mario…" she called. "I love you."

He grinned slyly. "Yeah, I know you do." Then he turned and went back to work, this time dismissing her for good.

"Come on, Stacy, don't let his sacrifice be in vain," Chad said as he pulled on her right arm. She held on to the corner of the wall, but then she let Chad pull her away. He made her run, Chad knowing their time was short, and he all but carried her up the stairs to the roof hatch.

Mario waited until he heard the roof hatch slam shut and then he looked over at the barred swing doors. The bar he'd slid across it was ready to break and he reached into his right pocket and took out a sixty-cent disposable Bic lighter.

"Come on, you fuckers, let's get this done!" he yelled with conviction, the feeling of dread in his stomach like a living entity. The feeling reminded him of something that happened to him when he was a child. He was eleven and his father had a drawer full of fifty cent pieces in his bedroom. His father had been tight-fisted and would never give him an allowance or money for the ice cream truck. Not wanting to feel left out, Mario had always snuck in and would take a fifty cent piece now and then. Only he didn't think that after months of doing this, the reserves would become vastly depleted. He remembered sitting on the stairs leading to the second floor in his house as his father and mother sat in the kitchen at the end of the short hallway. His father was counting the fifty cent pieces. He remembered the feeling in his stomach like it was yesterday, the dread that was like a thousand rats gnawing at his gut.

"I could have sworn I had more of these," his father had said, but then nothing had happened. Whether his mother had covered it up, as she was quick-witted and would have figured it out, or whether his father had just let it go, he never knew. But he always remembered that feeling, as if he was about to be shot or hanged.

This feeling filled him now, and as the bar on the swinging doors broke, he stood fast and watched the killers pour inside. He needed to get as many inside with him as possible, that way there would be less chance for pursuit of his friends. He waited so long he began to feel woozy from breathing in the gas. But when the first hands of a killer wrapped themselves around his neck and he was forced to the tile floor, his mind snapped awake and he flicked the lighter, while smiling so wide his teeth gleamed in the wan light.

He didn't want to die, but if he had to go, it was good to know he wouldn't be going alone.

The first time he flicked the lighter, nothing happened, and as he was stabbed repeatedly by a dozen blades, he flicked the lighter once more. This time a small spark turned into a smaller flame. The instant the flame appeared, the invisible gas in the kitchen ignited, the small flame becoming a massive fireball, until the entire room was nothing but fire and death.

Chad felt the air disappear and he heard a whoosh as the fire consumed everything in its path.

The last thought he had was that the feeling of dread was now gone, to be replaced by one of utter peace.

Chapter 25

Chad crawled out of the roof hatch seconds before the kitchen exploded. Just as he pulled himself onto the roof and slammed the hatch closed, the entire building shook. Stacy was only a few feet from him and she fell to the gravel-covered roof, crying out in fear.

Chad looked around the roof, searching for the others, and as the roof shook beneath him, he watched Martha, who was too close to the edge, lose her balance and tumble off. Her shrill scream lasted for almost five seconds before abruptly ceasing. Chad scrambled to his feet as the building vibrated under him and peered over the edge to see Martha sprawled on the sidewalk. Her head was cracked open and her brains were spread out like someone had dropped a plate of spaghetti. A halo of blood spread out around her head, and her arms were bent at odd angles, bone protruding from the torn skin. As he watched, five *changed* ran to her dead body and began hacking at it. In seconds, Martha was nothing more than unrecognizable meat.

Feeling his stomach heave inside him, Chad rolled back from the edge and got to his feet. He ran to Stacy and helped her up as the building heaved under them yet again.

Near the far edge, Roger, Jill and Tim were standing still, trying to figure out what to do next. Chad and Stacy joined them.

"It's too far, we can't make it," Tim said as he gauged the distance between the two buildings. It was a little more than ten feet, but the problem was the neighboring roof was higher than the restaurant. Once the divide was jumped, the person would then have to pull themselves up and onto the neighboring roof.

"It's not like we have a choice here," Roger said as he steadied himself. "This place is gonna burn and us with it if we don't get off this roof soon. Once those gas lines catch, this place is gonna be nothin' but rubble."

"I don't care, it's too far," Tim said again. "Don't do it."

Roger ignored him. "Look, it's jump or die, at least if we jump, it's a chance we'll make it."

"Then you go first," Tim told him.

Roger frowned and then set his jaw. "Fine, I will. You'll see, piece of cake." He backed up about fifteen feet, wanting to get some distance in before he leaped. He rubbed his hands together, breathed in and out a few times, and ran as fast as he could, looking like a sprinter at the Olympics. Tim watched from the side and he leaned forward to Chad and said, "He's not gonna make it, poor bastard."

Whether Roger heard him or just miscalculated, his shoe wasn't close enough to the edge when he leaped and he came up a foot too short. He slapped the side of the next building like something out of a cartoon and then fell straight down to the alley below. But it was only a one-story drop and he survived the fall. And if the alley had been vacant, he would have hobbled away to try again some other day with nothing more than a bad ankle. But the alley wasn't empty. It was filled with more than twenty raging killers who welcomed Roger into their waiting arms with cries of fury.

Roger landed on an old man, crushing him to the ground, killing him instantly. The cushion saved Roger from any real harm and he rolled to his feet, pushing and punching any who got too close. But he was simply outnumbered and in seconds was swallowed by the crowd. When they stepped away from him a full three minutes later, there was nothing left but a mangled mess of body parts and bloody clothing that resembled rags.

Up on the roof, the few survivors turned away, not wanting to see any more.

"Dammit, I told him it was too far," Tim sighed, brokenhearted. He had really like Roger, the two becoming good friends.

Behind them, the roof hatch popped open and the first of the rage-infected killers appeared.

These were the ones that had somehow survived the blast when the kitchen went up, but they didn't survive it unscathed. They were covered in burns, more than one practically naked thanks to the flames burning off their clothes. Almost all had no hair, and a few had no ears or only one eye. They suffered from burns that would have incapacitated a normal human but their rage-filled minds ignored the pain, wanting to kill and maim to the point that it overwhelmed their pain receptors.

"Oh my God, no!" Jill screamed as she stared at the killers pouring onto the roof. Some were crawling, their legs now useless, but with each passing second, more filled the roof.

Chad did the math in his head and saw he had seconds to decide what to do next. Turning around to stare at the side of the next building, he knew jumping to it was his and everyone else's only hope, despite what happened to Roger.

"We have to try," he said to Stacy.

"But Roger didn't make it," she said.

Chad shook his head. "He didn't put his foot right when he jumped. He screwed up. Look, Stacy, it's our only hope. We need to do this, Mario would want you to."

That woke Stacy up. Mario. He had sacrificed himself so she could live. She wouldn't simply lie down and be killed now, not after what he did for her.

"Okay, Chad, I'll do it," she said.

"What?" Tim gasped. "You're crazy, it's suicide."

"And staying here isn't?" Chad rebutted. He looked to Jill and Tim. "You two do what the hell you want, we're going for it." He grabbed Stacy's hand. "Come on, we need to get a running jump."

She did as he said, following him. The two of them ran almost to the crowd coming out of the roof hatch and to Jill and Tim it seemed like they were going to run right into them. But at the last second, Chad stopped, Stacy and him sliding on the gravel. He turned her around and pointed her toward the edge.

"You can do it, Stacy. You go first. I'll be right behind you. Don't try and reach the roof with your body, just your hands. Then you can pull yourself up."

"Okay," she said, her voice cracking.

"So, then what the fuck are you waiting for? Get going?" Chad said almost casually, smiling to calm her down. She nodded and took a deep breath, then began to run. Her arms swung out in from of her and she locked her eyes on the edge of the next roof. She tried not to think about Roger, and what happened to him. She ran as fast as she could, and when she reached the edge, she jumped, her legs swinging back and forth as her body went airborne.

Suddenly, she felt like she was flying. Her pulse pounded in her ears and she snatched a peek below her to see faces gazing up at her hungrily. Then she was hitting the side of the building. Her hands went up instinctively, and just as she began to fall, her curled fingers latched onto the edge of the roof. Metal cut into the crooks of her fingers, but she held on, her legs dangling as she tried to get purchase. Arms trembling, she tried to pull herself up, but she couldn't do it, her upper body strength wouldn't let her. She quickly realized her fingers were already slipping and she would fall in less than a minute.

The screams of the *changed* roared below her as they anxiously waited for her to fall. A few climbed on the heads and shoulders of others, but they still came woefully short of reaching her.

But then she caught a blur on her right and suddenly Chad was there. He hit the wall harder than her, but managed to get his elbows over the edge instead of just his fingers. Grunting with the strain, he began to pull himself onto the roof. Stacy felt her hands slipping and she let out a cry just before her fingers finally went numb and she felt herself falling. Her eyes were closed as she slid from the edge, and no sooner did she let go, then she was jolted to a stop.

Opening her eyes, she looked up at Chad's straining face as he struggled to hold onto her. He was too tired to speak, but his eyes told her volumes. She put her feet against the brick of the building and began to try and push herself up. An imperfection in the brickwork allowed her left shoe to halt her descent and then she was pushing upward. Chad was groaning with the effort, but she was rising, an inch at a time. Finally, he let out a scream to rival any of the *changed* as he hauled her over the edge. Stacy rolled onto her side and stared up at the morning sky, amazed she was still alive.

Chad was already on his knees and he gazed out over the divide to the restaurant's roof which was now becoming hidden in black smoke pouring out of the shattered windows below.

"Jill, Tim! You gotta jump!" he yelled, but as he watched the two survivors, he saw they weren't going to be surviving for much longer. While Chad and Stacy had jumped and managed to crawl to safety, Jill and Tim had become surrounded by killers, every side but the one facing Chad now swarming with burnt and bloody people.

"Come on, you can do it! Chad cried out, knowing the man and woman had only one chance to live past the next few seconds.

Tim and Jill were huddled together like refugees, and when a man with no face and one eye came at them, Tim kicked the man away. Then he grabbed Jill and the two dashed for the edge, wanting to join Chad and Stacy.

But Tim had waited too long and there was barely enough room to get up any speed. As he and Jill leapt into the air while holding hands, four of the *changed* leapt with them, arms grabbing them and pulling them far short of the roof.

Chad made eye contact with Tim as the man leaped into the air, and he saw the fear etched in Tim's eyes, the desperation and the hope to continue to live, to not cease to exist and know the world would just keep on spinning without you. That in the end, each of us is nothing; insignificant in the grand design of life.

Chad could only stare in horror and watch helplessly as Tim and Jill fell away to land heavily on the crowd below.

Both landed on the bodies of the crowd and were spared an instant death, which would have been a mercy that was now denied them. Like wild animals, the murderous crowd began tearing into them; with hands and weapons slicing them to pieces. Tim howled as his right arm was cut off by a saw and his testicles ripped off like they were nothing more than hanging apples on a tree at harvest time. Jill was luckier in her demise, and as she tried to fight, a blade came down and severed her jugular, the blood shooting out like a fountain to bathe the crowd in gore. She twitched and her eyes rolled back into her head as she bled out, and as she was gutted and torn apart, she felt none of it.

As for Tim, he wasn't so lucky and his screams went on for several minutes, causing Chad to cringe in revulsion as those shrieks of agony pierced his very soul. But thankfully, even those screams finally ceased.

Chad fell back onto his butt and stared out onto the restaurant roof. The crowd of killers was at the edge, howling and yelling at him. But they couldn't get him. A few were knocked off by their brethren who pushed and shoved angrily, and they landed on top of their brethren below, some dying from the fall, some merely wounded.

One killer fell head over heels and landed on his head. The crack was so loud Chad heard it from above. The body landed like a rag doll and flopped over, to be stomped into the pavement by the feet of the murderous crowd.

The smoke was thicker now and there were spots in the restaurant's roof where flames were poking through, the tar under the gravel now bubbling. The *changed* began to cry out in pain, but didn't seem to understand what was happening, while others had fallen over from smoke inhalation.

Chad began to cough as well and he helped Stacy to her feet.

"Come on, we need to go. This building's taller than the restaurant and should have a fire escape. At least if it's up to code."

"And what if it isn't?" she asked. Her eyes were tearing up from smoke and from losing Mario, Roger, Tim and Jill. She coughed repeatedly, her throat becoming raw.

"Then we're fucked," Chad stated simply as he pulled her across the roof, leaving the crowd of psychopaths behind.

* * *

At the far end of the roof, the fire escape was exactly where Chad hoped it would be. Down below on the street, it was deserted, every infected killer wanting to be where the action was on the other side of the building.

Chad went first and then, when he saw it was still clear, he waved Stacy down. At the bottom of fire escape was a metal ladder and Chad had to release it and let it fall. He cringed as the ladder rattled on its rollers, but the noise was lost under the cacophony of the crowd on the opposite side. Chad went first again, and when he peered around the alley's end to inspect the street, he nodded and then waved for Stacy to follow him. When she had joined him on the ground, Chad took her hand, pointed to a shadow-enshrouded alley across the street, and the two ran for it.

Reaching the next alley, Chad spun around and checked to see if they had been spotted. They hadn't.

"It looks like we made it," he whispered. "Every crazy bastard in a mile of the restaurant must be there now. We should be able to get out of here safely."

"And go where?" she asked, her eyes filled with the loss of her friends. True, she had only known them for a few short days but in that time she had bonded with most and felt sympathy for ones like Tina.

Chad didn't know what to say to her, and he told her as much. "Look, for now let's just get out of here, all right?"

She blinked in agreement and the two spun around and jogged away, while behind them, the restaurant continued to burn.

* * *

Brad shifted inside the air conditioning unit on the roof of the restaurant on the north side. It was heating up by the second and he wondered how much hotter it was going to become.

He'd thought it was such a great idea when he'd come up with it. When he'd left the others and snuck onto the roof, he saw how far the other buildings were and knew it would be suicide to try and jump to them. Then he spotted the a/c unit and had gotten a great idea. Why not just hide out in the large ductwork and let everything blow over? Let the others be the decoys for the mindless killers to chase, and when the commotion died down and the killers had wandered away, then he could come out of his hiding spot and head off for better pastures.

But there had been a hitch in his plan he hadn't thought of, and it was that the restaurant fire would burn so hot and so fast that it would consume the entire building. Unknown to Brad, the insulation in the building's walls and ceiling were outdated and very flammable, the entire structure going up like a massive candle.

He shifted position and the sheet metal burned him wherever it touched his skin. He was sweating heavily and the air was so thick with smoke he could barely breathe. He was coughing, too, though he covered his mouth with his sleeve so as not to make any noise.

Over an hour passed as he roasted like a chicken in an oven and finally he couldn't take it anymore; he wanted out and right now!

When his arm touched the sheet metal, his flesh stuck to it, the sizzle of his skin coming to his ears and the scent of cooked flesh filling his sinuses, he knew he couldn't take another second.

Kicking off the grate, he crawled out of his hole and onto the roof. The second he landed, he cried out in pain, the gravel scalding him worse than the sheet metal of the a/c unit had. He rolled to his knees and looked up through the smoke to see a bright sun shining down on him.

He could see large holes in the roof, tongues of fire licking out, and he knew he needed to go right now.

But as he turned to head to the edge, and from there he still didn't know what to do when he got there, he suddenly saw shadowy forms coalesce out of the smoke. At first it seemed like he was imagining it, but as the forms grew closer, he saw they were human-shaped.

Brad's face took on one of instant understanding as he stared at the burnt and twisted faces boring down on him. He realized right then that his plan had another serious flaw. He had assumed the *changed* would have left the roof once they had slaughtered Chad, Stacy and the others; he hadn't taken into account that their rage-befuddled minds wouldn't be able to allow them to figure a way off the roof. So they had stayed there, waiting to die, not understanding what was happening.

And then they heard Brad cry out when he landed on the gravel upon climbing out of the a/c unit, and they realized they had found fresh prey.

Brad's face took on a visage of surprise, which then quickly shifted to one of utter horror as the killers surrounded him; hands reaching out for his hair and clothes as already bloody knives and clubs began to find his body, slicing flesh and breaking bones.

Brad took a long time to die, and when he finally expired, his eyes now gone, torn from their sockets and his tongue sliced off, the roof opened up beneath him and swallowed him whole, taking two dozen killers with him.

The flames reached for the sky, consuming the sacrifice given unto it, but in seconds it was hungry once more. It would never be satiated, never appeased, and in many ways the conflagration was a lot like man.

No matter how much it consumed, it would never be enough.

Chapter 26

Chad and Stacy were three streets over from the restaurant when they ran smack dab into a massive crowd of *changed* people. As Chad and Stacy stared at the crowd coming toward them, he still didn't understand what they'd done wrong.

He had to rack it up to simple exhaustion and carelessness on both of them.

He and Stacy stood immobile at the end of the street as the rage-filled crowd slowly approached. Each held a weapon and more than one carried bloody body parts from past kills. A few kids screamed and tittered as they ran about between the adult's legs, the children also covered in gore.

Chad didn't understand why they weren't attacking until Stacy nudged him and told him to be quiet.

"Just do what I do and we'll be fine," she said out of the corner of her mouth.

"What are you..." Chad began.

"Don't talk. Look, I don't have a lot of time to explain it to you but we're both covered in blood from the fight at the restaurant. If we act crazy enough these bastards will think we're like them."

"What? That's ridic..."

"Shut up, no it isn't. I've done it before. Just don't speak. They don't talk, well, not really. Just growl and look like you want to kill everyone who looks at you funny." She began walking. "Now, follow me and do what I do."

Chad stared in shock as she began to walk towards the crowd. Not wanting to be alone and knowing there was no way to outrun them, he followed her, trying to look as unbalanced as possible. He found as he let himself go, it wasn't really that difficult.

All he needed to do was ask himself: How much death could one person witness before they lost all feeling?

Stacy went up to the leaders of the crowd and she growled at them, screaming unintelligible words. She pushed a woman away from her and smacked a man in the face. Chad couldn't believe what he was seeing, and though he was scared to death, feeling as if he was walking into the lion's den, he mimicked Stacy, yelling crazy nonsense and shoving a few crazies aside. His eyes were wide and his mouth was bent at an odd angle, and he thought of the horror movies he'd watched as a kid when the maniac killed the college kids at the camp or in the sorority house. He was absolutely amazed when he and Stacy were welcomed into the throng and not molested.

Stacy shot him a quick glance and then she turned and began walking with the crowd. Chad, ready to pee himself, did the same thing. He thought back to when he'd entered the church and how the people had looked at him at first. If he had acted more unstable, it was possible they would have taken him for one of them. But how was he to know this?

Chad and Stacy fell into step, walking through the destroyed streets of the city. They came upon the restaurant again and all the *changed* still milling around the building joined them.

Chad didn't know where they were going, but it was too late to do anything but play his part.

They walked for more than two miles, coming upon a furniture store.

Here, a group of normals were surrounded, and before either Chad or Stacy knew what was happening, the crowd surrounded the normals and began to kill them.

Chad was pushed and shoved forward, and before he realized it, he found himself next to a small child, no more than seven or eight. The child was normal and was screaming, the small boy so terrified he looked like he would pass out from sheer terror.

Suddenly, Chad felt hands on his back, and a few of the *changed* pointed at the boy and then to him. One used a knife and pretended to slide it across his throat, indicating Chad needed to do this to the boy.

Chad froze, not understanding, but at the same time understanding all to well. He had been told to kill the boy and if he didn't, he would be found out as a fraud and he knew what would happen then. First the *changed* would kill him when they realized he was normal, then they would kill the boy.

So in the end, though it was against everything he believed in, Chad knew if he wanted to live, he had no choice.

The boy had to die.

As he watched the slaughter of others around him, he saw many using hands and teeth to kill and maim.

And he knew what he had to do to keep his disguise up and save his life.

He was shoved forward again and a few faces glared at him, as if they were ready to pounce if he didn't do what was expected of him. With a heavy heart and a sob in his throat, Chad grabbed the boy and picked him up. Though terrified and shaking like a leaf on a tree in a windstorm, the boy kicked and screamed, crying out for his "Mommy".

Chad hesitated one last time, not knowing if he could go through with it. To do this heinous thing would be to lose what was left of his humanity. It bode the question, if a man will do anything to survive, are some things not worth living for after the deed is done?

He felt a knife press into his side in warning and a guttural growl at his ear and he knew if he didn't act now, he was dead. His own survival instinct took over and he pulled the child's body to him, his teeth sinking into the boy's throat over the jugular.

It was the hardest thing he'd ever done in his life.

Chad's eyes were closed as he ripped into the warm flesh, the taste of blood shooting into his mouth to cause him to gag. The boy screamed and kicked, one of his feet kicking Chad in the groin, which caused Chad to bend over in pain, which caused the crowd around him to roar in what seemed like laughter. As the child died in his arms, the boy's bladder let go and Chad felt his leg become warm. Then the boy was ripped from his hands to be torn apart by the others. He felt a slap on the shoulder by another killer and he fell to his knees in shame. He heard the boy shriek a few times as he was ripped to pieces, then when the head was severed from the small body, the cries mercifully stopped.

Chad spit out the blood, the taste mixed with his own bile as he fought to keep his stomach from heaving. All around him the normals were killed, some slow, others fast.

When a hand rested on his shoulder, he barely felt it, but then Stacy knelt down and whispered into his ear. "I saw what you did, you had no choice," she said.

Chad shook his head and cried, not feeling that way at all. He'd murdered a small child, how could he live with himself after doing something so inhuman?

She helped him to his feet and the two joined the raving crowd, careful to stay on the edge so they didn't have to get involved in any more killings. All the while, Chad cried, the tears washing some of the blood from his face. When Stacy saw this, she went to a body lying on the edge of the sidewalk and scooped up a healthy handful of gore, then splashed it onto Chad. He barely felt it, lost in a world of guilt and misery.

The killing and carnage went on for hours, but eventually it quieted down when a man stood on a car and held his hands aloft.

Chad and Stacy found out his name was Dean, and unbelievable as it sounded, this man was *changed*, but somehow could still talk and think. Chad and Stacy watched as this man directed his *people* to get ready to leave the city in the morning. They were going to the airport where other normals were believed to be holed up. Stacy watched Dean talk to another man, a normal man. He had blonde hair and was young and looked scared out of his mind.

When she thought it was safe, Stacy whispered into Chad's ear. "When we head to the airport in the morning, we'll pick our chance and sneak off. Then we can get as far away from the city as possible. Okay?" Chad didn't answer and she shook him hard. "I said, okay?"

"Yes, fine, whatever you want. What's the point?"

"The point is we keep on living," she hissed.

"Yeah, but at what cost to our souls?"

She didn't reply, not wanting to talk for too long and be discovered.

The rest of the day was nothing but horrors, as the *changed* fornicated, terrorizing and killing what ever they could find. Chad watched the crowd carry in a large German shepherd and as the gawkers hooted and hollered, the dog was gutted and skinned, one of the crowd taking the pelt for its own. This happened three more times before any more dogs in the area managed to escape.

Chad didn't know if it was more heartbreaking to see a human or an animal slaughtered. At least the humans understood what was happening to them. But the dogs all had trusting eyes; right up until the first blade slid into their abdomens and slit them like a roasted chicken.

When they eventually tired of the carnage, Stacy and Chad found a quiet spot away from the crowd and sat against a wall inside the furniture store. Dean was busy killing some normals his people had brought back to him while others had gone off to set fire to the opposite end of the city and thus drive any normals hiding right to Dean where they could be slaughtered like cattle. Stacy stayed away from Dean, the man far more terrifying than any of the killers she'd seen. This man was rational and yet he loved to kill and murder.

He was the Devil incarnate.

Later, when they had a chance to talk, Chad asked her once more, "Will it work? Do you think we can really find somewhere that isn't like Chicago?"

"We'll just have to wait and see," she said with a shrug. "All we can do is try."

The next morning, Dean gathered his people to him and they headed off to the airport. The blonde haired man walked next to Dean, and Chad wondered who he was and why Dean was allowing the man to live. Chad heard that the man's name was Mike, but that's all he knew.

The road to the airport was a long journey, as they all went on foot. Many times the massive crowd would meet others and Dean would gather them into his flock. By the time the airport was just a few miles away, he had thousands of murderous followers filling the highway from shoulder to shoulder.

Chad turned and look behind him to see a sea of heads and shoulders bobbing around the abandoned cars and trucks on the highway. The vehicles were like tiny islands as the heads flowed around them, some of the more energetic men and women climbing over them.

He didn't know what would happen at the airport, but he felt sorry for whoever was there. With this many *changed* going to attack; anyone at the airport was doomed.

He felt someone tug his shirt and he turned to see it was Stacy. She nodded to the shoulder of the highway and he let her lead him to it. Once there, she began to slow down, the two of them falling to the rear of the massive army of killers.

It took almost an hour, but eventually they were in the last section and then were in the trailing section, only a few dozen strong.

She bent over to stop, as if she was too tired to go on, and Chad knelt down beside her with his head down. The few remaining men and women walking behind just avoided them, swerving around them as they followed the army.

No one seemed to care if two more stragglers were falling behind. Chad glanced over his shoulder to see bodies scattered here and there across the highway. One was only ten feet away and he walked over and inspected it. It was a man, and when Chad rolled him over, he saw there was a bullet wound in the man's lower torso.

Stacy joined him and looked at the body, then gestured to the others lying on the road, some now only crawling.

"It looks like if they get hurt, they're too stupid to seek medical attention," she said. "These people must have gotten hurt at some point and either finally bled out or died from infection...sepsis maybe."

"Yeah, makes sense," Chad said. "They do seem to have one tract minds." He glanced towards the rear of the marching army, seeing the backs of the killers and then looked back to Stacy. "So what now?"

"Now we find a car that works and we go the other way."

He waved to the cars around them, more than a dozen just in their general vicinity. "Well, we have enough to pick from, what'll it be? Toyota or a Mercedes?"

How 'bout a Porsche?" she suggested as she walked back the way they'd come until she came upon a black Porsche with Italian leather interior. "I saw this when we passed it and that's why I thought this was as good a place as any other to stop."

Chad went to the driver's door and opened it. "You're in luck, the keys are in the ignition."

She placed her hands on her hips and smiled. "Actually, there was no luck needed. I saw the keys inside when I passed it. Like I said, that's why I picked this part of the highway to stop. If we need a car, it might as well be something nice."

"Might as well ride in style, is that it?" he asked with a slight grin.

"Exactly," she grinned back.

Chad reached inside and pulled the keys from the ignition and went to the trunk, opening it so see if there was anything worth it inside. There wasn't, only a spare tire. Then he tossed the keys to her. "Why don't you drive," he said as he walked around the car and climbed into the passenger seat. There was a splatter of dried blood on the seat and dashboard, but he only glanced at it, then it was forgotten. Blood didn't seem to freak him out like it once did. He was still covered in dried blood, some his, some from others, and he found with enough time, a person could get used to anything.

Stacy ran around to the driver's door and hopped in, shoving the ignition key back in and turning on the electrical. Both of them let out a small sigh when the dash lights came on and the beeping of seatbelts not fastened filled the interior.

She nodded to his seatbelt as she buckled hers, smiling like a kid getting her first bicycle. "Buckle up for safety."

He frowned, thinking it would be foolish, but he did as she asked. She, too, was covered in blood, some fresh, but most of it dried. They looked like a couple of serial killers who had orchestrated a massacre and were now going for a ride in the country.

She put the transmission in drive and swung around, driving the wrong way on the highway. When there was a break in the guardrail, she crossed the wide grass medium, and swung back onto the road with a spray of dirt and gravel from the shoulder.

She drove for a few miles until coming to an exit that looked promising. A large green sign was bolted to a silver pole, the sign hanging over the highway. On the sign, in clean white lettering, were the words:

INDIANA, INTERSTATE 32, NEXT EXIT, ½ MILE.

"Hey, how 'bout Indiana? Got any family there?" she asked as she downshifted.

Chad shook his head. "No, I don't have any family. Not really. You?"

"I've got a couple of cousins there," she said.

"Then let's go there, one place is as good as another, I suppose. If whatever has infected Chicago has also gotten to the rest of the country, we're pretty screwed no matter where we go."

"My, my, Chad, you're such an optimist," she joked.

Chad changed the subject. "So, what do you think is gonna happen at the airport?" he asked.

She shrugged as she downshifted again, getting ready for the exit. She drove in and around cars and wrecks, loving the way the high-performance machine handled. She could never have afforded a car like this on her salary, and now, here she was driving one.

"Not our problem, Chad, let's worry about us and the here and now, okay?"

"Yeah, good idea," he said.

Stacy slowed as she took the exit and Chad looked at her again. "Will it be better there?" he asked.

"Don't know," she replied. "But it has to be better than Chicago."

Coming out of the turn, she got on the new highway. The road ahead was relatively clear of wrecked cars and she changed gears and leaned back in her seat. Her window was down and the wind felt great on her skin, as the dried blood flaked off to be blown away. She glanced at Chad to see he was looking out his open window at the Chicago skyline in the distance. The city was burning like a massive funeral pyre and she saw he was lost in his thoughts.

Though she hadn't known him long, she liked him.

And if she had to go through this living Hell with someone, Chad was a good person to do it with. As if he felt her eyes on him, he turned to look at her. She smiled and held out her right hand which he took, squeezing it in a comforting gesture. Then he turned and gazed out the window, the wind ruffling his hair. Was it her imagination or did he seem at peace for the first time since she'd met him?

The engine revved when she shifted to a higher gear, the feeling of power filling her with strength and hope. Her life may be on a tenuous string at the moment, but at the same time, she felt strangely unburdened.

No more rent, no more nine-to-five job, no more taxes. For the moment, it was all gone.

For the first time in her life, she actually felt free.

And as she sped down the highway, the wind blowing her hair behind her, she believed that if she really wanted to, she could just close her eyes and imagine she was flying.

The world of the *changed* is far from over.

Find out what happens next in book 2 of
the Rage virus series:
Dead Rage
Available now.

DEAD RAGE
by Anthony Giangregorio
Book 2 in the Rage virus series!

An unknown virus spreads across the globe, turning ordinary people into bloodthirsty, ravenous killers.

Only a small percentage of the population is immune and soon become prey to the infected.

Amongst the infected comes a man, stricken by the virus, yet still retaining his grasp on reality. His need to destroy the *normals* becomes an obsession and he raises an army of killers to seek out and kill all who aren't *changed* like himself.

A few survivors gather together on the outskirts of Chicago and find themselves running for their lives as the specter of death looms over all.

The Dead Rage virus will find you, no matter where you hide.

CHRISTMAS IS DEAD: A ZOMBIE ANTHOLOGY
Edited by Anthony Giangregorio

Twas the night before Christmas and all through the house, not a creature was stirring, not even a. . . zombie?

That's right; this anthology explores what would happen at Christmas time if there was a full blown zombie outbreak.

Reanimated turkeys, zombie Santas, and demon reindeers that turn people into flesh-eating ghouls are just some of the tales you will find in this merry undead book.

So curl up under the Christmas tree with a cup of hot chocolate, and as the fireplace crackles with warmth, get ready to have your heart filled with holiday cheer.

But of course, then it will be ripped from your heaving chest and fed upon by blood-thirsty elves with a craving for human flesh!

For you see, Christmas is Dead!

And you will never look at the holiday season the same way again.

DEAD HOUSE: A ZOMBIE GHOST STORY
by Keith Adam Luethke
Welcome to Dead House

The old mansion on the edge of town, aptly named Dead House, has a history of blood, pain, and death, but what Victor Leeds knows of this past only scratches the surface of the true horrors within.

But when his girlfriend is attacked by a shadowy figure one rainy night, he soon finds himself caught up in a world where the dead walk and ghostly wraiths abound.

And to make matters worse, a pair of serial killers are fulfilling carefully made plans, and when they are done, the small town of Stormville, New York will run red. The last ingredient to open the gates of Hell, and plunge this small upstate town into madness, is rain.

And in Stormville, it pours by the gallons.

The Zombie in the Basement
by Anthony Giangregorio
Illustrated by Andrew Dawe-Collins

The spooky house at the end of the street was the one all the kids avoided. With its overgrown shrubs and weeds, the place was a modern day haunted house. Especially at night. So when Ricky sneaks into the yard to retrieve his favorite ball, he comes across something he'd only seen in movies and bad dreams. He sees a zombie in the basement window of the old house, but when he tells his friends, no one believes him. Ricky knows what he saw, that something lurks in the old house, something that isn't supposed to exist.

With his best friend Eric by his side,　Ricky will find out the truth and prove to everyone that zombies are real. And when the night is done, everyone will know about the zombie in the basement.

Note: This book is for young adults and for those who are young at heart.

DEADFREEZE
by Anthony Giangregorio
THIS IS WHAT HELL WOULD BE LIKE IF IT FROZE OVER!

When an experimental serum for hypothermia goes horribly wrong, a small research station in the middle of Antarctica becomes overrun with an army of the frozen dead.

Now a small group of survivors must battle the arctic weather and a horde of frozen zombies as they make their way across the frozen plains of Antarctica to a neighboring research station.

What they don't realize is that they are being hunted by an entity whose sole reason for existing is vengeance; and it will find them wherever they run.

VISIONS OF THE DEAD
A ZOMBIE STORY
by Anthony & Joseph Giangregorio

Jake Roberts felt like he was the luckiest man alive.

He had a great family, a beautiful girlfriend, who was soon to be his wife, and a job, that might not have been the best, but it paid the bills.

At least until the dead began to walk.

Now Jake is fighting to survive in a dead world while searching for his lost love, Melissa, knowing she's out there somewhere.

But the past isn't dead, and as he struggles for an uncertain future, the past threatens to consume him. With the present a constant battle between the living and the dead, Jake finds himself slipping in and out of the past, the visions of how it all happened haunting him. But Jake knows Melissa is out there somewhere and he'll find her or die trying.

In a world of the living dead, you can never escape your past.

DEAD MOURNING: A ZOMBIE HORROR STORY
by Anthony Giangregorio

Carl Jenkins was having a run of bad luck. Fresh out of jail, his probation tenuous, he'd lost every job he'd taken since being released. So now was his last chance, only one more job to prevent him from going back to prison. Assigned to work in a funeral home, he accidentally loses a shipment of embalming fluid. With nothing to lose, he substitutes it with a batch of chemicals from a nearby factory.

The results don't go as planned, though. While his screw-up goes unnoticed, his machinations revive the cadavers in the funeral home, unleashing an evil on the world that it has not seen before. Not wanting to become a snack for the rampaging dead, he flees the city, joining up with other survivors. An old, dilapidated zoo becomes their haven, while the dead wait outside the walls, hungry and patient.

But Carl is optimistic, after all, he's still alive, right? Perhaps his luck has changed and help will arrive to save them all?

Unfortunately, unknown to him and the other survivors, a serial killer has fallen into their group, trapped inside the zoo with them.

With the undead army clamoring outside the walls and a murderer within, it'll be a miracle if any of them live to see the next sunrise.

On second thought, maybe Carl would've been better off if he'd just gone back to jail.

ROAD KILL: A ZOMBIE TALE
by Anthony Giangregorio
ORDER UP!

In the summer of 2008, a rogue comet entered earth's orbit for 72 hours. During this time, a strange amber glow suffused the sky.

But something else happened; something in the comet's tail had an adverse affect on dead tissue and the result was the reanimation of every dead animal carcass on the planet.

A handful of survivors hole up in a diner in the backwoods of New Hampshire while the undead creatures of the night hunt for human prey.

There's a new blue plate special at DJ's Diner and Truck Stop, and it's you!

DEAD WORLDS: Undead Stories
A Zombie Anthology Volume 2
Edited by Anthony Giangregorio

Welcome to a world where the dead walk and want nothing more than to feast on the living. The stories contained in this, the second volume of the Dead Worlds series, are filled with action, gore, and buckets and buckets of blood; plus a heaping side of entrails for those with a little extra hunger.

The stories contained within this volume are scribed by both the desiccated cadavers of seasoned veterans to the genre as well as fresh-faced corpses, each printed here for the first time; and all of them ready to dig in and please the most discerning reader.

So slap on a bib and prepare to get bloody, because you're about to read the best zombie stories this side of Hell!

THE DARK

by Anthony Giangregorio
DARKNESS FALLS

The darkness came without warning.

First New York, then the rest of United States, and then the world became enveloped in a perpetual night without end.

With no sunlight, eventually the planet will wither and die, bringing on a new Ice Age. But that isn't problem for the human race, for humanity will be dead long before that happens.

There is something in the dark, creatures only seen in nightmares, and they are on the prowl. Evolution has changed and man is no longer the dominant species. When we are children, we're told not to fear the dark, that what we believe to exist in the shadows is false.

Unfortunately, that is no longer true.

SOULEATER

by Anthony Giangregorio

Twenty years ago, Jason Lawson witnessed the brutal death of his father by something only seen in nightmares, something so horrible he'd blocked it from his mind.

Now twenty years later the creature is back, this time for his son.

Jason won't let that happen.

He'll travel to the demon's world, struggling every second to rescue his son from its clutches.

But what he doesn't know is that the portal will only be open for a finite time and if he doesn't return with his son before it closes, then he'll be trapped in the demon's dimension forever.

SEE HOW IT ALL BEGAN IN THE NEW DOUBLE-SIZED 460 PAGE SPECIAL EDITION!

DEADWATER: EXPANDED EDITION

by Anthony Giangregorio

Through a series of tragic mishaps, a small town's water supply is contaminated with a deadly bacterium that transforms the town's population into flesh eating ghouls.

Without warning, Henry Watson finds himself thrown into a living hell where the living dead walk and want nothing more than to feed on the living.

Now Henry's trying to escape the undead town before he becomes the next victim.

With the military on one side, shooting civilians on sight, and a horde of bloodthirsty zombies on the other, Henry must try to battle his way to freedom.

With a small group of survivors, including a beautiful secretary and a wise-cracking janitor to aid him, the ragtag group will do their best to stay alive and escape the city codenamed: **Deadwater**.

DEAD END: A ZOMBIE NOVEL
by Anthony Giangregorio
THE DEAD WALK!

Newspapers everywhere proclaim the dead have returned to feast on the living!

A small group of survivors hole up in a cellar, afraid to brave the masses of animated corpses, but when food runs out, they have no choice but to venture out into a world gone mad.

What they will discover, however, is that the fall of civilization has brought out the worst in their fellow man.

Cannibals, psychotic preachers and rapists are just some of the atrocities they must face.

In a world turned upside down, it is life that has hit a Dead End.

BOOK OF THE DEAD 2: NOT DEAD YET
A ZOMBIE ANTHOLOGY
Edited by Anthony Giangregorio

Out of the ashes of death and decay, comes the second volume filled with the walking dead.

In this tomb, there are only slow, shambling monstrosities that were once human.

No one knows why the dead walk; only that they do, and that they are hungry for human flesh.

But these aren't your neighbors, your co-workers, or your family.
Now they are the living dead, and they will tear your throat out at a moment's notice.

So be warned as you delve into the pages of this book; the dead will find you, no matter where you hide.

BOOK OF THE DEAD 3: DEAD AND ROTTING
Edited by Anthony Giangregorio

WELCOM TO THE ZOMBIE APOCALYPSE!

In this, the third installment of the Book of the Dead series, we get right to the guts of the matter.
In these stories, the world has already succumbed to the zombie menace, whether by a week or years.

The action can only be topped by the gore, in these fast-paced tales of the dead.

So hold on to something, for this volume will top the first two and feed your undead brain with buckets of blood and gobbets of tender flesh.

Welcome to **Book of the Dead 3: Dead and Rotting**, where the dead rule the land and mankind is a dying race.

The Lazarus Culture
by Pasquale J. Morrone

Secret Service Agent Christopher Kearns had no idea what he was up against. Assigned on a temporary basis to the Center for Disease Control, he only knew that somehow it was connected to the lives of those the agency protected...namely, the President of the United States. If there were possible terrorist activities in the making, he could only guess it was at a red alert basis.

When Kearns meets and befriends Doctor Marlene Peterson of the Breezy Point Medical Center in Maryland, he soon finds that science fiction can indeed become a reality. In a solitary room walked a man with no vital signs: dead. The explanation he received came from Doctor Lee Fret, a man assigned to the case from the CDC. Something was attached to the brain stem. Something alive that was quickly spreading rapidly through Maryland and other states.

Kearns and his ragtag army of agents and medical personnel soon find themselves in a world of meaningless slaughter and mayhem. The armies of the walking dead were far more than mere zombies. Some began to change into whatever it was they ate. The government had found a way to reanimate the dead by implanting a parasite found on the tongue of the Red Snapper to the human brain.

It looked good on paper, but it was a project straight from Hell.

The dead now walked, but it wasn't a mystery.

It was The Lazarus Culture.

END OF DAYS: AN APOCALYPTIC ANTHOLOGY VOLUMES 1 & 2

Our world is a fragile place.

Meteors, famine, floods, nuclear war, solar flares, and hundreds of other calamities can plunge our small blue planet into turmoil in an instant.

What would you do if tomorrow the sun went super nova or the world was swallowed by water, submerging the world into the cold darkness of the ocean? This anthology explores some of those scenarios and plunges you into total annihilation.

But remember, it's only a book, and tomorrow will come as it always does. Or will it?

DEADFALL
by Anthony Giangregorio

It's Halloween in the small suburban town of Wakefield, Mass.

While parents take their children trick or treating and others throw costume parties, a swarm of meteorites enter the earth's atmosphere and crash to earth.

Inside are small parasitic worms, no larger than maggots.

The worms quickly infect the corpses at a local cemetery and so begins the rise of the undead.

The walking dead soon get the upper hand, with no one believing the truth.

That the dead now walk.

Will a small group of survivors live through the zombie apocalypse?

Or will they, too, succumb to the Deadfall.

DARK PLACES

By Anthony Giangregorio

A cave-in inside the Boston subway unleashes something that should have stayed buried forever.

Three boys sneak out to a haunted junkyard after dark and find more than they gambled on.

In a world where everyone over twelve has died from a mysterious illness, one young boy tries to carry on.

A mysterious man in black tries his hand at a game of chance at a local carnival, to interesting results.

God, Allah, and Buddha play a friendly game of poker with the fate of the Earth resting in the balance.

Ever have one of those days where everything that can go wrong, does? Well, so did Byron, and no one should have a day like this!

Thad had an imaginary friend named Charlie when he was a child. Charlie would make him do bad things. Now Thad is all grown up and guess who's coming for a visit?

These and other short stories, all filled with frozen moments of dread and wonder, will keep you captivated long into the night.

Just be sure to watch out when you turn off the light!

BOOK OF THE DEAD
A ZOMBIE ANTHOLOGY
VOLUME 1
ISBN 978-1-935458-25-8

Edited by Anthony Giangregorio

This is the most faithful, truest zombie anthology ever written, and we invite you along for the ride. Every single story in this book is filled with slack-jawed, eyes glazed, slow moving, shambling zombies set in a world where the dead have risen and only want to eat the flesh of the living. In these pages, the rules are sacrosanct. There is no deviation from what a zombie should be or how they came about. The Dead Walk.

There is no reason, though rumors and suppositions fill the radio and television stations. But the only thing that is fact is that the walking dead are here and they will not go away. So prepare yourself for the ultimate homage to the master of zombie legend. And remember... Aim for the head!

DEAD TALES: SHORT STORIES TO DIE FOR

by Anthony Giangregorio

In a world much like our own, terrorists unleash a deadly dis-ease that turns people into flesh-eating ghouls.

A camping trip goes horribly wrong when forces of evil seek to dominate mankind.

After losing his life, a man returns reincarnated again and again; his soul inhabiting the bodies of animals.

In the Colorado Mountains, a woman runs for her life, stalked by a sadistic killer.

In a world where the Patriot Act has come to fruition, a man struggles to survive, despite eroding liberties.

Not able to accept his wife's death, a widower will cross into the dream realm to find her again, despite the dark forces that hold her in thrall. These and other short stories will captivate and thrill you. These are short stories to die for.

REVOLUTION OF THE DEAD
by Anthony Giangregorio
THE DEAD SHALL RISE AGAIN!

Five years ago, a deadly plague wiped out 97% of the world's population, America suffering tragically. Bodies were everywhere, far too many to bury or burn. But then, through a miracle of medical science, a way is found to reanimate the dead.

With the manpower of the United States depleted, and the remaining survivors not wanting to give up their internet and fast food restaurants, the undead are conscripted as slave labor.

Now they cut the grass, pick up the trash, and walk the dogs of the surviving humans.

But whether alive or dead, no race wants to be controlled, and sooner or later the dead will fight back, wanting the freedom they enjoyed in life.

The revolution has begun!

And when it's over, the dead will rule the land, and the remaining humans will become the slaves...or worse.

KINGDOM OF THE DEAD
by Anthony Giangregorio
THE DEAD HAVE RISEN!

In the dead city of Pittsburgh, two small enclaves struggle to survive, eking out an existence of hand to mouth.

But instead of working together, both groups battle for the last remaining fuel and supplies of a city filled with the living dead.

Six months after the initial outbreak, a lone helicopter arrives bearing two more survivors and a newborn baby. One enclave welcomes them, while the other schemes to steal their helicopter and escape the decaying city.

With no police, fire, or social services existing, the two will battle for dominance in the steel city of the walking dead. But when the dust settles, the question is: will the remaining humans be the winners, or the losers?

When the dead walk, the line between Heaven and Hell is so twisted and bent there is no line at all.

RISE OF THE DEAD
by Anthony Giangregorio
DEATH IS ONLY THE BEGINNING!

In less than forty-eight hours, more than half the globe was infected.
In another forty-eight, the rest would be enveloped.
The reason?
A science experiment gone horribly wrong which enabled the dead to walk, their flesh rotting on their bones even as they seek human prey.

Jeremy was an ordinary nineteen year old slacker. He partied too much and had done poorly in high school. After a night of drinking and drugs, he awoke to find the world a very different place from the one he'd left the night before.

The dead were walking and feeding on the living, and as Jeremy stepped out into a world gone mad, the dead spotting him alone and unarmed in the middle of the street, he had to wonder if he would live long enough to see his twentieth birthday.

FAMILY OF THE DEAD
A Zombie Anthology
by Anthony, Joseph and Domenic Giangregorio

Clawing their way out of the wet, dark earth, these tales of terror will fill you with the deep seated fear we all have of death and what comes next.

But if that wasn't bad enough to chill your soul, these undead tales are penned by an entire family of corpses. The zombie master himself, Anthony Giangregorio, leads his two young ghouls, his sons Domenic and Joseph Giangregorio, on a journey of terror inducing stories that will keep you up long into the night.

As you read these works of the undead, don't be alarmed by that bump outside the window.

After all, it's probably just a stray tree branch...or is it?

ANOTHER EXCITING ADVENTURE IN THE DEADWATER SERIES!
DEAD SALVATION
BOOK 9
by Anthony Giangregorio

Henry Watson and his band of warrior survivalists roam what's left of a ravaged America, searching for something better.

HANGMAN'S NOOSE!

After one of the group is hurt, the need for transportation is solved by a roving cannie convoy. Attacking the camp, the companions save a man who invites them back to his home.

Cement City it's called and at first the group is welcomed with thanks for saving one of their own. But when a bar fight goes wrong, the companions find themselves awaiting the hangman's noose.

Their only salvation is a suicide mission into a raider camp to save captured townspeople.

Though the odds are long, it's a chance, and Henry knows in the land of the walking dead, sometimes a chance is all you can hope for.

In the world of the dead, life is a struggle, where the only victor is death.

BOOK 3 OF THE EXCITING DEADWATER SERIES!
DEAD CITY
by Anthony Giangregorio

After narrowly surviving an attack by a large pack of blood thirsty, wild dogs, Henry and his companions stumble upon an enclave that has made its home in an abandoned shopping mall.

Hoping for a respite from the perils of the walking dead, Henry and the others plan to settle down for the winter, safe in the company of fellow survivors of the zombie apocalypse.

But unknown to the group is the dark secret the enclave keeps, a secret that could threaten to destroy the companions and anyone else unfortunate enough to be caught in the trap.

In a dead world, the only thing still living...is hope.

THE CHRONICLES OF JACK PRIMUS
BOOK ONE
by Michael D. Griffiths

Beneath the world of normalcy we all live in lies another world, one where supernatural beings exist.

These creatures of the night hunt us; want to feed on our very souls, though only a few know of their existence.

One such man is Jack Primus, who accidentally pierces the veil between this world and the next. With no other choice if he wants to live, he finds himself on the run, hunted by beings called the Xemmoni, an ancient race that sees humans as nothing but cattle.

They want his soul, to feed on his very essence, and they will kill all who stand in their way.

But if they thought Jack would just lie down and accept his fate, they were sorely mistaken.

He didn't ask for this battle, but he knew he would fight them with everything at his disposal, for to lose is a fate worse than death.

He would win this war, and he would take down anyone who got in his way.

LOVE IS DEAD: A ZOMBIE ANTHOLOGY
Edited by Anthony Giangregorio

THE DEATH OF LOVE

Valentine's Day is a day when young love is fulfilled.

Where hopeful young men bring candy and flowers to their sweethearts, in hopes of a kiss...or perhaps more.

But not in this anthology.

For you see, LOVE IS DEAD, and in this tome, the dead walk, wanting to feed on those same hearts that once pumped in chests, bursting with love.

So toss aside that heart-shaped box of candy and throw away those red roses, you won't need them any longer. Instead, strap on a handgun, or pick up a shotgun and defend yourself from the ravenous undead.

Because in a world where the dead walk, even love isn't safe.

Blood of the Dead
A.P. Fuchs

Bits of the Dead
edited by
Keith Gouveia

Axiom-man
The Dead Land
A.P. Fuchs

Dead Science
edited by
A.P. Fuchs

Zombifrieze
W. Bill Czolgosz
Sean Simmans

Don of the Dead
Nick Cato

Snarl
Lorne Dixon

World War of the Dead
Eric S. Brown

The Lifeless
Lorne Dixon